Cold Fusion 2000

Karl Drinkwater

Organic Apocalypse

Compassion for all living things is the way to peace. Good work, Aber VegSoc!

Karl Drinkwater
September 2017

To my readers. Some stories are not so straightforward as they might first seem, and small details can be telling.

A Very Brief History Of Time

"This book is so important I never lend it out. In it Hawking takes us on a journey, a flight through physics that educates as it inspires, but you don't have to be a physicist, it can even be read by average people. It only includes one equation. So this is a starting point, somewhere to begin – a Big Bang book ha ha – and like that event its ripples shape everything we know, and everything we don't know. Mine's the first UK edition, hardback. It feels so solid. Look inside, it's dedicated to Jane, must be his first wife. Anyway, those ripples, they start here, and everything is built on them. Turtles all the way down, as Hawking would say."

1992 to June 2000

1992. The Shamen shouted "Eezer Goode, Eezer Goode". Alex listened; decided that MSc's 're good and started his postgrad in physics.

1993. MSc over, Alex started a PhD on the topic of ancient physics. UB40 sang "(I Can't Help) Falling In Love With You". Alex met a first year undergraduate called Lucy Spiers. He couldn't help himself.

1994. Towards the end of the year Lucy dumped him on a Saturday Night, much to Whigfield's surprise. D:Ream told Alex that Things Could Only Get Better. He didn't believe them and left the university, PhD unfinished.

1995. At the age of twenty-three Alex was living at home and started teaching in a Gangsta's Paradise (he had to explain to Coolio that it was really a UK further education college).

1996. The job was Killing Him Softly, he decided, seeing himself as a refugee from "proper" academia. "I Wannabe doing something different next year," he gasped to a sexy photo of the Spice Girls when his family made the mistake of leaving him alone in the house unsupervised.

1997. Natalie Imbruglia was Torn. Alex was just sexually frustrated. He didn't care about Aqua's Barbie Girl – he'd settle for any girl.

1998. Alex had his twenty-sixth birthday. He was still at the college. Madonna was Frozen. So was Alex.

1999. Alex was still living at home. Shania said, "That Don't Impress Me Much". Alex had to agree. Throughout 1999 he was tense and ready to snap at people.

"It's not a new millennium in 2000. There was no year zero. 1 BC went straight to 1 AD, therefore after twelve months we were in the year 2 AD. You always add a year. After a hundred years we were in year 101. A millennium is a thousand years, so a new one begins in –"

Responses varied, from "Shut up, Alex, don't confuse things," to "Don't care, I'm going to the party *this* year," to "Fuck off, ginger balls".

1999 was not a good year.

2000. Now. Will the Real Slim Shady please step forward?

Superdense Matter

"*Matter is everything physical. Every object, every star, every person. All made up of atoms, those teeny tiny magnetic Lego bricks that click and clack together to give things shape. And matter can become energy. We're all potential stars. But there are gaps between those building blocks. Something interesting happens when you pack them tighter. Things become heavier, harder, denser. Stars are some of the largest consistent entities we know, and when they die and collapse in on themselves the matter is crushed together. You get a neutron star. Something smaller than the UK but hundreds of thousands of times more dense than the Earth. And the largest are so dense that they pull everything else in, even light itself. And it then exists in this lightless world of weight, growing forever in its hunger for matter but existing as a distorted darkness that precludes life. Kind of like Manchester.*"

Mid-June. A Monday.

Struggling to breathe, tight-chested mumbles and cloth-filled inhales, slurred words "No, not an octopus" accompanied by thrashing, the being resisting the dream of suffocation with renewed energy, eyes opening, bleary, as face lifts from the pillow, "Urgh" it grumbled, turning to see what time it was according to Lion-O's pointing sword on the old Thunder Cats alarm clock. The Sword of Omens said it was 7.20am. Five minutes before the alarm would go off. Alex pushed the lever to prevent the bells from ringing.

A yawn. Stretch. Why was he –

Bang! "I'll write another article," he said.

Alex threw the duvet back and staggered to the window, almost slipping on the unmarked student essays he kept meaning to move. He made a mental note to knock marks off every one that had been put into a slidy plastic sleeve.

He drew back the curtains to greet the morning sun, revealing to the world the full glory of his white body in baggy-arsed briefs.

The world paid no attention.

He dived onto his bed, old springs creaking, and fumbled around on the floor amongst books and bits of paper until he found a notepad and pen. He bit back anger when the pen didn't write, tried another; that was running out too and he couldn't see any others – *where the fuck did all his pens go? everything went missing in this house* – so used the stub of a pencil, telling himself to stay calm. He frantically scribbled down ideas

6

for an exciting new article on particle collisions, even though he had four other pieces in draft form and two submitted to magazines. He bit the end of his pencil then made bullet point ideas for a lesson plan he could use with his science students, grinning as ideas sparked off each other and ignited the forebrain flame.

A snakelike slither to the floor and he started his press-ups enthusiastically, twenty with his face turned left, twenty to the right, then an extra ten for the five he'd missed the day before (the system required doubling as punishment) *then another few for good luck and ... and ... whiteness –*

. . .. *honest*. . . . .
.. . . *night.* . . .
.. . .
. .. . *fire*.. . . . .
.. . . *leapt*.
.. . .
. .. .
. . . . *smile* .. . .
.. . .
. . .. *butterflies* . . . .
. . ..
.. . .
. . . . *me*. . .

– and he was shaking his head to clear it as colour flooded back, like waking from a dream, aware of aching as the time bubble popped, no idea how many press-ups he'd done during his mind-blip fugue ("Too bloody many!" moaned his arms). He collapsed, cheek resting on yesterday's socks.

7

He'd not had an "episode" for a while. It always felt like a lot of time had passed and he'd experienced something intense, even though witnesses had told him he only blanked out for a few seconds. After it happened he retained no real memory of what his mind had experienced. Just fragments. Like sparks and drifting feathers and paper-thin fluttering wings.

Alex tried not to worry about it. No harm done. Better to think of the mini mind-blanks as creative jolts, as if his brain had temporarily overclocked its Pentium processor to light-speed frequency, but with the side effect of shutting his consciousness down to protect it from overheating. That theory fit the observable phenomena. Then again, the competing theories included: he was nuts; he had a brain tumour; aliens had temporarily abducted him. Perhaps he needed to open an X-File of his own.

He wondered where his mind had wandered this time, what life it had lived as a trail of neurons sped through networks of possibilities particle-fast, too rapid to catch without a hadron collider, causing super quarks of weirdness and leaving him with only a vague after-image like a melting dream. He had to accept that he couldn't catch all his thoughts, all the things going on in his body, the processes which slipped by in the background just leaving a shadow, an itch, a grain of sand that probably wouldn't become a pearl, a blazing after-trace that lives a second then is gone forever. All those possibilities occurring in a moment of frantic life: it never ceased to amaze him. The world was an incredible and beautifully constructed thing.

However, there wasn't really time for a wank.

He'd powered through the sit-ups, grunting accompaniment to the last ten, and then had a tentative feel while he lay on his back. There was potential for action there all right, his cock was as enthusiastic and energised as the rest of him, and he'd been about to spit into his palm when he caught Lion-O's mighty stare, his own sword also moving into the vertical now: discipline. Running late, get back on track. Have a shower before the others initiated the battle for the bathroom.

He had the brains. He had the energy. Last week had been shit, but that was in the past. Today was a new week. It would be brilliant and productive. His tingling Spidey-sense (or nighttrapped nerve) told him so.

The house was quiet when Alex left his room. The bathroom door was ajar so he walked right in.

A gasp. Natalie stood next to the shower, a small towel snatched from the rail and held against her front, but not before he glimpsed a slender body and dark hair above her legs.

He jerked his head away, stammering, "Sorry, didn't know you were in here …" then noticed he was now facing the large wall mirror, which revealed a condensation-dripping rear view of Natalie. A misty memory overlapped for a second like the shadow of a scudding cloud, but he rejected it and looked down at his slippered feet instead.

"It's okay, my fault, I didn't think anyone would be up," she said. There was the sound of another towel being removed from the rail. "Okay, I'm covered up now, safe to look."

He turned, and saw she had the big bath towel wrapped around herself. It folded across her chest and reached down to her knees, so only exposed shaved legs, feet with pink nail varnish on the toes, and bare shoulders and arms dimpled with moisture. Less than Natalie usually revealed when wearing clothes, yet he found himself reaching behind and fumbling for the damp door handle.

"You've gone as red-faced as Kelly does!" Natalie joked with a grin. "Ah, so sweet! All you Kavanaghs are the same. Don't worry, I'm not embarrassed." He was half backed out when she added, "Look, don't tell your mum. I *would* be embarrassed if she knew."

"I won't say anything. But ... best to lock the door in future."

"Yeah. I just forgot. I'm not used to getting up so early. I want to be first at the jobcentre." She grinned at him, appealing and discomfiting in equal measure. She stepped forward, he stepped back, through the open doorway – like poles repel – and retreated to his room, away from steamy visions.

He paced. 7.54am. There was plenty of time. Relax. She'd be out of the bathroom and he could nip in. Quick shower. Soon back on schedule. A brisk walk. Catch the direct bus. It would go like clockwork.

He'd left the bedroom door open so he could hear when she'd finished, but her footsteps came down the landing towards him, instead of to her room. He sat on the edge of his bed and grabbed some notes, pretending he'd been studying. She came in with jeans and a T-shirt on now. Still bare footed, obviously unconcerned about the high probabilities of treading on a staple or drawing pin. Alex didn't have time for a Health and Safety talk though. "I know you're busy, I just wondered if you'd do me a favour, Alex?"

He put down the sheets of paper, risked a glance at the clock. "Sure." *Please be quick.*

"It's just that, with my birthday coming up, I've been thinking. So I'm writing a letter to my mum."

"Are you two talking again?"

"Not properly, but I thought this might help, sort of having my say without it turning into another row. There'll be less slammed doors and shouting."

"Sounds like a good idea. I'm sure you'll move home again soon. Once people are calm they can sort things out."

"Maybe. You'll be glad to be rid of me, I bet. It's not fair to put you all out for too long. You're all so nice."

He shrugged. "It's fine. You're welcome. Did you …?"

"Oh. I wondered if you could read through it. It'd help me having someone clever look over it, you'd spot bits where maybe I wrote something Mum would take the wrong way which I didn't really mean, so might save us more arguments."

"Okay, I'll have a look. You know I'll always help you."

"I know." She leaned over and gave him a peck on the cheek. "I like talking to you, you're always caring, kind of like a –"

"Big brother?"

"Maybe." She seemed uncertain.

Lion-O waved his sword, doing all he could to distract Alex. "I'll read it later."

"Oh. Okay."

"Is that a problem?"

"Not really. I was just going to see my mum later."

He resisted the urge to sigh. "Go get it. Be quick."

Footsteps thumped away. He paced, avoided looking at the clock but counted seconds anyway. Returning thuds, then she handed him the letter, her face flushed and happy.

He skim-read it standing up, murmuring the words. It took thirty-five seconds.

"Seems fine. Tenses got mixed in the second paragraph and there's only one 'e' in argument."

"Yeah, I can change that, but what about how it'll make her *feel*? I don't wanna make her angry."

"Of course. Sorry. I think it's sufficient. You could maybe tone down the bit about the last disagreement – if it's in the past raising it again will just remind her of any bad feelings. If you're aiming to be conciliatory then stick to the positives. That help?" He handed the letter back.

"Yeah, I'll rewrite it and change that bit. Thanks! And if there's anything I can do for you ... Anything ..."

"No need, it's fine." Silly girl, she could do nothing to help him, unless she secretly had editing skills that weren't apparent from her letter writing.

She caught him looking at the clock this time, thanked him again, and left abruptly.

He was just exiting his room when he saw the bathroom door click closed. He ran down the landing and banged on it. "Who's in there?" he demanded.

"Me," his sister called back without opening the door. "I'm getting a shower."

"I need one, I've got to catch the bus!"

There was no reply. He heard the shower cubicle close.

"Kelly!" He banged again.

"Get a bath instead," she yelled.

"There isn't time!"

"Tough nuts."

"Fuck!" He kicked the door as water started hissing. "Fat arse," he shouted. No reply from within.

He would have to make do with a quick body wash in the other bathroom. It wasn't as good though. He hated feeling grimy. It always started the day off badly.

"Aaaargh! It's not there! Someone must have moved it!"

Kelly's screeching ricocheted down the stairs and into the kitchen where Alex rushed to combine cereal and milk without getting bits of rice all over the countertop. He was failing.

His mum gave him a look which combined "You're not a kid so why are you so messy?" with "Shit, Kelly again".

"What's up?" she shouted.

"My hairbrush is gone! I need it! For Christ's sake have you had it again, Natalie?" she shrieked.

"No I haven't, and I didn't touch it the last time either!" Natalie yelled back from the dining room where she was filling in forms at the big table.

"Well it can't very well have *walked*, can it?"

Natalie came into the kitchen and said, "I didn't, honestly, Hannah."

"I know," his mum replied, sighing and heading for the stairs. "Hold your horses, I'll help you look," she called up to Kelly.

The fridge door was overloaded with bottles and rattled as it opened. Natalie poured herself some orange juice then gestured towards Alex with the carton. He shook his head.

"She doesn't half go off on one, your sister," she said.

"And there's never a logical reason for it."

"She's probably stressing. She said she's got a music test this afternoon and it's important."

"Of course! She needs a good mark to get into the College of Music. So she'll be in a bad mood until the test is over." People were easy to understand. Easy to despise.

8.07am. He didn't have time to catch the 245 bus now unless he sprinted all the way to Trafford General Hospital. He would have to catch the 15 and change at Stretford. Shit. He shouldn't have agreed to cover the Information in Society double session at 9.

Banging down the stairs. "Got it," Kelly said as she rushed into the kitchen.

Natalie raised an eyebrow at her.

"Under my bed," Kelly mumbled, looking down. "Sorry."

"No problem. I know how annoying it is when you can't find things. Do you want me to do you some toast?"

"No thanks." Kelly was shoving items into her bag. She rooted through an old Roses tin full of odds and ends and retrieved two highlighters. "Oh, sorry about the shower, Al, it's just I'm in a hurry too."

He ran a finger around his shirt collar. It felt grimy already.

"You need to be careful with those pens," he told her as he finished his breakfast.

"Why?"

"There are radioactive elements in fluorescent pens. Small amounts of micro-particles – we're talking nano-level here – mostly isotope derivatives redacted from nuclear waste, half-life negligible."

"Bollocks," she said, but eyed the pens warily.

"It's true. You know it's a topic I've studied. How do you think they get the inks to glow in the day? All passed by the FSA as hardly harmful, just a forty per cent increased risk of cancer and infertility."

She dropped both pens in horror as he left the room. Natalie whispered something about him joking.

"You're a bastard!" Kelly yelled at his back, sounding hurt. "I don't need your shit today!"

He grinned. 8.10am. No sweat.

He checked his backpack – notes, papers, pens, biscuits, breath freshener, wallet. Something missing. He pounded upstairs, dodging his mother on the way. Plugged into his PC's parallel port was his Zip drive. There was a reassuringly chunky clunk as the disk ejected. Solid and reliable, unlike so many things in life. He stared at the rigid piece of plastic. Each Zip disk held 100MB of data: over sixty floppy disks' worth in one tidy package. Incredible technology, as if the future was here already. Into the bag with that too, tucked into a pouch beside his calculator.

He only had to walk slightly faster than usual. The 15 was never early, and he was soon standing alone at the bus stop, realising too late that the day would be hot and he should have taken a hat or sunglasses. A minor irritation. He squinted hopefully up the road at some movement.

Fuck. It wasn't the bus. It was his arch-nemeses. Kids that lived in the street behind his house. How often had he walked past them then had to put up with one of the brats making squelching noises with every step he took? Or one of them shouting something at him, like "backpack boy" or "ginger minge"? It wasn't right that teenagers could get away with doing that to adults. He thought he'd be safe today because they'd be at school, but had forgotten that the fifth years were doing their GCSEs now, and only had to go into school for the exams. Still, what the fuck were they doing out so early?

He hated them. Delinquent shits.

"Please, God, let them all go straight to jobs at McDonalds. Don't send them to my college next year," he pleaded towards the open sky.

There were no lightning bolts or burning bins to show he'd been heard.

"Thanks a bunch."

Today there were three terrors, and they'd spotted him. He recognized Floppy Feet first. A lad with blonde hair sticking out from underneath a woolly hat, wearing a grubby white jacket. Alex called him that because the lad wore black trainers with the laces undone to the point that his heels lifted out with every step, so he clipped and clopped as if dragging his feet.

With him was Tram Line Boy in his tracksuit bottoms and T-shirt, and Super Perm. The latter's long and incredibly curly ringlets were possibly natural, but there was no insult in thinking of her as Naturally Curly Girl.

The dragging noise was now audible, an accelerated shuffle of horror. They were getting nearer.

But so was the bus! It had just turned the corner, showing that some mumbled prayers were heard and acted on. The bus overtook the kids and Alex hopped on and dropped the exact change into the tray. Then he rushed to the back as the bus pulled out and felt brave enough to stick two fingers up at the kids. Take that you scud-monkeys! *Kapow!* He imagined Floppy Feet swooning from shock. *Two-fingered wham!* Another one down. Then a single middle finger for Tram Line Boy. Just as they realised what he was doing he turned his back to them so he couldn't see their return gestures, giving him the last laugh. Back on form! He was the master, the world his student, a super-tough mega-brave physicist cum lecturer who would *not* be pushed around today.

17

Then he moved to a middle seat so he wouldn't get travel sick.

Early physics by Alex Kavanagh [maybe submit to Physics Review this time?]

Physics is not something we stumbled upon in the 1940s as the West rushed to create ways of killing more people [too harsh for PR?]. It was not John Dalton's 19th Century arguments for atomistic interpretations of chemistry that began it. (See November issue for a biography of JD.) [Go back to Galileo? Must slip in "imponderable fluid" joke somewhere, that would be hilarious.]

The ancient world used physics in their attempts to understand the way things worked. Democritus, the long-lived Greek philosopher ("lover of wisdom") had an atomistic theory to explain the world. There were atoms, and there was void. Form and the formless. And between the atoms were random connections, impacts, and only the most stable atoms survived –

Alex was pulled back from the Other World – the one where he managed to sneak back into the realm of academia and garner respect from other theorists and researchers – into the world where the air was heavy, where he was sat on the Stagecoach 15 bus to town surrounded by sticky people made crotchety by heat. The world where teleportation was not yet a possibility.

The bus had juddered to a halt at Stretford Arndale's car-park-on-shops bare bones architectural brutalism. Perspiring commoners were dropping change into the money tray or flashing passes. Alex went back to his article instead of calculating the number of new passengers versus the number of seats and taking any necessary remedial action to make the empty seat next to him look uninviting.

Big mistake.

He was distracted by the mass of a wide body in a thin leather jacket pushing against him, squashing him against the window and knocking his hand, which left an unwanted swish of blue ink up the page. Alex looked up angrily and realised that the day continued to serve cow-pats onto the plate of his life.

It was the Glasgow Smile Man. GSM.

GSM was a regular drunk on some of the buses Alex caught. He looked about sixty, wide-bodied, with an overwhelming smell as if he'd smeared a Chinese meal on his body. Even if he was a few seats in front you would pick up that whiff. Sat here, now, it was worse. Like wafts of stale junk food rising on a draught of hot body odour. Alex felt queasy.

From this close Alex could see the scars clearly. They ran from the sides of GSM's lips across his cheeks and up to his sideburns, a Glasgow smile cut into his face from many years ago. Once you had seen those faint scars from a vicious and bloody disfigurement, your perception of the man changed: he seemed ominous.

The smell was not even the worst thing about him. GSM drew attention. Occasionally GSM would mutter and shout when near the end of the journey. He would sometimes rush up to help lift bags for a woman, creepily repeating "God bless, love, God bless". He would sit next to passengers while tipsy and whisper and make jokes conspiratorially whether people wanted to talk or not.

The man *intruded*. That was the worst thing about him in Alex's eyes. He intruded physically, but also intruded on your *mind*. That sacred place meant to be a haven from dirt, sweat, ignorance, noise, and all the other grimes of reality.

He skipped ahead to draft a new section.

> *Stoicism – a Hellenistic philosophy. About the duty to do things, even if they were painful. Stoicists sought knowledge. They wanted to know the end of life, the goal; what virtue and goodness were; how to protect yourself and achieve good in the world.*

GSM usually carried a plastic bag with booze in that he would surreptitiously sip from during the journey, before leaving the bag and empty bottle on the seat as he departed. Today he had what appeared to be a litre of dirty orange cordial. He took a swig then glanced towards Alex, who quickly jotted extra words on the page with a look of forced "don't interrupt me this is serious shit" concentration.

> *And on this they built a materialist cosmology. [cf. Democritus]. The creative force in formless matter creates "matter with form" via tension.*

"What're you writing?" asked GSM in his rumbling voice.

"Nothing much. Just something I've got to do." Alex tried not to look up.

"A writer are you?"

"No, just doing something …" Pretend to be caught in deep thought.

"A student are you? At the university?"

"No." Write words, any words.

"You look like one."

Alex pressed his pen harder on the page.

They knew that matter was everywhere, homogenous. They also believed that the force was benevolent and purposive, that it guided things towards ends.

After a minute of uninterrupted writing Alex's heart rate slowed as he tried to forget about the threateningly chaotic and grubbily odorous world that existed outside of his regular orbit.

"Here, try this, for inspiration." The bottle was brandished in Alex's face; he felt horror as that dirty-looking liquid sloshed around only inches from his nose. It smelt sickly and sweet at the same time.

"No, no, I'm fine." *What the fuck was in it?* "Look, I've got to finish this."

"Stuck up cunt," GSM mumbled, before getting up and moving next to another passenger.

Emotions (even piety) were seen as vices, since they disturb a rational mind.

Alex underlined the second clause, then sighed with relief. He could live with the nasty accusation of those three parting words if it meant he had the seat to himself again. He quickly moved his bag from between his feet and put it in the vacated space next to him.

His hand was shaking. *Shaking.* As if teaching wasn't stressful enough. All the prep he puts in, all the effort.

Maybe he looked like a target?

A group of kids passed the open staffroom door, giggling.

He banged jars, looking for one with coffee granules that hadn't hardened to a black lump. The kettle was taking ages to boil. *And did no-one ever wipe down the fucking sideboard?* It was spilt-sugar gritty and patterned with overlapping brown circles from cups.

The whole room was a barely-controlled mess. Box files leaning on biscuit tins; boxes of paper sliding on piles of magazines. Always one step away from falling apart.

And it was like an oven in the staffroom, the vast expanse of glass along one wall a sadistic magnifying glass. He thumped the stiff window latch with the palm of his hand until it gave, then fully opened the window. The reward was a smell of cigarettes from the smokers' gathering point outside.

The kettle rumbled, adding further humidity to the room while he finished preparing his drink.

"Steady on, you'll rot your teeth!"

He hadn't heard Elaine Marchant come in. She ran the PGCE courses and liked to make Alex jealous by talking about her imminent retirement.

"Mmm?"

"The sugar. You were heaping spoonfuls in."

"I need the energy." He let his teaspoon clatter in the sink. "It's cheaper than cocaine."

"Try poppers. That works a treat for a quick blast."

"I'll borrow yours later," he replied. "For now I'll stick with coffee. I need that too."

"You can't survive without the ritual and the routine. Like your snack from the Union each day – what is it you call it, your 'Flapjack Foray'? You have OCD down to a fine art."

"I'll take that as a compliment."

Alex flopped into his favourite seat amongst the random assortment of the room: a soft green chair with a hole in the cushion where a long-ago cigarette burn had got out of hand. It had wide wooden arms, good for holding cups or essays, and didactic bottoms had moulded the seat into an ideal shape over the last twenty years.

"Don't you hate teaching sometimes?" he asked.

"What's up with you?"

"Everything. None of them pay attention. Clueless about citation. Won't do any research if it's not in the core text. They don't even use proper fucking grammar."

"I take it someone's just had a bad session?"

"I was covering Information in Society. They ignored me during the talk and pissed about during the discussion. The room was a sauna."

"C22?"

He nodded wearily. She wafted a hand in front of her face as if feeling the heat there herself.

"Then some of the little shits changed the title of the presentation."

"To what?"

"'There is no need for fucking censorship in a democratic society'. I assume the word 'fucking' wasn't in the original title. And they used as many vulgar terms as they could to illustrate 'freedom of expression'. I didn't even recognise half of them. Is a poonanny a good or a bad thing?"

"What charmers. Don't take it to heart. Are you coming to the staff meeting later?"

"No. Afternoon off, so I'll probably go to the Cornerhouse and see a film. Something to look forward to, anyway."

"There you go. Focus on that. Nice to have time alone." She finished making her own drink and sat on a stool. "You look like you've had an idea."

"Yes: maybe Anne could be persuaded … I'll go and speak to her."

"Wahey, nearly summer!" said Isaac Rose as he entered the staffroom, his deep voice sounding genuinely cheery for once.

That was another thing to focus on, Alex thought. It was only two weeks before the college broke up. Time off and relaxation, and *absolutely no stress.*

His frown returned as the other teachers piled in, bickering about whose turn it was to get more milk. He'd had enough of being packed into small spaces with sweaty bodies.

Anne was teaching her GNVQ Business group. Alex spied through the glass of the door, watching her make an expansive floor-to-ceiling gesture as she explained a diagram she'd drawn on the whiteboard which – bizarrely – mentioned dead dogs and cash cows, as if she was pitching a horror film to vets and farmers.

He rapped on the glass then gave a little wave when she peered over, trying to see who it was.

He waited, hearing her give instructions before she slipped out.

"I'm teaching," she said, taking off her small glasses to polish them. "I don't like to be disturbed when I'm teaching. You know that."

"I know. I'm sorry. It's just that I'm off this afternoon. I was going to go to the pictures alone, but it would be nicer to go for a drink with you."

Alex reached for her hand but she flinched and looked nervously up and down the corridor.

"Not when we're working!"

"You're so professional. What about it?"

"Staff meeting."

"I know. Skip it."

"I can't."

"You can. You could come back later on, just a longer dinner. I need to have a whinge."

"Great."

"It'll be fun. Spontaneous."

"I wouldn't want to miss that."

"And I'll buy you dinner."

She sighed. "Okay. But get lost for now."

"I will. Meet me at The Pelican when you finish. I'll go there now, do some reading."

He leaned in as if to give her a kiss and she backed through the door with a glare. She was good at the strict schoolteacher look.

Alex sat on the other side of the table from Anne. Both were watching people through a window of The Old Pelican Inn on Manchester Road. People who smiled and looked radiant in the bleaching sunlight.

Neither Anne nor Alex smiled. Anne glanced at her phone sometimes as if wishing it would ring. She'd recently bought it. "Jumping on the teenage bandwagon," Alex had joked last week and only received a frown in exchange.

The good thing about the pub was the incongruity. Mock Tudor frontage facing one of the busiest roads in the area; dark wooden furnishings offset by the bleeping lights of a fruit machine and jukebox. Everywhere falsity was laid bare.

The bad thing was that, being the closest pub to the college, small groups of older-looking students could be found in here during the day. Alex had scowled at one group by the cigarette machine which included underage students of his. He was trying to make them leave guiltily but they ignored him.

He ran a finger around the inside of his shirt collar, separating it from his sweaty neck.

"Shall I buy another drink?" he asked.

"No! No thanks, I mean. I should be getting back." She had been hasty with the no, as if horrified at the thought of staying another half-hour.

26

"I thought you might take the afternoon off and spend it with me?"

"Oh, well, not this time. I should go to the staff meeting after all."

The pub was almost empty at the moment. Lifeless, quiet, still. It emphasised the awkward silences at his table.

"Yes, okay. I'm sorry, I'm not good company today, am I?" He exhaled, a huge breath. "It's been a shit day. Shitty last week too."

"It's not just you, it's … I don't know, it feels different doesn't it?"

"Different from when we first started going out?"

"Yes."

"You're right." He rotated his empty pint glass, watching the last drops of liquid slosh around, trapped by the endless curve. "Have I done something wrong?"

"Ha! So you *have* noticed it too! I wasn't sure, you're so head-in-the-clouds, like everything just goes on normally. I didn't know how to mention that we weren't having fun together any more."

"Well, you have now. It's probably best to be open."

For the first time since entering the pub Anne was smiling. It was not the full-illumination smile Alex used to see. This one started at the mouth right enough, but it didn't reach those almond eyes he'd been so attracted to four months ago. They weren't sparkling behind her glasses today.

She was just as attractive as when he met her but he suddenly realised he wasn't *attracted*. The same brown hair down to her shoulders framed the same face, and her clothes hinted at the same shapely body he'd come to know, but he had begun to look at her with more of an art dealer's eye than a lover's. Clinical numbness had seeped in.

And he knew what that meant. Once the numbness settled it was only a matter of time. He'd hoped, as ever, that this time would be different.

"Well, I've been thinking too," Anne said. "Perhaps I've been a bit too preoccupied with work, not putting my heart into this as much as I should. If so, I'm sorry, I didn't mean to do this to us, maybe if I stop thinking so much about work …"

"No, no, it isn't you, Anne. It's me. Believe me, I didn't want this to happen to us, but relationships and me just don't seem to work out. It's happened before but I hoped it would be different this time, I really did, I like and respect you so much, but it's like there's a timer in my head … and I think the alarm just went off."

"What alarm? You've lost me."

"The end of whatever was making me happy."

She raised her head, as if surprised, and he noted that a faint redness had appeared on her cheeks and neck. "The *end?* Is that what you think this is?"

"Isn't it?"

"I've been trying to think of what we can do to salvage things, I didn't mean they were already *beyond repair.*"

"Oh. I thought we were past hope." Alex stared at his empty glass, not at her. He couldn't stand to look at her. He had become an expert on damage limitation. "It won't work. I know it won't. I'm a serial insensitive. It'd be better for both of us to end it now."

Silence for five whole seconds. Alex didn't dare look up, but his peripheral vision showed that she was staring at him intently. He still didn't know what her reaction –

"Well you little *shit*, Alex. You stinking little *shit*. What a loser. You won't even look at me, huh? You'll drop me like this, mumbling pessimism into your glass? Won't even try at making things work? You're like someone who reads a newspaper and decides we're all doomed, no point doing anything about it. Well if that's your attitude *fine*, you can have your sulks and gloom, if you want rid of me you could have just *said so* without all this nonsense, I never realised I was going out with a closet fucking *nihilist*."

– would be.

Okay, anger.

"Sorry, Anne."

"Somehow I don't think you are."

As she stood up and grabbed her bag to leave, Alex looked up.

"I really am, but I hope we can still be friends."

"Still be friends? *Friends?* Grow up, Alex. Seriously. Think you're so smart, but you know nothing about people. It's fucking sad." She snorted and strode out.

That hadn't gone well.

It was only 12.15.

He'd had another pint.

He was so wrong.

Then one more drink.

He'd given in too easily.

He should be stronger. Should have realised he was in control of things, he wasn't a slave to emotions. Just because past relationships always fizzled out and he ended up with another person who hated him didn't mean it had to be that way. Things were always clearer after a few drinks. He would fight for Anne, regain her love and affection, and make it work. Nothing could go wrong with that.

Instead of going home he strode back to the college. He could just about make the staff meeting, speak to Anne before it started, resolve things, get a bus home with everything made right again and still have a nice afternoon relaxing in the garden. Just like flicking a switch on an electro magnet, he would reverse the day's polarity from negative to positive.

Easy.

It was the last staff meeting of the term. Teachers and curriculum managers sat at student desks in the first floor health and social care classroom overlooking the performing arts block. Most of the staff looked bored; the ones on the side of the room in direct sunlight slowly fried and grumbled.

There was no sign of Anne. Alex needed the toilet but was determined to see her first. He checked his watch. The meeting was due to start in a few minutes. He didn't want to be stuck here on his afternoon off.

"Seen Anne?" he asked teacher after teacher, only getting head shakes.

Isaac Rose was looking out of the window and rolling a cigarette for later. "Anne is outside. Looks like she's just relaxing. Must have forgotten about the meeting."

Someone muttered "grass" under their breath. It may have been the ICT co-ordinator.

Isaac knocked on the window, made beckoning gestures, then shrugged.

Alex pressed his face against the glass to see down to the entrance. Anne had already disappeared. A barbecue and bar were being set up in a pavilion tent outside for after that evening's performance of Tom Stoppard's *Arcadia*. Elaine Marchant joked about going down to the bar for refreshment. The hospitality course co-ordinator suggested she do one of his courses. She said, "I only wanted to drink in a bar, not run one, pillock." The beauty therapist tutor threw a rolled-up ball of paper at the hospitality lecturer, which bounced off his shoulder and made him say "Ow!" on reflex before looking sheepish as the others jeered at him for being a wimp.

Anne would be here in a minute.

Alex sat on the edge of Elaine's desk. She was writing a shopping list. He spotted graffiti by his leg: "only users loose drugs". He pointed it out to Elaine. "Wit let down by spelling. Hardly the most pulchritudinous sentence."

"Ooh. That's a long word," Elaine replied. "Is it real?"

"Of course it's real. I made it up last night."

"You look bothered."

"Next year has got to be different. Things have got to change," said Alex.

"Staff meetings?"

"No. Everything. I vow to get an article published this summer. Then refer the grotty students to it next year."

Elaine patted his hand. "Good boy."

Outside they heard a clopping noise, like coconut shells being banged together. A student voice drifted in through the open window, surprisingly loud, saying, "I'm a lame horse!"

Isaac muttered, "Not very convincing."

"Since you're staying for this, are you coming for a drink with the others after work?" asked Elaine.

"Not going for a drink." Quieter: "I didn't get invited."

"Just an oversight."

"I never get invited. Not staying either, I just wanted to see Anne."

There was a long pause. Elaine looked thoughtful. "I spoke to Anne when she got back from her drink with you. People seem to like confiding in me. Maybe they think I'm their granny."

Alex groaned. "The kind that lives in a gingerbread house. What did she say?"

"Enough."

"I want to try and talk to her again."

Elaine pulled a face. "Oh no. You would just upset her. I love you to bits and you're usually okay with teenagers: not so good with adults."

"Thanks. I feel empowered. I love our little talks."

She just smiled her "humour me, I'm older than you" smile.

The college principal came in, the only member of staff who always wore a suit. "All right, all right, sit down you horrible lot," he said in a Yorkshire accent. He used to teach in a school.

Alex stared at the door, willing Anne to appear as everyone settled at their desks. The principal looked over at him. He might as well wait here as anywhere else in the college. Alex sat next to Elaine.

Just after they got started Anne came in, glanced around, scowled when she saw Alex, and sat at the front.

The third item on the agenda was presented by the young, earnest male librarian: a report on some new electronic resource. Those who made stifled yawns were glared at by the curriculum managers.

Alex crossed his legs tight, hands between them. The need to wee was excruciating. All those pints. He couldn't help but fidget, despite Elaine giving him a funny look.

At first he thought of it as a sacrifice for love, a noble challenge. If he held on for the full hour then love would conquer all.

The librarian just kept talking.

Alex could imagine what an expanded bladder looked like, stretched to bursting by volumes of liquid. At what point would you lose control?

"... and then they can get a password list from the library desk."

He'd finished, a miracle, like the parting of the waters. Maybe that was the end –

The next agenda item was training.

Oh piss, the pressure and wriggling was giving him an erection.

He checked his watch, there were another fifteen minutes to go. Time was dripping by. He couldn't hold it, he couldn't hold it ...

"Have you got something better t'be doing, eh, Kavanagh?" asked the Principal. He always used surnames.

"Erm, no ... I just, well ... Please can I go to the toilet?" Alex almost added "Sir". The principal was that kind of person.

"Just go, man. If you can't hold it in then at least don't hold us up."

All eyes were on his back as he left the room with controlled dignity; once out of their sight he broke the hallway code and ran to the toilets on the next floor, filled with images of sweet release.

The room was emptying when he got back. They'd finished early. Anne had given him the slip. Maybe she would be out at the car park? Or heading the other way to the staffroom?

He hesitated at a junction, looking down each rubber-floored corridor. Elaine beckoned to him. He didn't have time for her.

Or perhaps Anne was in the college's new canteen extension. Elaine waved again. He frowned, looked in each direction, then pushed past teachers to get to her.

"What? I need to search the college."

"There's no fire, Alex," she said with some amusement. "When I spoke to her she said she had some photocopying to do."

Alex smiled his thanks and nodded. "I owe you one, Granny Marchant."

Alex decided the stakes were high enough to justify one of his advanced psychological theories. He knew all women liked cats. People liked things that resembled themselves. Therefore applying some of the rules for interacting with cats to the reality of interacting with women could only help.

Most rules were straightforward:

Admire their grace.

Don't interrupt them when they're grooming.

Back off if they hiss.

Don't approach cats, let them come to you.

This needed to look natural.

He turned a corner in the college, deftly avoiding a group of Access Ed students who weren't looking where they were going, and snatched some handouts from the cluttered office he shared with the other part-time lecturers. They really did need photocopying for a science group. He rushed back to the small staff-only photocopier room.

Anne wasn't there yet.

"We meet again, my adversary," he declared in an awful eastern European accent.

The multi-function, high-performance dry electronic photocopier did not reply. It waited for Alex to make the first move, its huge sorting rack looming over him.

It had once been a pristine machine of extraordinary power, capable of sorting, stapling, enlarging and reducing. It could do full double-sided copying by combining the Reversible Automatic Document Feeder and the Automatic Duplexing Unit. Its copying speed was once as high as sixty copies per minute without jamming.

That was once. It was now one of only a few quirky relics left in action in the whole country, since almost every business apart from his college had leased more modern machines. It frequently broke down but stubbornly refused to die, staying around to torture generation after generation of lecturers like a tenacious and malicious old soldier, gobbing splats of ink.

"I need to copy. You will make it so." He started the job running with a few deft button presses. He was entering the co-ordinates for a class two space anomaly that needed investigating by his intrepid crew. Every key had to be entered correctly, or it would spell disaster.

A whirr. A hum. A frown-making bang. But it was off. Paper flowed smoothly at warp factor four. This boded well. The machine was tamed.

The door opened. Anne was frowning at him with an armful of paper. "Going to be long?"

"No. Nearly done." He grabbed his copies and moved aside. "Your hair's nice."

"Hmmph."

She hadn't hissed yet.

"Sorry about before, Anne."

"Whatever."

"You're still not happy, are you?"

She slammed her papers down on a table. "Do you have any idea of how angry I am?"

The machine started to make grinding noises. He spared it a glance then looked back at Anne. "Pretty angry?"

"Pretty damn fucking angry." She moved closer. "It's been brewing in my mind: where'd this come from? I knew it couldn't be another woman. That would require some sign of life from you. Then I realised – you never loved me. You just strung me along, wasting my time. I've never been anything to you apart from a habit." She glared a challenge at him.

"That's not true. More than a habit."

"That good, eh?"

"Yes!"

"I was being sarcastic."

"Oh." Thankfully the grinding eased down to a wheeze. Paper still flowed.

"It makes sense now. Like you living at home. I fucking hated that. There was no privacy if I visited you, like being a teenager. That's you all over."

"You're angry. Now's obviously not a good time to talk. I was thinking, maybe we could meet up later, talk then, clear the air. When you're calmer. Do you want to suggest a time?"

She looked shocked. "How about never? Is *never* good for you?"

Clunking from the copier, more grinding, it was difficult to ignore it.

"But remember the good times we had?"

"No. Funnily enough, I don't."

"Well *I* do. I thought you would want to patch this up?"

"Don't believe everything you think. That applies to lots of people, but particularly you. Grow up, Alex, it's over. You're an emotionally immature teenager trapped in a man's body. I bet you've still got Homer Simpson socks in your drawer."

"Bart."

"Right. Fuck off, Alex."

She stormed away without collecting her papers.

Alex stared at the door after she'd banged it.

"What the fuck?" he murmured. Then, louder. "What the fucking fuck? I was being nice!"

The photocopier had jammed. He tried to remove the paper and it tore, brittle with heat. He kicked the machine, opened its guts, and somehow got toner on his shirt cuffs.

Cogs had ground to a halt all right. Not just in the machine. Everywhere he looked things were shitty and smudged.

He punctuated the repairs with growled curses until the pathway was clear.

"Maybe she's right," he muttered.

He didn't carry on with the handout copying. Instead he put the back of his arm on the glass and did one more copy. It came out beautifully – a scan of his hand with two fingers extended in a V.

He stuck it in Anne's pigeonhole before leaving the college. It was almost 3pm. The afternoon was wasted.

Kelly was sat in front of the mirrored vanity unit she had owned since she was twelve. It had childish pink hearts on the side but she couldn't bring herself to get rid of it. She'd spent ages persuading her parents to buy it for her – it was a satisfying memory of a juvenile victory.

"I could get my ears pierced again when the exams are over. A reward for going to uni," she told Natalie, who was lying on Kelly's bed, flicking through a magazine and drawing moustaches on the women. "We could spend the afternoon in Affleck's Palace."

"You're not cool enough for Affleck's. But yeah, double piercings could suit you. I'd still be winning, I've got three in my left ear."

"I'm not competing with you."

"Copying then," Natalie said lazily.

"Don't be so big-headed. Any luck at the jobcentre?"

"Not really. I popped in to see Elinor though, mentioned where I'd been, she said I can do some part-time work at Gregg's for now."

"Urgh. You'll smell of hot greasy pasties and cheese."

"Whatever. At least I'll be earning."

Kelly paused from brushing her hair. "Maybe I'll get a job over the summer too."

"You? In the real world? Doubt it."

"It's no weirder than you going back to college. For – what? – the *third* time?"

Instead of answering, Natalie picked up a hair band, took aim, and pinged it off the back of Kelly's head.

"Ow! You bitch!" snapped Kelly.

"Calm down, it didn't hurt. Hey, your cheeks are all red."

"Are they?" Kelly examined herself in the mirror.

"Yeah. Looks like you've had an orgasm."

"Screw you."

"No-one else is."

"Don't expect me to get the violins out. At least you're usually the one doing the dumping."

"There's no point going out with someone if they're crap."

"Craig?"

"Too greasy. Too much gel."

"What about Sanjay?"

"Too young."

"Same age as you!"

"Too young."

"You act so mature, but you're only one year older than me."

"One year's all it takes."

"Shifty Shane?"

"Too dodgy. It was bad enough him dealing, taking risks, but he never had any money because he smoked as much as he sold. He wouldn't listen to me about taking a step back. Anyway, he got sent down."

"Really?"

"Yeah. Strangeways. I want a better boyfriend. Something that isn't just lust. Someone with no meanness in him."

Kelly grinned slyly. "In that case you should go after my brother. He sounds like what you're looking for. If you could put up with a boring older guy who hardly ever goes out and doesn't know how to have fun."

Natalie smiled, her eyebrows raised a fraction.

"Oh, that's gross!" said Kelly, and they both laughed.

"Is it gross because he's your brother, or because he's older?"

"Both! Imagine if you married him, when you were thirty he'd be nearly forty, a wrinkly old man! But then again, it would be great to have you as a sister-in-law."

"Right. As if I'd want to join your family of freckle-faced freaks. The only good thing about you is that the carpet matches the curtains."

They paused, then both burst out laughing again, before Natalie rolled onto her back and grinned up at the ceiling.

The first bus hadn't turned up so he'd had to stand with college kids for ages, simmering; then at Stretford he got caught in the even more irritating school run. He hunched into his seat as school kids shouted, banged on dirty windows, or threw balls of paper.

Alex got off at Davyhulme Circle. He didn't thank the driver.

The other teachers didn't want him at their after-work drink? Fuck them.

He had other places to go, places that were more fun than a pub, places that welcomed him, where there was peace instead of inane jabbering.

He walked with his head down to keep the sun from his eyes, and was vaguely aware of passing two people sitting on a low wall. Alex was still trying to calm his anger with deep breaths when the wall-sitters began to follow him. He heard an ominous shuffle-drag.

"Backpack boy," said a sarcastically pitched voice.

"Mummy's boy, home boy," echoed another.

He walked quicker but they followed. The gobshites had been eating crap from the nearby takeaway. He should have looked ahead and seen the danger. It was too late to adopt Primary Tactic 1, as he usually did when faced with a threat: sneak off before the threat saw him.

At least it only seemed to be two of them, Floppy Feet and Tram Line Boy.

He tried to outpace them, looking nonchalant. Floppy Feet was forced to shuffle faster, but managed to keep up.

It was ridiculous. He felt trapped at some younger age. Fourteen maybe, suffering the nickname "ginger egg head" as he walked home at the end of each school day.

"Go-ing home to Mu-mmy?" one of them lilted in up and down notes.

His privacy had been violated! How did the kids know? Then his stomach sank: they probably didn't even realise they were right.

He took a detour down Old Crofts Bank, power walking towards the place of safety that was better than any pub, then rushing through the door next to the mirror-like wall of glass. It worked. They didn't follow him in. He got his breath back.

"Hi Alex, the science books you wanted came in," said the librarian as he approached the cluttered desk and left behind the outer noise of traffic, accepted into this calm refuge. This was *his* domain. Urmston Library had more staff and books than this small Davyhulme branch, but he preferred the quiet here. Even the after-school homework club hardly ever impinged on his reflections.

"Thanks, Yvonne. Is *New Scientist* in?"

"Not yet. How's the article going?"

"Getting there. I'll do some ref-checking at Manchester Central tomorrow."

After borrowing his books he had an idea, snatched the *Manchester Evening News* from the newspaper rack then found an empty table and rustled through the crinkly pages. Straight to the Properties For Sale section.

When he'd dropped out of the PhD it had been simple: live at home. Save money. But he was still there. Why'd he done nothing about this before? That was obvious too. It was easier to leave things as they were. He didn't want to be lonely.

After skimming the pages with diminishing enthusiasm he soon gave up, since the cheapest houses that looked inhabitable were over £62,000.

He tried the Properties To Rent section instead, but a quick calculation showed that most of his part-time salary would disappear. The ones he could easily afford to rent were in places like Moss Side and Hulme. And he didn't want to work more hours.

Even viewing places seemed like it would be a sequence of stressful events. How would he get to them? Who would he view them with? It was all too complicated.

Bugger.

And his fingers were smudged with newsprint.

Home at last, drifting in his own thoughts, Alex only reconnected with the world as he floated into a conversation in the kitchen between his mother and sister.

"... a bit inappropriate. Have a subtle word with her, Kelly. Baggy tops are okay but not so revealing and not so much bare leg."

"Okay, okay. Oh look, Professor Bore. Hey, Alex, did you break any cups?" asked Kelly.

"What are you on about? What bare leg?"

"Forget bare legs," said Alex's mum. "Did you break any crockery last night? You're not in trouble, I'm just trying to work out who chipped two cups."

"Not me."

"Funny how things in this house seem to break so often," muttered his mum as she turned back to the cupboards.

"Funny how me and Natalie always get the blame," said Kelly.

"Funny how I don't know what you two are on about half the time," finished Alex. "Have you eaten already, Mum?"

"Yes. Chips from Charlie's."

"Typical." Alex would have to fall back on one of his five recipes. He fancied number four: cheese on toast. He took a clean knife from the draining rack then started rooting through the fridge to see if there was any Cheddar left.

"Mum, can I borrow some money to go ice skating with Natalie?" Kelly wheedled. "I did pretty well in my practical, so …"

"Sorry, love. We used my notes at the chippy and there's only a bit of change left. I'm not going out again today just to drive to a cash machine. You should have asked before."

"I didn't know we'd be going out *then*." She turned to Alex with a sigh. "What about you? Could you lend me some cash?"

"Lend? How will you pay me back?"

"Could I have it then, and I'll pay you back with sisterly affection?"

He ignored her as he finished slicing cheese, neatly cut and ready for once he'd changed his clothes.

"I'll do your share of the dishes for a week."

It was tempting. He hated washing up. It seemed silly for a twenty-eight-year-old to do household chores for his mother. Still, he didn't want to encourage her. He shook his head. "Revise instead."

"That's all I do!" yelled Kelly, storming out.

Exceptional heat, even for June. Alex decided he'd eat tea in the garden on the old bench. A mature apple tree shaded it from the worst waves of heat.

He was glad to get his shirt off but dismayed to see how grimy the collar was. Into the wicker wash basket on the landing. Putting a clean T-shirt on, and swapping his trousers for a pair of shorts, made him feel better. By the time he slipped on some spotless white socks and his sandals he'd finally discarded the events of earlier along with the old clothes.

He was grilling the cheese, watching it melt and brown, empathising with it in this stifling summer heat when he heard giggling from behind. When he'd returned to the kitchen Kelly was there, past exam papers spread over the wide pine table while their mum washed up.

"Hey, Mum, we should have got chicken legs from Charlie's."

Brief laughter from his mum. "Chicken legs are thicker."

That set Kelly off even more.

Alex wished the grill would hurry up. "Just revise," he said without turning round. "As the resident mong you need to do lots of that."

"Alex, don't call your sister that!" snapped his mum.

"I can't revise with your legs shining at me like that," said Kelly smugly. "They're distracting. Worse than white, like tinfoil reflecting the sun."

"You're just jealous because my legs are thinner than yours."

"I'd rather have a fat arse than *those*," she replied, her voice rising.

"Well congratulations, because you *have!*" Alex jabbed the grill pan handle towards her empty bowl. "Too much ice cream. Don't you want to be slim? So you don't look like an elephant next to Natalie?"

Her chair scraped back. "Why are you always mean?" she demanded, almost shaking with anger. "You're fucking horrible to me!"

He was ready to relent when he noticed she was crying. "Sorry, I didn't –"

"Fuck off! You did! You're a horrible brother." She ran up the stairs and slammed her door. A few seconds later there was loud music from her room, heavy bass.

A slow clap from his mum. "Oh, well done, Alex," she said sarcastically.

"Well, *she* started it."

"Can't you learn to take a joke? How old are you anyway? For fuck's sake, I can't put up with you two going at each other all the time. It's getting worse and it's doing my head in."

"Sorry."

"Don't just *say* it, do something about it. It won't kill you to be nice to her. She's all stressed, the exams are important."

His mum left the room and went upstairs without waiting for a response.

"I'm stressed too," he mumbled, snatching his burnt food from the grill.

Unpacking his bag, spreading things out on the desk in his bedroom, Alex came across the Zip disk.

Hot proton *shit*.

He'd meant to download physics datasets while at college; on the 56K dial-up connection at home things took forever to download.

He enjoyed running the datasets through equation software or spreadsheets on his Pentium II PC. Watching numbers crunch and evolve was almost as mesmerising as the Windows 98 disk defragmenter. Apart from lesson plans and Minesweeper he didn't use the PC for much else.

Chaos. His *life* was fragmenting.

Alex tidied his bedroom impatiently until a semblance of order was restored. Then he lay on his bed and emptied a folder of newsletter printouts – the Brookhaven Bulletin. It was another thing he did in the college, downloading and printing PDFs or documents from Usenet sites like sci.chaos and alt.sci.physics.

Research for the new article. That would fill the evening. A summary of major particle physics experiments. He had a good feeling about this one: it might be his breakthrough piece.

The Brookhaven Laboratory was on Long Island, New York. They did all kinds of research but it was their grand-sounding

Accelerator Division that interested him most. They were the ones in charge of the Relativistic Heavy Ion Collider, or RHIC to its friends. Alex usually read every piece in the Bulletin, enjoying the quirky mix of hard science and Valentine's messages; updates on projects alongside those on the Ballroom Dance and Classic Motoring Clubs. It reassured him that some physicists had exciting lives outside of work.

And it *was* an exciting time. The laboratory had installed the 3,000 ton PHENIX detector. He wished he could experience the wonders it would measure.

Dense ions of gold fired into a two and a half mile track of criss-crossing rings and accelerated up to almost the speed of light, a micro-glitter of ions kept in a tight beam of particles by over 1,700 huge superconducting magnets. The mind spun at the thought of them coursing the track a hundred thousand times every single second, incomprehensible velocity, driven to such speed that when they collided at intersections they would shatter: an explosion of worlds in blinding light, generating temperatures hotter than the core of the sun for a micro-second and fragmenting into thousands of molten particles within a swirling plasma soup resembling those first seconds after the universe was born,

(why did all this make him think of cremation?)

the height of technology birthing the first existence, and finally viewing the great mysteries, those alien subatomic particles such as quarks and gluons. All measured by massive detectors like PHENIX. Beauty could rise from those ashes.

He opened his eyes, letting the majesty of the particle trickle away.

The controversy filled its place. Some scientists had said the experiments were dangerous because they could lead to the creation of new types of "strange matter" with unforeseen effects. Maybe even the end of the world if a black hole opened on Earth. One of the photocopies in the pile was an article from the *Sunday Times* the previous July, where the potential dangers had first been made public and launched the debate. Knowing the recent problems at the RHIC – faulty power leads, obstructions in the particle chambers, overheating, misaligned magnets – it meant anything could happen.

The first collisions would start later that evening.

As he skimmed facts and figures something nagged at his mind. Reiterating patterns. A repetition of numbers.

It was inevitable, he told himself; silly even. Whenever there were lots of numbers then some would recur.

He pulled over a notepad and started scribbling.

The RHIC track was 3,834 metres long. The sum of that was 18. It was also divisible by 18.

The *Sunday Times* article had been on the 18th July.

The focussed beam of gold ions would travel at almost the speed of light, c. 180,000 miles a second. He wrote it out at 18×10^4.

The RHIC had six interaction points, six straight sections, and particle injection at the six o'clock position. 18.

The experiments would start that night at 9pm Brookhaven time. It was the 12th June. Twelfth day, sixth month. 18.

One of the undiscovered elements these experiments hoped to find was element 117. 11+7 or 1+17 both equalled 18.

It was meaningless.

He looked for other numbers. 72 stood out. The experiments could reach temperatures of up to 7.2 trillion Kelvins, the temperature at the birth of the universe.

Even the RHIC's location on the globe was 72 degrees west.

Alex scribbled out other examples of 18 and 72.

It was very, very silly. He should stop.

But his mind was dense with ideas, and high-mass processes couldn't stop instantaneously.

Instead he pulled reference books from his shelves, almanacs and encyclopaedias. Flicked from index to referent and back again.

18 and 72 seemed special for mathematical reasons. 18 equalled twice the sum of its digits, which applied to no other number. 72 was the sum of two sets of consecutive primes.

Delving deeper, 18 was associated with life. The coming of age in many cultures. In fact, the Hebrew word for life had a numerical value of 18.

72 also tied into cycles of life. The Earth's axis moved one degree every 72 years when viewed against the endless stars. The life duration of a sperm in the uterus was 72 hours. 72 was also his birth year.

He laughed. "Useless numerology crap." Pen tossed aside.

He rolled onto his back, forearm over his eyes to block the glaring bulb, a micro-sun of filament heat.

The heat of the day. One long, sweltering, sticky mess.

Anne's face. She glared at him, dark looks matching hair. He changed her expression to a smile. Almond eyes and parted lips. That was better.

She licked her lips.

His free hand slid under the elastic waistband of his shorts.

Anne when they first kissed, eager with her tongue, dominating his mouth, making him hard from the tiniest touch.

And he was. So hard.

Just a finger and thumb, an O like an open mouth, the tiniest eager friction of an enclosed space.

Making love to Anne that same night. Clumsy and too quick but eager, yes, eager, both, tongues and hands and rubbing legs.

He pulled his shorts down, shrugging them from his hips, one side then the other, eyes still covered in dark arm shadow, freeing the end, hand enclosing, hard grip, not too quick but eager, yes, eager.

Anne's face when she wanted him, but then a lubricated slide as it altered, merged, another face, a strong face with blonde hair, a face that jabbed his chest with pain even though he made it look like love, he wanted to see the face and love both, gliding into his mind from the dark-shadowed past and eager, so eager, he wanked harder for her, sweltering resistance building up for a sticky mess, it was her, *her*, and when –

A knock, rapid; a door, opening; he pulled up his shorts and stared, blinking spots from sudden brightness, pulling up his legs to hide the erection; the blur resolved to Kelly stood staring.

"Does no-one fucking knock then *wait* for an invitation any more?" he yelled at her surprised face. "It's my fucking room!"

She threw a letter at him, it landed amongst all the other bits of crumpled paper on the bed.

"I'm sorry … This came today and I forgot to give it to you … It's from a magazine or something … Sorry," she repeated as she closed the door behind her.

He punched the bed with his fist, papers bounced and slid to the floor like crumpled tissues, and even when he'd stopped thumping, his jaw stayed clenched.

Alex's wallet was by the bed. Velcro rip revealed some notes. Things hastily thrown into a rucksack. Long trousers put on. He caught Kelly on the stairs, shoved the crumpled paper into her hand.

"Here, go ice skating or whatever." He ignored her surprised thanks and rushed past her, heading down.

His mum was in the living room with her feet up on a foot rest.

"Mum, will you tape *Weird Science*? It's on tonight."

"Where are you going?"

"Out."

"You never go out at night."

"Are you saying I have no friends?" he asked, too loudly. "How do you know I'm not meeting some right now? For all you know that's *exactly* what I'm doing. I have lots."

He slipped the rucksack on, too fraught to pretend he was putting on a Ghostbusters Proton Pack. When the door slammed behind him he grimaced at the realisation that he was "doing a Kelly".

Alex walked up and down the road twice, glancing over the grass field until he was sure that it was deserted. He'd guessed correctly: at 7.45pm in the summer it was too late for parents to still be entertaining their little darlings, yet the teenagers wouldn't descend on the place with bottles of cider until it went dark in a couple of hours.

He jumped the fence and made his way through the playground to the climbing frame. It was orange pipework in the shape of a tilted rocket leading up to a large red nose cone you could sit inside.

He turned, walked backwards, scanned the field to make sure it was still clear, and almost tripped over the see-saw, arms flailing for balance. He remained upright and the park was safe. He scrambled up the rocket, easy and familiar movements, metal still hot from the day-long heat-sear.

He had to scrunch up to fit into the cone but it was cosy rather than unbearably cramped. The open circles of viewports gave an early-warning view in every direction, and he could dangle his legs from the trapdoor if he wanted.

He didn't need to stay here all evening. Just long enough to make sure Kelly and Natalie had gone out.

He removed the letter from his backpack. It had the logo of *The Physics Teacher* so must be a reply to his proposed article on the safe use of fireworks in teaching about explosives (his other pending article about demonstrating gravity using an OHP was for *Physics Education*).

It wasn't heavy, considering how much hope he had in it. He opened it reverently, sliding the watermarked sheets – *oh, just one sheet?* – out, then unfolding carefully.

Dear Mr Kavanagh,

Thank you for your submission for our consideration

but then the dreaded words seemed to leap of the page at him. The "but" and the "regret", standing out from the polite formalities as if marked in red. He crumpled it up and leaned back, banged his head against the hard metal a few times, a hollow echo.

Rejected. Again.

Would it have been different if he'd been *Dr* Kavanagh? If he'd stayed on to finish his PhD and followed it up with a few supervisor-backed dissemination articles?

He knew the answer to that.

Mr Kavanagh.

He was going nowhere, success was retrograde, negative, minus, T-minus even. That's how he could go somewhere! Bolts blown. Auxiliary Power Units running at 72,000 rpm. Propellant ignited, aluminium burning silver fire down the length of the rocket and kindling the solid fuel in a fraction of a second – Alex waved goodbye as the ground launch stage was over and he left for the endless stars. He could glance out of the porthole, watching the Earth recede, the glittering solar fires of space becoming clearer as he sailed into darkness.

Unfortunately the climbing frame remained cemented to the dog-shitty ground. He saw litter speckling the field and park, polystyrene and paper constellations with names like KFC and McDonalds, while wrappers from Mars Bars and Milky Ways and Galaxys rolled in the hot breeze.

He knew that even if he had launched into a trajectory around Earth it would be no escape from people. Millions of pieces of man-made rubbish floated up there, orbiting litter from broken and smashed shuttles and satellites, bits of solid rockets, nuclear coolant leakage. So much for physics. In every way.

Because we're chained to matter, we're chained to laws. Linearity. Cause and effect. Time. Sunlight takes eight minutes to reach us. It takes light more than four years to reach us from the next nearest star, Proxima Centauri. We don't see things as they are now, we see them as they were. We live in the past. And we're stuck there.

"I've lost my sparkle," said Alex.

He wouldn't cry though. He never cried any more. Even after a burning day tears stayed cryogenically frozen, always.

Kelly skated over and braked sharply in a scrape of ice. Natalie had been taking a break from fast laps weaving in and out of bodies. After the action it was fun to watch people – skating newcomers falling over, or recognizable by the damp patches on their bottoms; experienced skaters gliding effortlessly; lovers supporting each other as they learnt a new skill together. Half her attention right now was on a young man who was practising doing cherry flips and managing to dig his toe in, jump and spin without falling. Natalie had tried it a few times, and always landed on her arse. She had vowed to only attempt it again when the ice rink was man-free.

Music played and echoed around the massive room. She held the rail behind her and dug the point of her blade into the ice, chipping small pieces out.

"Just heard some news from Jemaine. Quality gossip," said Kelly, leaning against the bar and readjusting her scarf which always seemed to expand to cover her mouth.

"Yeah?"

"It's about Lissa Pilton. She's pregnant, the slag."

"Shit! I bet she doesn't even know who the daddy is!" Natalie turned her back to the rink and slid her feet back and forth. "Check this: a smart guy plus a smart woman equals romance. But a thick guy and a thick woman equals pregnancy. Or something. I'm glad we came out. Lucky break, your brother giving you money. You need to let off steam when you revise. You bottle it up too much."

Kelly checked that no-one was near enough to overhear. "Talking of … I think Alex was having a shady one before."

"Give over!"

"I think he does it when he wants to cheer himself up. It was gross."

"Nah. Everyone does it."

"I hope you don't do it in our house?"

"No. I do it on the bus. What do you think? I do it in the shower sometimes. With the high pressure water jet. Makes the room all jungle-steamy."

"Too much information, freak."

"Come on, Kel. I bet you tickle it too."

"Only when I'm stressed."

"So that's once a day? Ha, I can tell from your eyes! At last, a smile from that pretty face!"

"I'm not pretty compared to you."

"We're all different. Hey, forgot to tell you, Alex saw me in the shower this morning, maybe that was what he was wanking over. You think?"

"I think you're sick. That'd be gross too. He's horrible all the time. He has been ever since he left uni."

"You've got to respect him though, he always seems to be writing stuff, posting things, planning lessons, going to the library. A real brain."

Kelly stifled a snort.

"He is, isn't he?" Natalie insisted. "Didn't he go to university for years?"

"I suppose. He were always a brainy bod really. He did some degrees. I think he was a mature student – that's a laugh – doing his PhD thing. Always old in the head. Mum says he's 'twenty-eight going on forty-eight'. And she's right."

"If he did a PhD doesn't that make him a professor or something?"

"He dropped out. I think it was to do with the bitch he was going out with. So he never became the family's first doctor. Dr Kavanagh would have been too weird."

"I bet you wish you were as smart as him."

"No! He's more like the guy in *Rain Man*, the one that can do huge sums but can't talk to normals!"

"He can talk."

Kelly sniffed. "Yeah. Fucking Dustin Hoffman. Alex is a walking coma."

"He just needs cheering up."

Natalie had been half watching a group of girls who'd skated past a few times, the one at the front wearing make-up and glittery tights with a red skirt, her own skates, long blonde hair in a plait. They were aiming to get attention, seeing themselves as queens of the ice. The girl sneered at Natalie and Kelly as she approached.

"Do you know her?" Natalie asked. "She keeps looking at you,"

"I know her, she was always tight to me. Called me names." Kelly frowned, obviously remembering something unpleasant.

"What like?"

"It doesn't matter."

"Posh arrogant bitch," Natalie muttered, glaring at the skaters. The group were all slim and attractive. She could imagine what names they'd called Kelly. They were lording it up like they owned the place.

"Leave it," said Kelly.

"Don't worry about them, they're nothing, Kel." Natalie waited until they neared again then pretended to launch herself towards the lead girl who'd been staring her out. Natalie kept hold of the bar and swung back round but it was enough to fluster Blondie who lost her stride and almost fell. Natalie held up her middle finger and laughed at Blondie's discomfort.

"You're mad," said Kelly, laughing too.

"I know. But I stick by my friends."

When a gap opened up Kelly kicked away with a shake of the head and a grin, sliding unsteadily off but then gaining balance and moving smoothly over the ice.

Cherry Flip Man was gone. Natalie pushed on the bar and followed Kelly.

Making minimal sound, key turning slowly in the lock, Alex entered the house. No lights on, no sound of conversation. The house was asleep.

No teenagers had invaded the park tonight, so he stayed there and read a book he'd thrown into his bag: H.G. Wells' *The Time Machine*. He'd lost himself in mechanical brass and ivory devices until he realised that his limbs were cramped and he was reading by orange street light. By then he'd definitely remained long enough to make it seem plausible that he'd been *socialising*.

He removed his shoes then carefully navigated up the stairs, avoiding the creaking centres, a Morlock feeling his way along the banister until he reached his room.

With the door closed he could put the lamp on. It was 12.32am. He dumped the bag on the floor. He was grubby. He felt as though he had cold grease on the back of his neck. Sticky armpits.

He stripped off, took his towel from the radiator and fastened it round his waist. He'd sleep better after a long shower; would shave too. Tomorrow he could get up early and leave the house straight away without seeing anyone. Spend his free day doing something which had no connection to Kelly, his mum, Anne, the college, or fucking FE students.

The water was purifying, washing surface grime away. He fumbled amongst all the shower gel, shampoo and conditioner bottles collected by the household but got the wrong one. It was his dad's Grecian 2000 lotion, used when he was home from the rig. Worried about grey hair. Was that the future for Alex too?

Alex looked through the shower door, catching multiple reflections of himself in mirrors. It unnerved him. When his parents had designed the house they incorporated a few features that were different or mysterious, such as the secret panel in the hall where important paperwork was kept. However, their pride was this bathroom, which seemed much larger on the inside than you would expect from the outside, an illusion created with tricks like a raised ceiling, large frosted windows, walls that encroached on nearby rooms, and lots of mirrors. *Lots.* They extended the room into multiple dimensions. Dad always called the bathroom "The Tardis Room".

It just made Alex feel small.

He turned his back on the disturbing sight of lots of naked Alexes, faced the tiled wall, scrubbed himself. From the edge of his vision he saw steam filling the room, sneaking and unreal, diffusing the light until he was enveloped in fog. The shower had transported him to no man's land. A wet Tardis with no controls.

The cubicle suddenly felt claustrophobic. He needed something positive to counteract the angry surges he kept feeling in his body, an electric eel in his gut that was getting more and more frantic ... The RHIC! The first collisions had been due at 9pm in Brookhaven. They were four hours behind, so would only start at 1am his time. A miracle of technology that could end us all with the beginning, a hope for answers fuelled by precision. The scientists there would be running safety checks, warming up machines, excited at the prospect of launching things in two directions to collide and see what happened, a child's train track set on self-destruct in an explosive particle pile-up that could make new matter.

He should be there, not here. He had the wrong life. He'd been swapped at birth.

He grabbed some Body Shop shower gel, not caring whose it was, and rubbed it in briskly. Angrily. He didn't even stop for a stroke between the legs. He tried to calm himself. He wished he could go back in time and do things differently.

Beams on a track, converging, and he wanted to shout "Fuck!" but gritted his teeth to keep it in.

Being dead had to be better than this.

He kicked the shower door, not hard enough to damage it. Frustration and heat, all focussed, running haywire through his body along nerves, synaptic pathways, arteries, all unstoppable once committed, criss-crossing speed of light; he pushed on his eyes until he saw spots, a micro glitter of ions and fears followed the tracks, particle-fast, fears of the unknown despite reassurances, courses that can't be stopped once set in motion, can't be changed, inevitable and foregone conclusions with no deviation, no way to break free, mind spinning – he panicked, thumbed the cold button and was drenched, so cold, he could take it, "Uh uh huh" he repeated, gasping and unable to catch his breath, the cold water only 18 degrees but dropping his body from 36 rapidly, sympathetically, bodies being 72 per cent water anyway, amazing and beautifully constructed things, and as temperature fell his heart rate rose from 72 bpm, soaring up towards 180 bpm as he stayed for a minute, two, teeth chattering and brain ice-cream-frozen so it couldn't think any more, molecules slowing into crystalline structures like brass cogs freezing, halting, dizzying ice pain from above bringing faintness, *the coldness of death, an explosion behind his eyes as time folded in and ... and ... whiteness –*

Broken Parities

"Parity. Equality. Finding a balance. In the Big Bang there were equal amounts of matter and antimatter, though now the universe is dominated by matter – why? Can a left-handed person become right-handed, positive change to negative, co-ordinates invert? If so the Law of Parity (or symmetry) has been broken. Maybe that's what happened in the Relativistic Heavy Ion Collider experiment that created a bubble in the Quark Soup. (See the appendix for my Quark Soup recipe – best use of sweetcorn ever). Breaking the balance is a big thing. Restoring it is just as big."

Mid-June. Tuesday to Friday.

Fluttering pigeons took off in a scatter of feathers as Jane stepped away from the coach. The sun stung her eyes and she had to blink it away, turn, see the bustling, living crowds through the remaining flashbulb aura of the star's brightness. She smiled at them, stood and watched for minutes as people brushed past, recovering from her sleep and the remains of a travel headache. Despite it being the terminus she was the only person who'd got off this bus. The driver gave her a wave and pointed upwards at the number on the display above him, made up of red dots: 72. She nodded and waved back then covered her mouth with a hand as she yawned. She felt like she'd slept a long time. Buses did that, with their soporific rumblings and warmth, window scenes repeated like sheep jumping a fence until your eyes closed in relief.

The crowded station was covered in signs and noticeboards, yet she wasn't sure which direction to go in. It didn't matter for now. There was no immediate hurry. She could just take it in, enjoy this experience, let the post-sleep confusion dissipate like mist.

She picked up her only bag and made her way past rows of buses and concrete pillars, tannoy announcements echoing behind, and finally stepped through automatic sliding doors into the real world. She had to cover her eyes and squint as she adjusted, everything seemed washed out and unreal, concrete almost white, glaring reflections from glass, cars backed up along the road. A sign said Chorlton Street. Steel stick men climbed the side of a building opposite, sculptural folly that made her smile.

There weren't many trees in sight; the only visible ones seemed to line a car park to her right. She would have liked her first view of the place to include more of them. Grass, flowers, butterflies. Never mind. She was still excited to be in a new place. Confident. As she looked up and down the road she felt that anything could happen. She was not the same; not that Jane who'd lived in London. She could remake herself for a few days. The sun burnt down, endless flame. She shaded her eyes and squinted up. Everything has two sides. Fire cremates, but it also supports life. Without it there would be no phoenix.

She turned right and began walking. After a while she looked behind, noting the location of the National Express coach station. It would be easy to find again, since it was at the base of a multi-storey car park that dominated the block. She would be back.

She wandered almost at random, zigzagging streets, following a canal for a bit, stopping to admire the towering red brick buildings that channelled her along, manufacturing heritage trailing along the water. Some were over eight storeys tall, solid behemoths that would outlast whatever food outlet had set up shop on the ground.

Looking up always changes things. Here it revealed all the details on the old buildings: secret towers, spires, turrets. They were castles in the city. Rewards for those that saw beyond their shuffling footsteps. This was a city made for looking up, she thought.

She realised she didn't have a camera with her and would have to commit the sights to memory alone. As she stepped from the shade of one old warehouse she noticed a tall industrial chimney peeping shyly over the top; something hidden but wanting to be discovered, acknowledged. That made her smile too.

This short escape was precious. An escape from someone else's shadow.

"That is fantastic, I'm so proud of you!" said Mrs Spiers. She leaned over the coffee cups and empty plates to kiss her daughter's cheek; then tutted and used her napkin to remove a smudge of lipstick she'd left on Lucy's face.

"Thanks, Mummy," Lucy replied. "And it's not just the promotion and perks – my salary increases too. So this lunch is my treat. For all three of us." Lucy smiled at Jane; Jane immediately felt her hackles rise, but Lucy's patronising tone was so subtle there was no way of drawing attention to it without seeming paranoid.

"I'm pleased for you," Jane answered, letting her voice merge into the lunchtime murmur of the cafe.

"You don't sound it," said her mother curtly. "You could show more enthusiasm for your sister's success. And even let some of it rub off on you. I mean, being a nurse – I agree with the sentiments of course – but one would think you might be working beyond that by now, maybe become a doctor?"

"It doesn't work like that."

"You could have done the same as Lucy, studied business, have something to fall back on. You know my friends would have helped you afterwards."

"I'm not Lucy."

Her mother just huffed and turned her attention back to Lucy. Jane stirred the coffee, though the sugar had long since dissolved, and stared at the comforting brownness. They were sitting inside Café Rouge by the window looking onto the busy little square outside. It was Mrs Spiers' favourite cafe, tucked away from the noise of the main road. Jane's enjoyment of the food was spoilt by Lucy paying for it. Lucy the Golden Girl.

It was easy to understand why Jane had been sidelined. Lucy and Mummy both liked to dress in the same expensive clothes; go to the same places; mix with the same people; talk about the same subjects. They could never understand that it bored Jane stiff. Even now they talked about Mummy's new hairstyle, a French twist updo, something that Lucy had spotted and praised straight away.

"I'm going to the National Portrait Gallery next week," interrupted Jane.

"Sorry – what?" asked her mother with vague irritation.

"It's strange that I've never been. That you never took us. Yet it's so close. I'm going with Claire."

"Ah yes, I remember when she visited. Not very smart, is she?"

"You mean you thought she was common," snapped Jane with a flash of anger.

"Well, she did get dinner and lunch mixed up, didn't she?"

69

Jane stood. "I'm going to the loo." She saw Lucy and her mother glance at each other conspiratorially.

The things she wanted to talk about never seemed to count.

The memory needled away her good feeling. She needed a drink. The canal had led her to a choice of pubs, as if looking out for her, a guardian in a strange city. She chose the pub on the left, passing through an impressive orange-tiled entrance. Real sun and Mediterranean colours were swapped for coolness, light for dark.

She'd picked this one because it had a funny name and flower baskets hanging outside. No better reasons were needed.

He was fuzzy-headed, face squashed into a pillow. Eyes gritty. After-trace of a dream. Noises in the house, footsteps and muffled voices. It was light. He'd overslept.

Alex stumbled out of bed but couldn't face doing any exercises, so he got dressed, opened his door, and listened. Kelly and his mum were talking, then the front door clicked closed. He rushed to the landing window and looked out to see Kelly walking up the path. Safe. The morning was cool and calm, but the clear blue skies would soon burn down again. He descended the stairs to get breakfast.

His mum made a comment about it being "all right for some" when you could stay in bed for part of the morning. He grumbled about still being tired. She said he should appreciate how lucky he was. He told her that recently he'd had no luck at all.

"Rubbish. If you fell in the canal you'd come out with a fish in your pocket," she replied.

"It'd be diseased. Half piscine, half bicycle. I'd catch crabs from it." He splashed milk on his Ricicles. She left him alone.

He decided he would still go into the city centre. He could live it up on his Tuesday off: treat himself to some new stationery then visit the central city library. The thought of being alone *all* day depressed him though. He wanted to get things off his chest, speak to someone who didn't live in the same house.

He looked through the shared address book by the phone in the hall. Very few of the numbers were in his handwriting. Of those, many hadn't been used in years. Faded friends. He didn't feel like calling any of them.

A connection fell into place. Work; city centre; Aytoun Business Library.

He flicked through the Yellow Pages, found the number for that library.

"Can I speak to Suzannah Smith please?" he asked.

"One second." A crackle, then a different voice. "Hello?"

"Hi Suzannah."

"Who's that?"

He gripped the receiver tightly, resisted the urge to bang it on the wall. "Alex!"

"Oh, hello." She sounded surprised to hear from him.

"I'm in town today. Will you come for a drink with me at dinner time?"

"Oh, I don't know about that, Alex. I don't really like to drink during the day."

He said "Fine" and exhaled heavily through his nose. He was about to hang up when she changed her mind and agreed to meet him. He smiled. Arranged a time. Hung up. Decided he was good on the phone after all.

Into the living room. "Mum, can I have a lift to Stretford please? I want to catch the Metro."

"No."

"Why not?"

"Don't whine. I'm not taking the car out there twice. I've got to drive up there later for my cleaning." She went back to sorting through the mess of magazines on the coffee table. "And I wish someone else in the house would learn to drive," she grumbled. "What are you going there for, anyway? Library?"

"I'm meeting a friend," he said, emphasising the last word and hoping she'd be impressed.

"Who?"

"Just a friend."

"Who, though?"

"Suzannah," he mumbled, defeated.

"Cousins aren't friends. Why don't you hang around with people who aren't related?"

He slammed the door as he left.

Charles Street, by the canal, in the Lass. Alex liked this pub. The signs outside said "The World Famous Lass O' Gowrie Manchester's Original Brew House"; "Fine ales brewed on the premises"; and "Here was the site of Manchester's oldest pissotière. Last used AD 1896." Any place that made a combined virtue of function, history, and biological necessity, could not be all bad.

Inside there were wooden floors and irregular spaces, separated by raised platforms, bare brick walls, or low wooden barriers. Knick-knacks and books on shelves, walls plastered with pictures. Bar crowned with taps honouring different breweries, holy symbols calling the faithful.

"We all have days like that," Suzannah told him, cutting off his list of recent problems. She cradled a glass of lemonade in her hands as they stood by a wooden ledge. He'd tried to persuade her to have something alcoholic but she had seemed horrified by the idea.

"I know. Sorry to be a bore."

"I didn't mean it that way, Alex."

She had seemed worn-out though, ever since arriving. A charity case, maybe that's how she thought of him. Maybe all his cousins thought that way.

She was wearing some kind of pink rectangular shawl which folded over her shoulder and around her neck, like a wide, soft scarf. She kept readjusting it. A form of fidgeting.

"Do you want another drink?" he asked. "My turn this time."

"No, just the one." A false laugh. A fidget. She looked around the room.

He decided not to have one either. It was too reminiscent of yesterday.

"I am boring you, aren't I?" he blurted out. "We're related, you can be honest with me."

"I already said I *wasn't* bored. You get some funny ideas, Alex. It's just because I need to get back to work soon. Why don't you come out with me and Dave later on? He said he was going to take me out for a drink, I know he wouldn't mind if you came too. I'm sure you two could get on a bit better."

Alex almost laughed at that. He remembered the last time Dave had been to his house with Suzannah. His name was Dave Chambers but Alex always thought of him as The Football Hooligan. They certainly weren't going to be best friends.

"So there he was, in the bog – that was after he'd had six pints – and he was looking around, as you do, and turned to Tommy Nuttles and said, 'Twin streams?'"

The Football Hooligan prattled on with his tale about the local bogyman. Why did Suzannah have to go out with someone like this? As Alex's cousin she should have more refined tastes. And she shouldn't leave Dave and Alex together while she had a natter with his mum and sister. Just because they were both men didn't mean they had anything in common.

Dave was leaning back against the door frame, arms folded in a way that seemed calculated to show off his biceps. Alex hated that too.

"So Tommy said, 'I'm in a hurry'. Classic! Then he added: 'And stop looking at my fucking cock.'"

Alex gave a weak smile, since The Football Hooligan seemed to expect it at that point. It was like patting a dog on the head to encourage it. In this case a squash-nosed bulldog. Alex wished he would hurry up and finish the tale so he could make an excuse to go up to his room and read.

"He mustn't have realised who Tommy was, or he'd never have looked down at his cock again. Shit, the poor bloke was asking for it."

"What do you mean, 'it'?" Alex asked before he could help himself.

"A punch."

"So he said to this Nuttles person, 'Give me a punch'?"

Dave stopped smiling and slowly eyed Alex up and down in a way Alex didn't like. "No. You knew what I meant, so why be arsy and pompous about it? Want everything to be literal, eh?"

"Sorry. I just have a problem with phrases like 'he was asking for it'. It's like the challenge 'are you looking at me?' It's irrational. It irritates me because I'm so used to hearing language getting mangled by students."

"Jesus H. Corbett." There was an awkward silence. Finally Dave shrugged away from the door frame. "By the way, I'm not crazy about talking to you either," he said under his breath, staring. "But I do a better job of hiding it than you do. Think on that, professor." Dave tapped his temple for emphasis then left the room.

"It won't work," said Alex. "We're too different."

"It seems a shame to me, you're both smart – Alex? Are you listening? What?"

But Alex wasn't listening. His eyes were locked on to a woman on the other side of the pub. Suzannah wore glasses that never seemed powerful enough and squinted in the direction he was looking, targeting the girl with blonde bobbed hair wearing a tight red short-sleeved top and long skirt.

"Someone you know? You've gone a funny colour, Alex."

"Yes, I know her. It's the girl I went out with at university. Lucy."

"Oh. *Her.*"

"Yes. *Her.*"

Jane sat on a wooden stool at one end of the bar, her back to the busy lunchtime clientele, an untouched glass of wine in front of her.

"Yeah, and you could go shopping, there's shitloads of places to buy clothes."

The girl behind the bar talked to Jane between customers, as if sensing that Jane was alone and somehow jet-lagged and culture-shocked. Jane mostly just listened. The girl was fake-tanned and friendly, pouring words over her without a break, not offended by only receiving a smile in response to her latest suggestion of things to do in Manchester.

"Do you ever wonder why you're here?" asked Jane, interrupting.

"What, in work?"

"No. More generally than that."

"Nah. You just get on with life. No point thinking about it as well, is there?" The girl seemed pleased with her answer, then suddenly she hissed, "Predator alert! Don't look round!"

Jane ignored her and immediately glanced back, not liking games, and saw someone staring at her intensely.

He was familiar, but hard to pinpoint. Jane frowned; then it clicked, present view colliding with past memory; overlap and connection. Curly reddish hair. An image on some of Lucy's university photos. Stories told. A face once seen from a window.

"I know who it is."

"A friend? You do know someone here after all!"

"No. He's the ex of someone I know."

The girl behind the bar had caught Alex staring and told Lucy, who had turned around straight away – Lucy had never believed in subtlety. When she'd seen Alex she had appeared puzzled for a few seconds before recognition dawned on her face and she looked quickly away again.

That she hadn't recognized him immediately just made him more annoyed.

He turned back to Suzannah, determined not to look over at Lucy again: he wanted to make it easy for her to slip out without having to speak to him. That would be best for all concerned.

The girl leaned over the bar on crossed arms, conspiratorial. "So why is he staring at you?"

"I look identical to his ex."

"Identical? You related?"

"We were born at the same time. We grew up together. Most people would call her my sister."

"Wow, identical twins. Not sure if I've met any before."

"I don't really like anyone calling us identical. When a single fertilized egg splits in two," here Jane put two fists together then peeled them apart, before holding up her palms, "you get two people with virtually the same genetics. Personalities though ... that's on the inside. We're not identical in here." Jane patted her chest as she said the last words, picked up her glass of wine, took it to her lips, hesitated, then put it down firmly. "I hate her. She always leaves a mess. She was horrible to him. Two-timed him. Does he look angry?"

"Yeah. He's turned away now, but doesn't look too happy. Now you've told me all that, it does look more like hate than lust."

"Hatred means hurt. Even after a couple of years? Oh, Lucy. Another problem caused."

"Your sister sounds like my brother. Great at breaking things, not so good at fixing them. If he gives you any grief just tell me: I'll get him to leave."

"No need. It's not his fault." A thought. *She was not the same; not that Jane who'd lived in London. Anything could happen.* "You might be on to something though. About the fixing things."

"What?"

Jane tapped a lip with her fingertip while she thought aloud. "Well, there's an idea. It could be nuts. It's not me to think like this. But I could go and apologise for my sister. I'm sure *she* never did. Say she was out of order, and wasn't worthy of anyone nice. That would be a good thing to do, wouldn't it? Just let him know that it won't have been his fault: Lucy is a bitch to everyone."

The girl laughed. "Yes. That is crazy. Go and do it. And if you can get his phone number for me I'll give you a free drink. He's cute."

Jane took a deep breath then headed over to Alex and his friend.

"Alex? Can I speak to you for a minute? Sorry to interrupt."

Alex spun round, surprised.

"Oh, that's okay," said the woman he was with. "I've got to go now anyway." She seemed eager to leave them.

"Oh no, don't go, I'll only be a minute," Jane pleaded, wanting this to be quick.

Alex seemed to agree, trying to persuade his friend to stay, but she insisted she had to leave. Then she said, "Nice meeting you, Lucy."

Nice meeting you, Lucy.

Of course, Alex would have thought she *was* Lucy. A memory: Lucy joking that Alex hadn't even known about her sister. Jane had asked "Why?", shocked. Lucy had laughed infuriatingly, then just shrugged and said, "I wouldn't have wanted him to fall in love with *you*, would I?"

A nonsense answer, of course. An example of Lucy's evasiveness as much as her ability to easily irritate Jane.

Alex didn't know Lucy had a twin.

She could put him straight. Explain all that; possibly cause greater hurt when he found out that Lucy had kept even more secrets from him; make him feel he'd been laughed at behind his back.

Or …

She could just tell a little lie, a minute of dishonesty that would make another person feel better in themselves. She could live with that if the aim was to benefit someone else, not herself. The opposite to Lucy; a positive charge to counter her negative.

She could remake herself for a few days. Ignition.

They were alone.

"Hi, Lucy."

"Hi, Alex. How are you?"

"Not so bad, thanks. You?"

"I'm fine." Now she had started it, she was trying to sort out in her head the best way to approach this.

"What are you doing around here?" Alex asked.

"I'm staying for a bit. There are some things I want to do and see."

"And you couldn't leave without saying hi to old Alex, huh?" She could sense anger. He really was still wounded. Lucy had a lot to answer for.

"Well, I don't want you to think I'd avoid you."

"That's rich. Shame you didn't think like that when you first dumped me," he said in a raised voice, people glancing over.

"Then you ignored all my calls and letters, refused to see me until I gave up and went away, you were happy enough to avoid seeing me then huh, while you and Ted waltzed off together leaving me like a sad fool for having piled up my dreams in … oh forget it!"

So much bitterness. How had Lucy damaged him so much? And why couldn't it be *her* here, having to deal with this?

The reason was simple, though. Lucy would make a mess of it. It had to be this way if it was to actually make someone feel better. Time to eat someone else's humble pie.

"I'm sorry, Alex. I know I didn't handle things well. I'm sorry for the way I behaved, honestly. I know it was all me at fault, I was wrong and selfish and I've often regretted what I did. In fact," she added, warming to it, "I was a total bitch. Complete and utter. Mad, maybe. A horrible woman. So I just want you to know that."

There. Every word he might need to make it clear that it was not his fault for loving the wrong person. She turned to leave, wanting to get out for some fresh air and leave this silly idea behind.

Lucy had looked nervous, which was something new in Alex's experience. Her face was as pretty as ever but her voice seemed softer. Perhaps because she was trying to be nice for once.

He had been shocked at the venom in his own voice, and Lucy had recoiled. When she spoke next she'd apologised with apparent sincerity. Her smile had none of the superciliousness of the old Lucy. The apology robbed Alex of his anger. He was impressed.

She was halfway to the door when he moved after her.

"Lucy!"

She seemed hesitant, but stopped and turned to face him.

"Lucy – I'm sorry if I seemed bitter just then. It wasn't very noble of me. And I'm grateful for what you said."

Her expression relaxed, and her face once again looked like his happiest memories of it. He could not let that be the end, even if it would have been a better finale than the cacophony of 1994.

"So we're okay?" she asked, trying to hide her surprise.

"Yes, we're okay."

His anger seemed dissipated, and instead he was just a gentle-looking man a few years older than her. Chestnut hair and a cute whimsical look. She nodded towards the door and was about to leave on that high note, but he interrupted her escape again, moved closer.

"Lucy, you can't just go like that after all this time, when I don't know anything about what you're doing with yourself now, and you don't know about me! Can't you stay for a while? Catch up a bit, show there's no bad feeling?"

She hesitated, unsure of the best excuse.

"If not today, how about tomorrow? This week sometime? Soon, anyway?" he asked.

When she didn't reply immediately a look of realisation crossed his face. "I understand if you don't want to." Such a pitiable look. He expected her to say no.

She could be a new person if she wanted. For a time. She could avoid excuses that would look just like that: excuses, rejection, undermining what she'd achieved. She could spend a bit of time with him and maybe do some more good.

"Okay," she said. His face lit up. She could handle it.

"Great. When? How long are you here for?"

"Not long. A few days."

"Are you free now? I was only going to do some research at the central library."

"As long as you're not missing anything important."

"It was going to be some fact-che— sorry, no, it's not important," he said with finality. "Not compared to this. Do you want another drink?" He was relieved when she said no. Drinking with a girl, during the day, was obviously the kiss of death for him.

"We could go for a walk if you like," he suggested. "Where are you staying? Just in general, I mean."

"Rusholme. A friend's letting me borrow their place. I haven't even seen it yet; only just arrived, really. At the bottom of Oxford Road?"

"It's near there. We could walk down to Whitworth Park. It's not too far. Then you're in the right direction."

"Okay." She shouldered her pink sports bag. It seemed quite light. He offered to carry it anyway, but she shook her head. "I always carry my own."

"That all you've got?"

"Yes. It's everything I need."

"You never used to be able to pack light. It's impressive."

She didn't answer.

Once they were outside the pub the unshaded heat was fierce. Lucy didn't seem to notice. She eyed everything with interest.

"Have you been to Manchester before?" Alex asked.

"Never. I should have come. There's so much to see. So much history. So many great old buildings."

"You're right. I suppose I take them for granted. This isn't the best bit for buildings though. Up near the Town Hall and around Saint Peter's Square is better."

"I don't mind. I'll see the Square tomorrow."

They were soon walking down Oxford Road, past the concrete of the BBC edifice and opposite the windowed expanse of one of the ManMet University buildings. As she looked around he wished there were things he could point out, little bits of history, something worthy of her curiosity. He normally walked A to B with head down, maximum speed, journeys an unpleasant connection between two nodes of interest. Things looked different as he followed her gaze.

"So, er, what do you do now?" he asked. "Your job? You wanted to go into something corporate, big company, didn't you? Put the business degree to good use."

"I work in the promotions section of a PR firm. It's competitive, but it pays well. Too boring to talk about. What about you?"

"FE teacher, West Trafford College."

"What do you teach?"

"Physics, mostly. They were begging for science teachers, it didn't matter that I didn't have a PGCE. I cover other science too, some ICT." At her blank look, he added, "Computers."

"Do you like it?"

He gave a bitter snort.

"It's that bad?"

"It's not where I'd planned to end up."

"What went wrong?"

"I didn't finish my PhD, did I?" Lucy pulled a face, so he added hastily, "I wasn't having a dig."

"It's okay. You must get time off at least, if you can be in town drinking during the day. Unless you're on holiday too?"

"Not holiday. I work part-time."

"Part-time?" She laughed. "You should be ecstatic! I always seem to be working. I know people who'd kill to be able to just work part-time."

"I suppose."

"No-one likes their job all the time."

"I know."

"What's so bad about it?"

"The kids."

"Ah, so teaching would be better if there was no-one to teach? You're pulling my leg."

He didn't answer. Whatever he said would sound petty and silly. He knew it wasn't, couldn't be, but didn't want to argue about how difficult things were. She wouldn't understand.

"Are you hungry?" he asked instead as they passed On The Eighth Day. "This is a nice cafe."

She shook her head, then pointed across the road. "Is that Whitworth Park?"

"No, that's just some park for All Saints Library. We're in the education area. Whitworth is further down. Loads bigger."

"Can we walk through it anyway?"

"I suppose."

There was a pelican crossing here. Instead of waiting for the lights to change she darted across gaps in the traffic as it slowed. But then she had to wait for Alex. He'd missed his chance.

"Dangerous," he shouted at her across the road. "This is Manchester, y'know."

"Don't follow all the rules, be spontaneous," she shouted back. "This is life, y'know."

It was good to get the shade of some trees, if only for a few minutes. As he walked he kept having to tug his shirt away from his sweaty back.

"What's that?" Lucy was pointing to the huge green and cream building on the corner of the junction ahead. Ionian columns supported a stone balcony with a bronze dome beyond.

"Great building, isn't it? Used to be a cinema. Look at the stones above the entrance. 'The Grosvenor Picture Palace'. Long ago. Just a studenty pub now, The Flea and Firkin. We can go in if you want?"

"No. I prefer to be in the sun. It feels good to be alive."

"You make it sound like a rarity."

"People often take life for granted."

"I meant the sun." He wished Oxford Road wasn't so long. He'd misjudged. "So, did you, uh, get married?"

"No."

"Me neither. Do you live in London?"

"Yes. I love cities."

"I remember."

When they reached Manchester Museum that was it for Lucy – she was absorbed in its cathedral-like neo-Gothic points, arches and narrow decorated glass windows, part of the university complex.

"Same architect as built the Natural History Museum in London, I think," Alex said, but Lucy didn't reply. She was craning her neck up. He followed her gaze. The pale sandstone walls seemed to extend up to the cloudless sky.

"Reaching up into the blue," she said.

"Every bit inspires you," he added.

"Rhyme."

"Oh yeah. I'm a poet blah blah blah."

White vapour trails drew lines in the sky. Humans had reached even higher.

"Imagine looking down from up there, people must look so small," Lucy said.

"We are."

They walked on.

After that she was apparently happy to just stroll without speaking, without asking him anything further. At first it was unsettling, he kept feeling he should ask questions, but then it became somehow relaxing.

The environs got greener as they neared Whitworth Park, trees lining the pavement and making it feel as if the city centre was now long behind them.

"This is it," he said as they followed one of the footpaths and left Oxford Road behind. Mature sycamores and willows extended their protective shade over patches of grass where people sat and talked, or lay reading, or leaned against tree trunks to eat food. Lucy left the path and led him across the short grass and he was embarrassed as he noticed the litter strewn around, carrier bags and cartons and melting chocolate. One of the newly planted trees had been snapped just above the support but was still attached so the tree's crown rested against the ground in an unnatural reversal. Little details like that worried him. Lucy didn't seem to notice but he couldn't ignore it. He wanted the park to be beautiful for her.

While she was in front he took his sunglasses out of a pocket. The lenses were greasy so he wiped them on the chest of his shirt. He put the sunglasses on but felt self-conscious so quickly returned them to his pocket and squinted instead.

They sat on a bench in the sun. She leaned back, stretched her arms out like a huge sun-welcoming yawn, and nearly touched his shoulder. There were six inches between their legs.

"So you're here on holiday?" he asked.

"There are some things I need to do while I'm here. But it's not work. I'm just going to take each day as it comes."

"You sound very relaxed."

"I am. It's amazing."

"If you lived here the feeling would soon wear off."

"I'm not going to live here."

"Who knows, maybe your firm will set up a branch nearby, you could end up ..." It sounded lame and they both knew it. She didn't reply.

He could see the shape of her thighs through the grey material of her long skirt.

"I'm sorry the park isn't nicer," he said.

"Don't be silly."

"Do you want to walk round some more?" He rubbed the back of his neck. She noticed.

"You look a bit red. Forehead too."

"Always burns. Our family curse."

"It's too hot for you."

"I don't mind."

"No, I'm being selfish. I mind."

"Wow."

"What?"

"Nothing. It's just ... interesting. You've changed."

"Because I don't want you to get sunburned?"

"That and other stuff. Please don't go, I'll be fine," he added, too hastily.

"I wasn't going to leave. But maybe we should do something indoors."

"What about one of the museums or galleries? We could go to the Whitworth just over there. They've got all sorts of textile stuff. You were always into that, right? And it's free." He hadn't visited for many years, but it used to be a place he loved. Their steps had led him here, and it was right to take that further step into the past.

"Okay. Let's get you out of this sun." She stood, then pointed towards Rusholme, asking, "What's *that*?" He followed the direction she'd pointed but couldn't see what she might be referring to; then realised she was running away from him towards the red brick of the gallery. "I'll race you!" she yelled back.

Alex stared at her. She was way ahead of him by the time he gave chase.

Maybe she always had been.

The gallery entrance was tiled and glass-domed, cafe tables nestled between marble pillars. They began with the textiles section, looking at Indian brocades and Chinese imperial costumes. Jane was amused by a reference to Manchester as "Cottonopolis", an old name from the manufacturing past.

And then they came to their first find of the day, an exhibition of Hannah Smith's casket. It sat there behind glass, an embroidered seventeenth century double casket, the front doors open to reveal drawers and a locked panel. The rich embroidery had been hand-stitched when Hannah was a girl, and attached afterwards. The images portrayed many topics: scenes from the Old Testament such as the stories of Jael and Sisera, and representations of summer and winter embroidered onto the fine linen side panels. The summer scene on the right showed a female figure harvesting corn, while the winter scene on the left showed an old man sat by the fire with his large cat.

Jane joked, "Typical – the woman does all the work while the man lazes by a fire!"

She was amazed at the detail; and the patience this girl must have had. What child nowadays would show such diligence? When she said as much to Alex he agreed, though he pointed out that it probably wasn't healthy for a girl to pursue such a lonely pastime with such fervour. She almost laughed that he would even think such a thing – but stifled it when she realised he was serious.

While Lucy admired the quality of the little embroidered drawers, Alex was more interested in the secret compartment at the rear of the cabinet, in which a letter had been discovered:

the yere of our Lord being 1657;

if ever I have any thoughts about the time when I went to Oxford ... my being there near two yers; for I went in 1654 and I stayed there 1655 and I cam away in 1656; and I was almost 12 yers of age when I went; and I made an end of my cabinete at Oxford ... and my cabinet was mad up in the yere of 1656 at London; I have ritten this to fortiffy my self and those that shall inquir about it;

Hannah Smith

This was what pulled at his thoughts, because it reminded him of himself as a child, when he'd loved to put secret notes in various places, like talismans of power. Secrets he could only keep from telling other people if he wrote them down and hid them in the earth; messages for imagined boys a hundred years from then, not realising that a paper note buried in a cigarette packet would have long since broken down into the soil particles, the secret being known only to the dark silence of the underworld.

But Hannah's message *had* been found, and he wondered why she wrote it. Why was Oxford so significant to her? And why did she leave this note in a secret drawer to be discovered over 300 years later?

to fortiffy my self and those that shall inquir about it

That was her answer but it wasn't enough for him. It just raised more questions. Why did a girl need to fortify herself? Perhaps she'd been lonely, and this was her note to an imaginary friend of the future. Her note to say "I lived too, once. And this is something to remember me by."

Could he say as much?

They moved on to the Historic Collection, principally Victorian paintings, Alex's favourites. Lucy's eye was drawn to a vivid watercolour by Samuel Palmer, *The Sailor's Return*. It portrayed a gorgeous sunset fading over sea lapping into a cove. A ship bobbed on the horizon where the sky was at its most bright, burning orange and yellow fading into the blue-grey heavens at the top of the painting.

"That's beautiful," she said, head tilted. "I'd love to have been there. Wouldn't you? It looks like the most perfect end to a day, ever. You can almost feel the cool breeze coming in off the sea, and hear it whispering through the branches of that tree on the left."

"Yes. It's got a kind of pull to it. The sunset is fantastic. I don't think the painting would work as well if it was dawn, would it?"

"Why not?"

"Well, it's the fact that something pretty is ending which gives the painting its extra power. A beautiful ending, because it's the ending of beauty."

"That's a very sad way to look at it. But you could be right."

"Of course I am. I'm a teacher."

She grinned at him. "And you can't stop being one, I see. Still, you seem to know a lot about art for a physics teacher."

"You've forgotten?" He frowned at her, puzzled.

"Forgotten what?" she asked, apparently surprised at his accusation.

He had to bear in mind what Lucy was like. She rarely remembered details she didn't think were important. There was no point in getting irritated over it. "Nothing. I just love beautiful things. Finding out about them. I'm from an arty family. Sister plays the piano, Mum draws, Dad plays the harmonica. That's why my undergrad degree was joint honours, physics and English lit. It was only when I did a Master's that I had to pick between the subjects and went for physics. Remember how you used to sneak up on me in the library and catch me reading poetry instead of working on my thesis?"

She nodded.

"I sometimes wonder what I'd be like if I'd chosen to do a Master's in literature instead of physics," he continued. "Would I be spending time in the science museum instead of here? Wondering what would have happened if I'd made the other choice? It does your head in."

"Don't let it. We could all ask 'What if …?' but then you just spend time looking back instead of forward."

"Don't you ever ask that? Don't you ever wonder about the choices you made?"

She gave him a thoughtful look.

"That wasn't a dig," Alex said quickly.

"I never said it was."

"Sorry. I'm still getting used to you." He smiled apologetically.

The next painting they were interested enough to stop at was *Springtime*, by James Thomas Linnell, another oil, which glistened in the light cast by the lamp above it. It showed a field, with deep woods in the foreground and sides. On a flowered woodland path in the fore was a beautiful woman with children and a dog. A glow on the horizon suggested early morning, casting a golden tinge on the tops of the trees' leaves which contrasted with the long shadows below.

"I'm beginning to see a pattern in what you like, Lucy. You love the light in paintings."

"Not just the light though: nature too. Peaceful scenes. Like a moment of escape from the world."

"But the world keeps growing, and the places for escape get smaller, and we're forced to look at captured images of escape rather than the real thing."

"You say sad things, Alex."

"I don't mean to."

She eyed the painting a moment longer before moving on.

Alex spotted the drawing he favoured above all others was nearby, so rushed her to it.

"This ... this was always my favourite thing in here. *La Donna della Finestra*, by Rossetti."

"That was done in 1870 wasn't it?"

"Yes! How did you know that?" he asked, impressed.

She pointed to the date Rossetti had drawn in the bottom left, next to his brown monogrammed initials.

"So you *can* read."

"So you *have* mastered sarcasm. Lowest form and all that." She leaned in for a closer examination. "It looks familiar."

"Rossetti did more than one drawing with this name, it was like an obsession for him. This is one of the earliest though, the purest."

And then Alex's gaze drifted into the drawing proper, and straight to the woman's eyes, the starting and ending point of any exploration.

He could not say conclusively why he loved it so much. On the surface it was nothing spectacular – a woman in dull and loose clothing leans against a balcony, and gazes just beyond the point where the artist stood. All the power was in that face, resting on a graceful neck and partially revealed shoulder, her complexion warm as if reflecting summer-evening sunlight, beneath a mass of curly and thick glowing chestnut hair. Her face portrayed an emotion Alex couldn't identify.

"Was she a real woman?" asked Lucy.

"Yes. Jane Morris. A beauty of her day. Rossetti fell in love with her sometime before he did this drawing, and began the sequence. His wife had died in childbirth, and Jane became the object of his affections. They were said to sit silently with foreheads touching for hours. But it wasn't to be."

"Why not?"

"Jane was married to Rossetti's friend, William Morris. I guess it couldn't work. Too dishonest."

"Oh."

"Are you okay?"

"Yes, fine. Just reminded me of something."

It had reminded Alex of something too, but he kept silent about that.

"What do you suppose she's thinking?" Lucy asked.

"I've never been able to decide. She looks philosophical, but sometimes I think I see a bit of cruelty in her eyes. But then it's gone, and instead I see someone loving. Like two people in one."

"I think she's worried. She's definitely thinking about something difficult. Maybe she's feeling something for Rossetti that she shouldn't?"

Alex stared into the eyes again, and they stared out of the canvas, but past him.

"Sounds likely, but no," he said. "She looks through you. If she were contemplating Rossetti she would have been looking at him; then when we looked at the drawing she would appear to be looking at us. But she isn't. It's ... disconcerting."

"So what happened?"

"That depends on when a story starts or ends. When his wife died Rossetti had buried a stack of unpublished poems with her. Consigned to a cold grave, but not forgotten. Stuff comes around again, gets dug up. His friends persuaded him to publish a book of poems so Rossetti had his wife's grave opened and he reclaimed the poems."

"Urgh. The dead shouldn't be disturbed."

"Perhaps he came to agree. The same year Rossetti did this drawing of Jane, he also published the recovered poems. And even though they were an amazing achievement, the collection got panned. He had a mental breakdown in June 1872. Later that year he shared a country house with Jane, their retreat from the world. But nothing lasts forever." Alex turned from the drawing. "I don't want to talk about Rossetti any more. Maybe the past is best left buried, sometimes."

Lucy was silent for a while after *La Donna*. It seemed appropriate. The gallery's subdued lighting and hushed voices reminded him of a church.

They ambled around the modern art in the South Gallery but neither of them were into it. The biggest reaction anything drew from them was a geometric painting that Lucy thought would make nice curtains.

"We can sit, if you're tired," Alex said. They'd done a lot of walking.

"Okay. Though I don't feel tired. The opposite. I'm really awake. Happy. I feel good."

"Me too."

They headed over to the bistro near the gallery entrance. Alex had a sandwich but Lucy just wanted a drink. She was talkative, full of enthusiasm for the things they had been looking at. He loved that fervour in her. It was infectious.

The men's toilets smelt of chemicals, but were reassuringly old-fashioned with their two blue and white striped towel machines, and a soap bar at each sink. The round mirrors gave a distorted reflection. How many faces from the past had gazed at their subtly twisted appearance over the years? In this place the past was a physical presence.

When Alex came out, Lucy was by the sales counter, putting something into her bag.

"What have you got?" he asked.

"I meant to buy some postcards. These ones were nice."

"Which did you buy?"

"I'll show you later."

They carried on and explore the upper areas. On the way up the stairs to the Mezzanine Floor there was a backlit pair of stained glass windows by that other notable Pre-Raphaelite, Edward Burne-Jones. As soon as Lucy spotted them she let out a gasp of surprise and rushed over.

"*Angels with musical instruments*, 1890," she read from the plaque, before looking back at the coloured glass which towered above them. "Wow, they're fantastic! I'd love windows like this, why don't people have stained glass windows any more? These are beautiful!"

"I guess you *can* have stained glass windows. They're just not standard with Barratt Homes."

She ignored his crappy sarcasm.

"I love the colours when the light shines through the frozen angels, the blues and the reds and the pinks, they're all so vivid."

Alex laughed. Lucy looked at him, puzzled.

"You're great!" he said, as explanation. "I love it when you're so enthusiastic!"

"Well, aren't you enthusiastic?"

"Yes. I love the angels' faces, so oval, so pretty."

"There's a pattern in the things *I've* liked and the things *you* have."

"What is it?"

"I prefer landscapes and colours. You prefer girl's faces. What does that say about us, Alex?"

For once Alex had no answer.

While Lucy was engrossed in a picture, Alex stole the opportunity to look at her profile with its determined chin leading to full lips, on to an aristocratic nose and past grey-blue eyes to a smooth brow. The dead paintings could not captivate him so easily.

She turned to say something, and caught him staring at her rather than the painting.

"Alex! What are you watching me for? Have I got something on my face?" She ran fingertips over her cheeks.

"Sorry, no, nothing at all. I was just looking at you ... because I haven't seen you for so long. I'm sorry, I didn't mean to stare."

"You seemed so intense ... stop it now, you're making me feel uncomfortable! Look at this painting, it's much more interesting than me."

It was a colourful piece, but painted impressionistically, so the details were hazy, and the subject was unclear. The name on the plaque didn't help to pin it down – *Ambiguity 3*, by a modern painter he'd never heard of, Reily Breen.

"I don't like this," Alex said. "It's just pigments on canvas."

"No, it's more than that. It's amazing. It's like a translation of emotion."

Alex tried to see an image, to force a shape on it. Then something glimmered, a configuration perceived below the surface. It reminded him of patterns of atoms, different chemicals and their molecular shapes, protons being shared.

"Maybe there is something in it ..."

"Ha!" Lucy laughed. "Got it."

"What?"

"At first I thought it was completely abstract, but then I saw a pattern of leaves. But I realise that was wrong now. No, it's butterflies," she said with confidence.

Alex looked again. Yes, they were butterflies. He reassessed the painting and decided he liked it, even though it wasn't his usual sort of thing. There was something undeniably attractive about it, something that woke the merest flutter of wings in his stomach.

"Okay, I admit it is a pretty painting. Remember the poem I wrote for you once about butterflies?"

"No, which was it?"

She'd forgotten. Sudden disappointment, a reminder of what Lucy could be like. Something of great importance to him once, something he had crafted carefully and with love, had become insignificant to her.

"Nothing. Doesn't matter."

"I've offended you haven't I, because I've forgotten? Tell me, I want to hear it."

Alex shook his head.

"*Please.*"

He looked at her, then took a deep breath, and spoke slowly, trying not to rush the words, uncomfortable as he was at speaking them.

"I loved you in cool honest darkness, at night,

When we were together my fire burned bright.

Each day I was reborn, my heart leapt anew,

And then it was night-time and thoughts turned to you.

We lay in near-darkness and your smile set free

All of the butterflies living in me."

Lucy just looked at him, silent. Heat erupted on his face.

Suddenly a male American voice piped up behind him. "That's a really perty poem, it's real nice to see someone who ain't afraid of being romantic nowadays."

A middle-aged American couple had been looking at the same painting.

"Erm, thanks," he mumbled.

"Come on, Hank, you're embarrassing the youngsters! A good day to you both, lovely poem by the way!" The woman tugged at Hank's shirt, and he followed her away with a quick wave.

Oh God. By now Alex was so self-conscious he could crawl under a bench and die.

At last Lucy spoke.

"They're right, you know. That poem is special. Don't take my denseness and poor memory to heart – take my words now. That's one of the most beautiful things I've ever heard."

There was a hesitation about her, and Alex thought she was going to kiss him, and he felt detached from his body even as his heart raced. But the moment passed and she turned back to the painting, a strange expression on her face. He couldn't speak.

He had written that while full of love for Lucy. And despite the emotional mushiness he liked it, because it had come from his heart, not his head.

He hadn't given the full story though.

After Lucy had finished with him he had added two more stanzas, and they weren't so nice. Eighteen lines of accusation. Remembering that time hurt.

They leaned against the railings outdoors, backs to the traffic, and looked through the trees at the balconied gallery entrance. Alex wished they were inside again, repeating the circuit. So fresh in his mind, yet already in the past. A warm breeze gusted from nowhere, tousling their hair, one to the other.

"I should go now," Lucy said.

"I could walk you there if you want?"

"Thanks, but I'm feeling a bit tired. We've been on our feet a lot. Could I catch a bus?"

"Sure. You can catch one over the road. It's only a few stops to Rusholme. You could tell the driver where you're going, he'll tell you which stop to get off."

"It might surprise you, but I know how buses work."

"Sorry. I just remember the time you were trying to catch the bus to Silverdale and ended up in Stoke."

"I'm better now. Walk me to the bus stop?"

The road was busy with rush-hour traffic. Lucy carried on talking about things in the gallery, and Alex listened and nodded, amazed at how contented he felt just being in her company again. She'd filled a gap he hadn't known existed.

"That one goes to Rusholme, I think," he said, indicating the double-decker crawling along in the queue of traffic.

"Great." She rooted through her bag for a purse.

"It's been a really nice day," Alex said. "I didn't expect this."

"I loved it too." Lucy smiled at Alex, her face warm and bright from the sunlight.

"Lucy, I've just thought, I haven't got a phone number. In case I need to ring you." He realised it sounded lame – he wouldn't *need* to ring her. And they had agreed to meet this once to catch up on things. Then again, isn't that just a way of covering your bets? If things don't go well you can fall back on the original agreement, and use that as the basis –

"Sure. Have you got any paper? Pen?"

He fumbled in his pockets even though he knew he hadn't. The bus edged closer and his heart sank.

"No! I meant to buy some pads and pens this afternoon. Shit. Haven't you got any in your bag?"

She shook her head. "No."

"Catch the next bus then."

"Don't be silly. Can't you remember a phone number?"

"Not a full number."

"Yes you can. Think of it as a test. If it's worth remembering, you'll do it."

"Why are you messing around? I don't like games."

"I have a mobile phone, so ring me on that." She told him the number, making him repeat it. The bus pulled in. She was ushered on board with the other commuters, and Alex lost sight of her. He craned his neck out, bobbing around to try and get a view. She appeared at the back window, kneeling on her seat and waving at him. He waved back. She was laughing. Then she drew reversed numbers on the dirty bus windows with her finger.

Alex watched, and recited the numbers in a panic as the bus drove away. So many variables, so little to hold on to. She'd brought chaos to his life again! But then it clicked, gateways in the brain opening and pattern-matching taking place. The code was easy, it was the same as Anne's. Plus … yes, the first three digits of the speed of light in metres per second, followed by … the atomic numbers for calcium and oxygen. It wasn't even worth sweating over. A simple visual mnemonic of those elements blasted through space from a dying sun and it was assured.

He strolled into a newsagent down the road, bought a biro, and calmly wrote the number on the back of his hand.

When Alex got home he took a deep breath before entering. The house was busy. His mum was in the kitchen on the stone-tiled floor, folded towel under her knees, cleaning the inside of the cooker. Auntie Louise was talking to her at the same time as reading *TV Quick*. Two of his young nephews, Richard and Martin, were chasing each other around the living room pretending to be having a Pokémon battle. Kelly was watching TV, occasionally shouting at the kids to "Mind the piano". Natalie was throwing paper aeroplanes at his niece, Melinda. The usual familial chaos.

His parents had built the house back in the 1970s, and because of their gregarious lifestyle they made it large. They didn't have much land around it but the house had a tremendous feeling of space inside; even when there were lots of friends and family around you could usually find a quiet room if you wanted to be alone or to sulk.

People dropped in, or stayed overnight; or sometimes for longer, as with Natalie. It was an open house. Dad was the only one who tended to be missing. He worked on an oil platform of the Douglas Complex off the North Wales coast, so would be gone for months at a time. That meant Alex was nominally the man of the house for most of the year.

Auntie Louise looked up from her Top Tips. "Did you have fun in town? Hannah told me you were meeting Suzannah." Suzannah was one of Auntie Louise's two daughters.

"Yes, it was nice."

His mum turned, her reddish hair slightly bedraggled. "You didn't waste the afternoon in the pub, did you?"

"No. I went for a walk, then visited the Whitworth Gallery."

"Always got your head stuck in a book or a museum or something. You're the brains of the family," said Auntie Louise. Alex found her face disconcerting – she shaved her eyebrows off then drew them back on in brown pencil. It was spooky. As a child he was convinced she was a witch.

"I'll take that as a compliment. What's up with the cooker?"

"Your sister had a go at making bread but put it on too high a shelf, so when it rose it stuck to the top," mumbled his mum, scrubbing at the insides again.

"How come you didn't get her to clean it then?"

Mum looked round, and Auntie Louise echoed her words as she spoke: "Because I want it doing *properly*."

Alex grinned at the common refrain, but Kelly shouted, "I offered!"

"I did too," said Natalie, who was now reading Melinda a story.

"Well, I know you'd do a good job, but you've already done us a favour by collecting Melinda from school."

"When's Mummy coming to collect me?" asked Melinda.

"Soon, sweetheart," replied Natalie, tickling her. "Alex, I've run out of things to read, can I borrow one of your books?"

"Yes, just take something off my bookshelves. Not *A Brief History of Time* though, I'm using that."

"Erm, thanks."

His mum shook her head and pursed her lips for no reason he could discern. He didn't understand his family sometimes.

"Anything you want me to do, Mum?" Alex asked.

"No, I don't think so. Though I've got a surprise for you."

"What?"

"Choc ices in the freezer."

"Thanks, nothing better on a hot day. As long as Natalie and Kelly don't eat them all first."

"*I* wouldn't!" smirked Natalie.

"I know," said Alex. "You don't look like you ate all the pies."

He left the room, and as he approached the stairs Natalie stuck her impish head around the dining room door frame.

"What, am I too skinny?" She stepped into the doorway, hands on hips. She had shorts and a cheeky look on. Her bare legs were slender.

"No," he said. "Your proportions match the golden mean."

Natalie blew him a kiss and smiled as she went back into the dining room.

Alex knew he was impatient. Foolish, maybe. It didn't matter. He walked down the sunny, eavesdropper-free tree-lined road. His steps became smaller and smaller as he neared the phone box. He began to sweat under his armpits, uncomfortable hot wetness, and he hoped someone would beat him to the pay-phone so he'd have to wait.

No-one did.

It smelt of cigarette ash. He lined up his twenty-pence pieces on the shelf and tried to rehearse what he would say. None of the openers sounded natural, or right; many were moronic or borderline psychotic.

"Hi, Lucy, did you really like it before, or were you just saying it?"

"Hey, how's it hanging? Wanna chill out with me again?"

"Lucy, maybe you're The One."

"Fancy a shag?"

Where the fuck did that one come from?

"Lucy, I wanted to talk but not sure what about, what do you think? Not stressed I hope, maybe we could do something but you might not want to anyway, based on past experience, and –"

He jumped when someone knocked on the glass. It was a woman with a greasy face and too-revealing top, and a young snotty child in a pushchair.

"Are you going to be all day in there? If you're not going to use the phone, get out!"

"All right, all right!"

Scary Woman was his spur. He would try and be natural. He dialled. It rang three times, and with each ring his nervousness grew. He was worried it would be a wrong *(or false?)* number. He wouldn't bump into Lucy again before she left Manchester for good.

End of story.

Or not.

Click. "Hello?"

"Lucy?"

"Hi, Alex. I didn't think you'd ring so soon. I didn't leave long ago."

"I know, sorry, erm, did you get to the flat okay? Oh, of course you did. You answered. Though it's a mobile, so you could be anywhere. As long as there's a signal, I don't know about coverage from different –"

"It was fine. Easy-peasy."

Awkward pause.

"I don't want to pester you. But … I really enjoyed today. I think I said that. I enjoyed it more than I'd have imagined."

"What, because you think I'm a bitch?"

"No! Oh God, no, I'm –"

"Only joking, calm down. I enjoyed it too."

Sigh of relief. "And I know you're not here long."

"That's right."

"So I wondered if you wanted to do something else? Tomorrow? Though if you don't want to, you know, if you're busy or something then no pressure."

"Weeeeell … I'm not fully booked up. I'd *like* to meet you again, but I've got some reservations." A cloud must have passed over – the phone booth was slightly colder, slightly darker. "I mean, we get on well, but I'm not sure where it might lead … not that I'm saying you mean anything by it, sorry, it's more me that I'm thinking of." The sun was shining on him again. "I, well, I don't know what I'm saying. Do you? It's complicated."

He almost laughed with relief. She'd felt it too. "I'm not thinking ahead. I just really feel like spending some time with you. That might be good or bad, I have no idea. I'm just acting on what I feel right here and right now. I'm – being spontaneous? Ha. The only thing I'm sure of is that I'm scared in case you leave without me getting to know you again, that I'd have lost out in some way ... oh sack it, this is difficult."

She sniggered, but sounded happy. "Sack it? Is that some weird Mancunian saying?"

"Yes, sorry."

"I like it. Okay, sack it. We'll meet up. What shall we do then?"

"Anything. On Wednesdays I start late and finish early, I could leave after the last student group and be in the city centre around four. Pictures? There'll be something decent on either at the Odeon or the Cornerhouse. They're close by each other. Go for a meal or drink afterwards?"

"Sounds good to me."

"I could check what films are showing, and print out a shortlist with ratings."

"No, we'll just meet and then decide. If you're going to be spontaneous, do it properly."

"Okay. I'll try. I'll meet you at Saint Peter's Square, by the statue, just after 4 o' clock."

"Yes. See you tomorrow, Alex."

"You will, Lucy."

His heart thudded. He put the unspent coins back in his wallet. The sun shone and all was good; he smiled at Scary Woman as he left the box. He untucked then re-tucked his shirt into his trousers, straightened the front, and walked briskly down the road with his chin up.

Jane jerked as if she'd been dreaming. This kept happening. Memories trickling through an almost-closed sluice gate, captivating her, relived in the now, intensity followed by dazzled awakening. Her hands rested on the worktop.

The kitchen was austere, ultra-modern, all furnished in white. The windows were frosted and revealed only vague shapes, possibly tree branches, and antiseptic brightness washed over Jane, ebbing and flowing around her as the branches or clouds moved outside.

She opened the cupboards one after another, but as she expected they were bare, not even a solitary packet of flavoured noodles. She didn't feel hungry anyway.

It wasn't romantic. Meeting Alex. The date.

No, it wasn't a date. Just because she liked him didn't make it that.

"Did I do the right thing?" she asked aloud, closing the cupboard door. She glanced around. There was no answer from the empty room.

She could chicken out, just not turn up. He was almost a stranger.

Immediately an image came to her mind: Alex stood by a statue, looking around for her, eyeing every face hopefully and waiting patiently; an hour passes before he finally gives up and leaves, looking like a lost boy in man's clothing.

She couldn't do that. Wouldn't be as callous as Lucy.

Jane could still smell rich incense on her clothes. The ghostly smoke from the priest's thurible had drifted throughout the church as he swung it by its chain while walking around the coffin. Bitter sweet smell. Bitter sweet feelings.

"I'm glad that's over. I hate that kind of atmosphere," Lucy said, breaking Jane's inner peace.

"What kind are you talking about?" Jane snapped. "The atmosphere of people feeling sad that someone has died?"

"No. The atmosphere of people pretending to be sad. How many of them in there really gave a hoot? They're just wondering what will happen to all the stuff." Lucy gazed off at the line of cars, already losing interest in the conversation.

"I can't believe you've just said that. And now, of all times."

They were standing at the base of the steps outside Our Lady of Victories church dressed in identical black outfits, at odds with the May sun beating down. Lucy was removing the small black hat which had been pinned into her blonde hair. Nearby a group participated in the ritual of hand shaking and condolences.

"It's just the way of the world." Lucy jutted her chin dismissively towards a group of their relatives. "I bet they're talking about wills and such now. 'Ooh, how much was her house worth?' Grasping pigs."

"You can be such a bitch."

"Do you hear that, Jane?" Lucy cocked her head, hand to her ear. "That's the sound of no-one caring. You need to drop some of your misguided romantic fantasies about the world and grow up."

Jane knew she shouldn't have been surprised. Knew she shouldn't rise to the bait. But at the funeral. Insults punched their way to the front of her mind, jostling to be picked, but it wasn't worth it. Lucy wouldn't change. Best just to keep a distance between them. Jane turned her back and inhaled deeply, trying to let the smoky scent recall peace.

Awake from a dream again. It was so vivid, as if it was happening at that moment. And equally easy to see Lucy here now, sat at the small breakfast table which was bolted to the wall.

"Playing with fire," Lucy said. She looked solid enough at first, but then Jane noticed she could see the top of the seat through Lucy's torso.

Jane folded her arms. "I didn't ask you."

"Just saying. I know you. Doing good little deeds. Then seeing them backfire. The question is, why continue with it? It can't go anywhere, can it?"

Jane looked down, wishing she'd never conjured Lucy up.

"Or can it? I know that face. You *fancy* him!"

"We're just friends."

"Liar."

"He's got depth."

"He's *different*. That's not always good." A smug look. Lucy suddenly clapped her hands like a spoilt little girl being told she could have a party. "This is great! It'll be fun watching."

"I just feel like he needs help."

"That's your maternal nature. Why you wanted to go into nursing, wasn't it? But men who inspire that don't always make good boyfriends. I know."

Jane looked out of the window, wishing there was a more hopeful view than ominously morphing shadows. "It's all from good intentions."

"Doesn't matter. It's still dishonest. I can tell you're uneasy about it. Not so pure after all, eh?"

"I'll tell him the truth when I see him."

"No you won't."

Talking to Lucy never made her feel better.

"How will you deal with it when discussions of the past come up? Or – even better! – discussions of your *intimate* past?" Lucy seemed to relish that word.

Jane put her face into her hands, only half in jest, and moaned. Once Lucy had stopped cackling, Jane said, "I'll play it by ear. I'm an intelligent girl. How hard can it be?"

Lucy resumed laughing, more energetically than before; Jane put her face back into her hands. This could give her nightmares. She clicked her fingers and Lucy faded away.

Alex put a CD in his PC and the rising notes of Gershwin tinkled from the speakers. Uncle Derek and Auntie Pauline had turned up for the evening so he'd left most of the family playing Monopoly. Alex's nephew and niece had brought their PlayStation round and, judging by the squeals, shouts and crunching noises, they were playing Tekken 3 in the living room. He knew he wouldn't be disturbed for a while.

He felt like looking through one of the photo albums from university. He hadn't looked at them for a while – too much of it hurt – and the idea of opening it tonight seemed clandestine. He hadn't told any of the family that he'd seen Lucy again.

He had to drag a box out of the built-in storage space in his room, crammed with relics of the past. Childhood toys, diaries, his red 3D View Master from the '80s with its round stereoscopic slides, all jammed in with poetry books he'd not opened for years. Not since he left university and lost his taste for verse. He flicked through one of the abandoned poetry books, the words forming familiar shapes on the page, especially in a well-worn Tennyson collection he used to adore. They could live again. He turned and put them in a space on his bookcase then lay on the bed with an album. The window was open and the lace billowed gently in the warm breeze that carried the scent of cut grass, and the mingled sounds of traffic, birdsong and lawnmowers.

"Keele" it said in golden pen on the photo album's black cover. A collection of memories from his many years there, running from his undergrad days up to his physics PhD time. The photos ended in 1994, the year Lucy split up with him and he gave up on his studies.

The photos were generally chronological but there were some strange lapses in coherence when events were out of place, photos mixed in with those of a later or previous year. Back then he wasn't always so rigorous in his organisation, and since then he'd rarely had the heart to open up the creaking album, let alone reorganise things.

He began near the end of the book with the ones he looked at least. The photos with Lucy in. And he surprised himself by smiling.

There was a formal photo from their first ball together. He'd never worn a dinner jacket before, and she kept saying how sexy he looked, seeming to mean it: running her hands around his waist, feeling the shiny material of the green cummerbund that matched his bow tie. Before the ball they had gone for a walk by the lake as the sun set, holding hands and stopping to kiss every few minutes. Her hair had been longer then, and she'd had it tied up at the back in a twist with a few loose tendrils escaping. She'd worn a pastel-pink little dress which exposed her shoulders, and he hadn't been able to resist nuzzling her neck at every opportunity.

A photo of Lucy and one of the girls she'd lived with throwing their hands in the air, faces shocked at something beyond the field of view. Alex couldn't remember what had been going on.

Then a creased picture that included only half of Lucy but most of a bathroom.

He leapt into the bathroom to take the picture, catching Lucy by surprise. She had a towel tied around her torso and her skin glistened, dimpled with moisture, the room steamy and smelling of soap.

Snap of the camera.

"*What are you doing, you idiot? Get out!*"

Grabbing another towel she beat at him and he retreated, laughing; but he stopped laughing when the door closed behind him and the lock clicked in place.

The photos had all been developed. They were sat together on the sofa shuffling through them when Lucy came to the bathroom picture.

"*Intrusion! Destroy!*" Before he could stop her she snatched it, began to tear it in half. He grabbed her wrists, yelling "*No!*" and managed to retrieve it before she'd done too much damage.

"You're beautiful in this," he said, smoothing it out with gentle precision. "Like half a Greek goddess in a toga."

He showed it to her again, wary of renewed attacks, but she was calm now and studied it with interest.

"You should have taken the photo with me in the centre, not off to one side."

"I didn't get the chance. If you pose for me one time, I will. I'll capture the moment forever. A beautiful goddess to haunt men's dreams. Let me take that picture?"

A pause. "Okay," she relented.

The new photo had never been taken.

Scrawled in the album's white space, in an angry deeply-pushed biro that indented even the next page, were some words paraphrased from Tennyson's *Locksley Hall*:

I'm mad.

She bears but bitter fruit.

She never loved me.

Love is love forever more.

Fucking traitorous bitch.

The last three words were purely Alex's addition.

He reached some earlier pictures of a party in one of the hall bars. The start of it all. He held the album to his nose and inhaled. Yes, there was something there. An aroma. Maybe a hint of perfume behind the surface mustiness. Particles from that time, trapped between pages, fibrous amber, and released again now. A form of time travel. He recalled the smell of her. Unique, like her fingerprint. Delicate, like her eyelashes.

The bar was called the Pig and Rat, and the night had been the craziest thing of that year. Everyone was dressed up, even the less-rowdy PhD crowd: some had pyjamas or nighties on, others had army clothes and camo face paint. Alex had worn a short skirt, padded bra and make-up. He chuckled at the photo showing his younger self. How uninhibited he'd felt back then.

The party had seemed a perfect combination of people – almost everyone there knew each other – and timing, since the undergrads had handed in their final assignments for the first term. The memories were smudged by alcohol but he remembered dancing on a pinball table with the captain of the rugby team who was wearing schoolboy shorts, shirt and tie. He remembered someone climbing on the roof and running around naked at one o'clock in the morning. One friend had canned cream squirted into his underpants by a trio of giggling girls from the hockey club. And there was lots of dancing.

Lucy had worn a short scarlet nightie. They weren't going out together at the start of the night, but had been moving in that direction since they'd got talking at one of the pub quizzes: their friends had declared it only a matter of time. She had said she liked him in a skirt. He had said he liked her in a nightie. And the consequence was that a few drinks later they were kissing in the ladies' toilets. She'd got Alex's lipstick on her face and refused to leave the room until she'd removed it.

His gut twisted at the next picture – Alex and his best friend at the time, Ted Withall, standing by a blue-baize pool table in the Students' Union bar. They each had an arm round the other's shoulder, cue in hand, smiling at the camera from the scruffy room.

Ted was the one Lucy had gone off with. He turned the page.

There was a knock on the door. Alex ignored it. Another rap. "What? Who is it?"

Kelly came in. "Knocked first. Truce? What are you doing?"

"Just looking at some old photos. Finished really." He closed the album and got up to put it away.

"No, wait! Which album is it? Can I look?"

"It's my uni pictures. Pretty boring."

"No, let me see. I'll be going soon, I wanna see what I'm in for." She flopped down on the bed and held her hands out. He hesitated. "Oh go on, I'm bored. Natalie's gone out, I thought I'd do something with you. Don't be an old fart."

He threw the album gently towards her. She caught it and started looking through from the start. He lay next to her, identifying people, talking about the parties, describing the views of the Keele campus, and the house he'd shared in Silverdale, until she told him she didn't need a commentary on *everything*.

They laughed at one picture taken by a housemate at about 4am. A view down the stairs of a communal hall with breeze-block walls that resembled a prison: Alex looking bleary eyed, wobbly legged, haggard, being supported by two laughing friends. Below that was a photo of Alex covered in flour and eggs after the last exam of his undergrad course.

There was also a picture of a group of his MSc friends on a picnic in a field near the campus. Everyone who didn't have sunglasses on was squinting. They had stayed until it got dark. At the edge of the picture was a blur of bright plastic – the water pistols they'd used during a lengthy water fight. He was part of something back then. They had fun.

The next page had a photo of Kelly and Alex when she'd visited him once at uni. They both had the trademark chestnut-coloured Kavanagh hair, with a slight curl to it. But in this picture they'd both dyed their hair green. They had looked like two walking peapods, and he'd been glad when it finally washed out.

"That was fun," Kelly said, her fingers lingering over the photo. "Doing things together." She looked at him; he ignored her and turned the page.

Inevitably they came to a picture of Lucy. In this one Alex was sitting with her on a sofa. That was when they had first started going out. He had a can of beer in his hand and was pretending to look glum while she appeared to be whispering something into his ear mischievously. He had a big pair of 14-eye Dr Martens on and some green and red baggy trousers tucked into them. Those were the days before he switched to shirts and proper shoes.

"Ah, the bitch-queen herself. Should've known she'd be in here," Kelly said.

"That's not nice. The past is past."

"Yep, past is past, so why'd you keep these pictures of her?"

"I keep all my pictures. Memories don't always have to be good."

"But isn't it better to dump bad ones? Why have reminders of bad things?"

"It makes life interesting. You fancy Joaquin Phoenix don't you?"

"Not half. He's sex on a stick."

"Would you prefer him without the scar on his lip? I'm sure he could get it removed if he wanted."

"No, I think he's fitter with it."

"So sometimes things should stay, be remembered. They become part of you."

"I still can't believe you're saying that about *her*. She was horrible."

"People change."

"What's that supposed to mean?" She seemed angry.

"Nothing. Just forget her."

"You never did," she said under her breath.

"What?"

"Nothing."

"Don't chicken out. You mean something."

"Just that you've never been the same since you dropped out of university. I blame her."

"I didn't change."

"Fucking did. You're a zombie."

"Your imagination —" He tried to snatch the photo album, desperate.

"Used to always get on well, never argued, then suddenly we fought all the time, I blame her, hate her —"

"Shut up!" He pulled but she gripped it too tightly.

"She's a cunt!"

Alex kicked out before he was fully aware of what he'd done, feet pushing at her. Kelly let go of the album and fell off the side of the bed with a huge thump, scrambled up clumsily and stared at him in surprise. "You only ever do that once," she said hoarsely, while tears spilled down. She ran from the room, ignoring his shouted apology.

Alex couldn't face any more of the photo album. He crammed it back into its box. For now he needed something to calm him down, something sure and reliable and satisfying.

The idea of a wank had been tainted by yesterday so instead he collected together his bank statements, payslips, hand-written notes on transactions in his chequebook, and rather than try out all the biros again he found an unbroken pencil. He would check the recent transactions against each other. Making the numbers match up reassured him that the world still worked in predictable ways.

He'd only got through a handful of items when the piano in the living room started up. It was right below him. Worse, Alex recognized the hard jangles and alternating notes as Prokofiev, the same sonata Kelly always seemed to play when angry. She couldn't play it as fast as it should be played but it was still pretty fast and discordant-sounding, and every time she made a mistake she started again. It drove him nuts as it climbed up and down scales. It was impossible to concentrate with it banging out below you like a demon on speed had got into the piano and was taking revenge on black and white keys.

She would play for at least an hour if she was that angry. There was no point doing anything here. He gathered the paperwork up and carried it bundled in his arms.

Alex climbed the narrow, steep and deep-shadowed staircase to the top floor. Up here were several small rooms mainly used as storage space. Hardly anyone came up here. It was ideal. The creaking floorboards marked his progress down the top landing that was only lit by the flickering windows of a pottery lamp in the shape of a fairy house.

He ducked to get through the little door and switched on a light with a yellow shade that made everything appear sepia-tinged. The dark wooden furniture, some of which was antique, added to the feeling of stepping into some room from the past. On the dresser were dolls and teddy bears that his mum had owned as a little girl: old and (frankly) ugly dolls with little white teeth and threadbare dresses; faded bears with dull orange-bead eyes that glistened. Alex found them repulsive. The bed's heavy wooden frame was covered with a sheet and stitched blanket rather than a duvet.

Still, it was a relief. He could barely hear Prokofiev up here. No cars on the road, no voices, no footsteps. For once, peace.

As he moved down lists, ticking off neatly ordered items, he noticed that his hands looked dry. At first he thought it was the light, but as he looked more closely then prodded the skin experimentally, he saw there were small wrinkles. All over. The closer he looked, the scarier it was. Cellular decay was a reality. His skin no longer fit properly.

It was letting him down.

He tried to forget about it and went back to the sums but was soon asleep with his head on a pile of crinkling statements.

He was alone in a room with a large grandfather clock. It was growing all the time, its dark wood stretching. He could hear the wood creaking, threatening to split or crack but always finding some new level of elasticity. And it ticked: marking out moments that were already over by the time he heard their noise. He was living in the past.

The rest of the room was dark. There was a door somewhere but he couldn't see it. He sat in a faded armchair watching the clock growing. He didn't know how big it could get before it reached the ceiling because above him was only darkness that went on forever.

Tinkling laughter came from behind him but he wouldn't acknowledge it.

The face of the towering clock was intricately decorated, though it seemed too small to host all that detail. Fractal-like, the more he stared the more he saw, and with each growth new patterns appeared, impossibly fine. Worlds of detail on a face that grew with the seconds.

Cracks appeared in that face, the stretching forces proving too much. As they widened he realised it was approaching the hour. In the blackness of the cracks a noise was preparing, a fluttering final chime that would signal some horrible departure.

Wednesday in work dragged. He let his groups leave early. He kept checking his watch. When he saw Anne he hid in a book cupboard, pretending he was tidying it. Once he'd finished he rushed for the bus then changed at Stretford to the Metro and trundled into town.

He got off a stop too early, blinked in the sunshine, confused about how it had happened, then alternated between walking

briskly and running. By the time he reached the pointing obe-
lisks of Saint Peter's Square he had a damp patch up the back.
He was still early though. And she always used to be late.

Maybe she wouldn't show up. She'd always been passive-
aggressive too.

He sat on a step near the war memorial, the dome of the Co-
rinthian-columned city library on his left, next to a strange
combination of curves and spikes that made up one end of the
Town Hall. Just in front was the playground that always seems
to be locked, and within that a brick hut with no windows, ru-
moured to be the entrance to a bunker for councillors in case of
nuclear war.

Hot wind swirled the litter in gusts.

It was silly to be nervous. This would be just another pleas-
ant evening, a chance to chat and see a film. Just like with any
friend. Nothing more.

The square was busy with people catching the Metro home
from work. Alex normally enjoyed trying to guess their lifestyles,
interests, occupations, and level of educational attainment, but
he couldn't concentrate. Then he saw a poster. A woman's face
staring at him from the nearby bus shelter. In the corner it said:

Follow heart. Follow love. One love.

It was a perfume poster of a model's face with her skin painted green. It annoyed him, since the slogan was missing a
possessive pronoun. But there was something amazing about the
model's dark eyes.

All nonsense. Just a beautiful woman, painted and tastefully photographed. Random.

It was difficult to tear his eyes away. His mind lingered on the words.

The town hall clock struck the hour, four sonorous booms that contrasted with the friendly toots of the trams. Alex looked around and saw Lucy a few seconds before she saw him. He had to compose himself quickly. She was wearing cargo pants and trainers, and a small bag was slung over one shoulder of her blue top. Her blonde hair was tied in a ponytail. In one fantasy he'd pictured her in a dress, all done up for a formal date or a ball. He was glad she wasn't dressed like that. This was just friends going to see a film.

He waved; she saw the movement; gave an honest and lovely smile when she recognized him.

They didn't embrace, just said hi. Like friends. Which they were.

She wasn't hungry so they headed straight to the cinema. As they chatted on the way he seemed to be on autopilot, floating along, responding where appropriate, laughing on the surface yet somehow detached inside.

They entered the massive Odeon cinema but didn't fancy any of the films. They all seemed to be violent action: *Mission Impossible 2*, *Gone in 60 Seconds*, *Gladiator*. Neither of them were into that kind of thing. So they walked down the road to the Cornerhouse which showed arty and international films, as well as galleries and exhibitions.

A different atmosphere. Jazzy music, refined hubbub; unexpected white angles and open balconies above wooden-floored classiness. A bookshop and a cafe. This was better.

Alex suggested *Sixth Sense* but Jane said she'd read a spoiler, and didn't like things with ghosts or twist endings. They debated watching a Swedish film called *Fucking Åmål*, but in the end Lucy made a decision and they got tickets to see *American Beauty*. Alex hadn't heard of it, but knew he liked beauty.

They followed winding stairs to one of the basement screens, and traffic noise faded away as they descended. The cinema was black walled and cosy. They sat near the back on comfy red seats, honorary brass plaques embedded into some.

The lights dimmed and they slouched down. As the film began he was conscious of how close they were. Sometimes their fingers brushed together on the single armrest. Every time it happened he got pulled from the film into the solidity of his seat.

Yet the film captivated him too. It was as full of beauty as he'd hoped. Images, music, ideas. At the end of the film, as he realised what had happened to Lester he hoped he wouldn't cry and look unmanly, trying to open his eyes wider to dry them out, when Lucy grasped his hand. Hers was hot and moist. He looked at her but she was watching the film, her profile softly lit by the reflection from the screen, glistening tracks of wetness down her cheeks.

He couldn't move his arm. It was too heavy, not part of him any more. When the scene passed she let go of his hand and wiped her eyes, still facing forward. *She had held his hand when she was upset.* Something that to her had been natural, not needing comment, not expecting to be rebuffed.

She'd changed. We all get older.

He began to see clearly, and it scared him.

He was still in love with her.

"Loved it!" she exclaimed as they came back out into the city, the sky still disconcertingly bright.

"Me too."

"There's so much beauty in the world. Yet it's too easy not to see that. Not to see what's right there." She grabbed his arm, linked him, eyes wide as she took everything in.

"Yes."

"Even in Manchester!"

"Even so."

"Why are you staring at me?" She let go of his arm.

"Just seeing what's right here." *Take it as a compliment*, he thought, but she changed the subject.

"What now? Would you like to go for a drink?"

"Does Americium have ninety-five protons?"

She punched his arm lightly.

They headed back up Oxford Road. Being in the underground cinema had reminded Alex of something.

"Here we are."

Lucy stared at the canopied steps stuck right in the middle of the road that resembled a Paris Metro station entrance leading down into darkness.

"This is a *bar*?"

"Yes. The Temple of Convenience. It used to be a public toilet."

She wrinkled her nose in a way that struck him as girlish.

"Don't worry, Lucy, it's much nicer now. Your delicate sensibilities won't be affected in the least."

They descended the steep stone steps, gripping the wooden rails fastened to chipped tile walls.

"Is it safe?" Lucy asked jokingly.

"Oh, yes. Except the toilet is unisex, so isn't the cleanest. And the stuff on the toilet walls is a mix of funny, insightful, offensive, and biologically unlikely."

It was a dark, tiny, subterranean bar that was easy to miss if you didn't know where the steps led. Alex only knew about it because one of his cousins, who was into indie music, had brought him once. He hoped it would impress Lucy, show her some semi-bohemian "real Manchester". It was the only rock and roll thing he knew.

"You're not claustrophobic, are you?" he asked, suddenly worried.

They were lucky to grab space on a long vinyl seat in the garish orange alcove. They had their own table, which held fresh flowers and a flickering candle in a red jar.

"Cosy," said Lucy, as they were squashed together in the gap between other bodies.

"Cramped," replied Alex. "But with shabby charm. Might even see some musicians in here later."

Lucy surprised him by asking for a pint rather than the gin and tonics or alcopops she used to drink. He didn't comment on it though; he'd said "But you used to ..." far too many times already.

They talked about the film some more; then films in general; then music, since the jukebox was always playing choice rock and indie music. Lucy shamed him by recognizing many of the Manchester bands or songs which were only vaguely familiar to him.

"Oh, this is classic Charlatans, look how everyone's nodding to the beat ... You must know this band! That's Bernard Sumner singing ... Have you really never heard of Ian Brown?"

His response to each was a head shake.

"You know New Order, right?" she asked, as if desperate.

He was relieved when conversation turned to food. There were too many tunes in the world. Thousands, apparently.

It was like discovering each other again. They agreed and disagreed, joked and chided, and seemed to be on the same wavelength. The exception was when they discussed jobs – Lucy appeared cagey in talking about hers. Alex got the feeling she was somehow embarrassed about earning a high salary, like it wasn't what she wanted any more. She changed the subject and that suited him. It saved him being ridiculed for complaining about his own job again.

Another topic Alex avoided was focussing on the past. He had decided earlier on that he wouldn't drift into conversations based around "Do you remember when ..." or "What about the time that we …" It could lead too easily into accusations and bad memories.

The bar was full now, the room hot, filled with soft laughter and friendly hubbub. The different scents people wore intermingled and there was a faint fog of cigarette smoke. In his slightly inebriated state, the bar reminded him of a Tolkienesque hobbit-hole.

"Pretty crowded, innit?" he asked after a pause.

"Yes, but I like it here. Changing the subject, I've noticed you sometimes sound different. It's hard to pin down, but most of the times you sound … normal, I guess … but other times you sound really northern. It's a bit weird the way you change."

"We can't all be posh speakers from Kensington."

"You mistake me, sir," she said in an exaggerated tone.

"I do not. You've got a lovely soft southern received pronunciation accent."

"It's just that I speak properly."

"So do northerners."

"Rubbish. You don't have rules on how you speak in Manchester, you *break* all the rules!"

"It seems that way to you, but there's rules."

She snorted. "There's nothing clever about saying 'Here's me book' instead of *my* book, or 'I don't fink so, bruvva'. It just sounds daft and ignorant."

Alex laughed. "When you put it like that … And it does piss me off sometimes that letters get missed out. 'It's my 'ouse', 'I'm goin' pictures 'n' pub, love'. Sounds too much like my sister. Well, not really. But teenagers, the way students talk. They also seem to hate the letter T. 'I like i- a lo-', 'sor-id'. The last one, 'sorted' seems to mean 'arranged to my satisfaction'. My students end every sentence that way."

"Okay. So we agree. Let's change the subject."

"Just one thing where it works better. Down south people only have one word for 'you', for singular and plural. We're more accurate, we have 'yous' as the plural, meaning 'you all'. So 'What do yous want?' It's more like traditional usage where 'thee' and 'thou' made that distinction."

"Yes, very colourful, cheeky charm etcetera. Enough though. Let's talk about *something else*."

"I haven't even covered our speciality, local colour. Expressions like 'is it eckers like', and 'I don't steal owt' are de rigueur."

Jane studied him as he continued. He could be a slightly pompous bore when he became this Frankenstein's monster of an academic. He didn't realise, maybe because of the drink, and it was obviously a topic he warmed to. He spoke loudly. There'd been a few looks over from other customers as he sounded pretentious.

What saved him was that there was no meanness in him. She felt it. Lucy was more keen on thrills and looks than inner qualities, but Jane knew she was more mature than her sister.

Anyway, it was better than having to negotiate a minefield of past memories she inevitably wouldn't share, and removed the very real danger of verbal traps.

"That's enough, Alex," she said. "Honestly, that's getting boring."

He looked surprised, then nodded and apologised. "Thanks for being honest. I appreciate that. I get carried away."

"Sorry, I feel bad now, didn't mean to hurt your feelings."

"No, no, you haven't … It's much better to be honest. I see that. Too serious. How about this: there are two kinds of scientists in the world. Those who can extrapolate from incomplete data."

Lucy waited for him to finish. He didn't. Then she got it. "A bit intellectual but it's a start."

"I don't do jokes normally."

"So I see."

"And before, what you asked about me swapping between two voices, leading me to waffle on – I know I do it. It's because I teach. I think it ends up giving me two personalities, since I try to speak … erm, more *formally* when I'm teaching –"

"You were going to say 'properly' weren't you?"

"And I speak that way with teachers. So I get in the habit of it. But when I drink –"

"You go back to how you used to speak."

"Precisely."

"You could have just said that originally."

"I know. I agree."

She reached up, held his face in both her hands and gave him a ghost of a smile. "I'm understanding. Starting to, anyway."

"What?"

"You. Everything. What I can do. Never mind. I feel good."
She dropped her hands.

"So do I."

They had another drink. She encouraged Alex to talk about
his life now, letting him give her facts and details that made it
easier to impersonate Lucy, and saving Jane from having to talk
about herself.

And as she listened she wove the threads into mental fabric,
forming a picture, a psychological tapestry called *Alex*; one with
skewed edges and blurred details which stopped it achieving perfection. He saw problems everywhere. And her background was
in caring, so it was easy to diagnose the problem.

He was worrying instead of living.

"You take things too seriously," she told him.

"I'll take that as a compliment."

"It's not, though. It's good to think, but life's too short to do
it *all* the time. You've got to be able to relax too, enjoy it. People
will like you more."

"It's easy for you, you've always been outgoing and inde-
pendent. You can just be yourself and people still accept you."

"It might look that way, but you'd be surprised."

"Well that's how I remember you." He stared down at his
hands, saw through them to the memories. She was moving,
doing something, but he ignored her, temporarily lost.

"Don't get too hung up on what I used to be like. Just look
at me now."

"I will," he said, looking up, then seeing that she'd torn the corner off a beer mat and lodged it beneath her nose like a moustache. He couldn't help grinning.

"That's better."

"Your look isn't. You just don't care what people think, do you?"

"Most people – no." She dropped the cardboard moustache on the table. "So no pessimism from now on, right? Glass half full instead."

"Mine's empty. Want another drink?"

"Now you're getting it!" She patted his shoulder.

"You're good at being patronising. You should be a teacher."

"Maybe I should. Do teachers get paid more than nurses?"

"Nurses? What have they got to do with it?" Alex gave her a puzzled look.

"Nothing, both just worthy jobs," she said quickly. "I wondered if they get paid the same."

He shrugged. He was flush-faced and happy despite the way the room seemed to sway, like in the hold of a galleon. It was affecting Lucy too, he thought – she was increasingly touchy-feely. After a bad joke on his part she elbowed him; she wanted to feel the soft material of his shirt (and he moaned with exaggerated satisfaction when she did, only partly in jest).

"I'll get us another," he said, standing with a slight wobble.

"No, I haven't bought one yet, it's my turn. And I need the toilet. We'll make it the last one. Same?"

"Yes," he said, falling back gratefully. As she walked away he muttered to himself, "You never used to be able to drink so much."

He watched her move. Could imagine her thighs beneath the cargo pants, the way her legs looked in a skirt – then interrupted himself. It wasn't appropriate for two friends. Just two friends having a drink.

The toilets were as bad as she'd expected. Going into a cubicle after a man just felt wrong.

At least it gave her a breather. She'd almost slipped up before. It was so easy to make a mistake, she could kick herself. It would be silly to mess things up now.

She entertained herself by scanning the graffiti in the stall. She guessed that it was mostly done by men as her eyes passed over drawings of misshapen penises and unrealistic cartoon breasts. The messages told her that "sausages are cool", "I need new underpants" and "Fuck hippys". One message said "We are all beautiful" in bold marker but scribbled underneath in red pen was "bet a fat girl wrote that".

Amongst a jumble of doodles was a number 37 with wings, flapping over "Jon's birthday". 37.

She checked her watch.

"I know," she muttered, before returning to the bar.

Alex watched her order the drinks. There were rowdy drunken lads nearby. One spoke to her. Alex had to lean forward to see properly.

It was nice being out with a friend. Having a drink with a friend.

The lad was younger than Alex, had the right hair, the right looks, cockiness, could be a model for Burton.

We all get older. We all change.

Lucy was ordering. She'd turned from the guy, who was gesturing something to his friends, and Alex felt relief.

He looked at his hands. Even in this light he could see small wrinkles.

Drinks in front of Lucy, she was paying. A tap on her shoulder from the lad, she turned, and the lad reached out, chest-height palms moving towards her breasts, his face an idiotic cock-sure gurn; but Lucy moved quicker, a flash, amazing, both her hands came up the centre and slapped his arms away, leaving the lad looking surprised; she said something aggressive to him and he stepped back; all over in seconds as she grabbed the drinks and left the idiots. She was a warrior, a force, perfection with two pints, instinctive and incredible. She walked away and left the lads being told off by the bar staff. Nothing could touch her. Lucy.

She put the drinks down and sat, smiled at Alex, her face told him she knew he'd seen and it was nothing.

"That guy ..."

"An idiot. Offensive arsehole. He'll probably get chucked out."

"You were so quick, the hand thing."

"It's nothing, automatic defence. He was drunk and slow. And lucky I did that rather than knee him in the bollocks."

Alex didn't laugh.

"Are you okay, Alex?"

"I don't know."

"You didn't need to do anything."

"Shouldn't a guy protect a girl's honour?"

Lucy shrugged. "They're leaving. Look."

He turned. The group's exit was being watched by a surly bouncer.

"No need to do anything, see?"

"I care –"

"I know that. But no point creating trouble. Stick up for yourself when you need to – you can't live a life in fear – but otherwise let it go. I assume you'd have been there if I needed you."

"Yes. Yes, I would."

"There you go then. Cheers."

But he was quiet while she sipped her drink and nodded her head to the song playing on the jukebox. He even recognised the band this time, Oasis, but he didn't feel like saying so.

You can't live a life in fear.

No, but he could make a good attempt at it.

They were just friends having a drink.

It rang hollow.

You can't live a life in fear.

"Are you in a relationship with anyone at the moment?" he surprised himself by asking.

"No."

"Me neither."

She didn't answer, so he added, "What do you think about second chances?"

"They're all too rare. Better to move on, sometimes."

His head ached when he processed her words. It wasn't what he'd hoped for. "Do you really think that?"

"You've just not met the right woman."

"Oh yes? And who is that 'right woman'?" Sarcasm invaded his voice.

"A strong woman, someone sensible and down-to-earth to balance you out."

"You seem sensible and down-to-earth."

"And someone with a future."

"What the fuck is that supposed to mean?"

"It means I'm not making sense."

"I don't believe that. You've been on my case. Subtly, I know. But you have been anyway. 'Alex, do this, do that.' You think I should be wild, not be afraid, all that crap?"

"What's got into you?" Lucy looked worried at his flash of anger.

"I'll tell you what's got into me, what's bothering me." He paused, took a deep breath. "Tonight's bothering me. Yesterday's bothering me. You know why?"

She shook her head.

"Because it showed how good we could be. And while I'm on the topic, I've never had an explanation. It's a thought that's been buzzing around in my head, stinging, I can't think of anything else! Why the fuck did you ever leave me?" The question hung in the air, as much a surprise to Alex as it apparently was to Lucy. His heart beat too fast. His ears burned as he spoke. Conversation in the room continued, no-one paid any attention, yet it felt like all eyes in the room were staring at him as he asked her. "I thought of this again and again," he added, when she didn't answer. "Always frustrated by not being able to think of a reason that made any sense. Is something wrong with me? Had I done something wrong? Was I pushing you too much when I wanted us to live together? The row we had was tiny. We didn't have to commit to anything … and suddenly it was over? And you, with Ted … I lost both of you in one go. I can't believe that you're just a horrible person, can't believe that at all, not now."

She looked horrified. "I … I can't explain it well. I wasn't myself … no, I couldn't have been. The reasons don't make sense any more. I won't lie to you about this. I feel bad enough about things."

"That's *it*? Your answer?"

"Does it really matter after all this time?"

"It matters to ME." A few people looked over. "It matters to *me*," he repeated, more quietly.

"I don't know what to say. This has bothered you for so long that whatever I tell you will just sound weak. All I can say is that

I was a different person then. Used to getting what I wanted. Not evil, just selfish. And I grew up."

"That's the best answer?"

Lucy nodded. "I'm sorry there isn't any revelation from that. Just … let it go. You don't need to know why sometimes. We're stronger if we can see that."

He looked away from her. Up at the corner of the room where there were no faces, nothing to accuse. In his mind he weighed what she'd said. "Okay," he said softly. "I'll play along." He rubbed the palms of his hands against his eyes angrily, determined not to let them run. He couldn't lower his gaze until they dried properly. Lucy turned his face towards her and he stared, a challenge, *he wasn't crying*, she hadn't made him cry, he wasn't embarrassing himself, he wasn't afraid, he could overcome it and he tried to smile at her but the muscles didn't work properly.

"Oh shit, Alex, did I hurt you so much?" She held his face, rubbed a thumb against the wet edge of one eye, and he saw that her eyes were wet too, she was crying, and something cold deep inside him was warming, softening, so he leaned forward and kissed her, soft lip memory, past overlaid on present, and the present was the sweetest; damp cheeks touching, lips hot, his hand in her fine hair. There was only each other.

And as the moment passed and they separated, a look of surprise – hell no, *shock* more like – was painted on her face in open eyes and parted lips and slack expression, that was a mirror of how he felt.

"Shit," he said.

"Shit indeed."

"I didn't expect that, Lucy."

"Perhaps we should have seen it coming."

"Yes."

Their voices were softer now, the humour gone.

"I want to explain something," Alex began. "Being around you – I'm feeling things I haven't for ..." He inhaled. "We're different now. This might just seem like some moment of madness to you, but it means more to me. There, I've said it. And ... and I can't read your face. I've embarrassed you? Oh shit, I didn't mean to say any of that yet. Oh shit. I'm sorry. You can forget what we did. I'll leave now if you want."

She shook her head but said nothing at first. She took his hands instead. It seemed like a minute before she spoke. Just breath and thought.

"That meant something to me, don't take it away. But the situation is very complicated."

"But simple in other ways. Can't you see that?"

Their clammy hands were still together. Alex squeezed hers in encouragement.

"There may be things to work out," she said.

"We can do something again before you go, can't we?"

"Tomorrow."

"Not great for me, the day after is better, I could probably get all Friday off work."

She bit her lip, shaking her head slowly. "Tomorrow night is my last one in Manchester."

"*What?*" Alex let go of her hands. "That soon? It's not the end of the world, but …" The weight of disappointment pushed his mood down until his body slouched. But looking at Lucy's face brought him back up. "Can you stay longer?"

"No. There are places I have to be. It's all fixed and can't be changed, no matter what I want, so it's what we've got. How about during the day tomorrow?"

He grimaced. "I'm contracted for the full day in work, revision sessions for science students, plus covering for another part-timer. I can't get out of it at this short notice."

"Tomorrow evening?"

"I can't. A family thing. All the clan's coming round, and a stack of friends. They're totally mad doing it on a weeknight but it's Uncle Derek's birthday, so I can't get out of that either. Shit."

They looked down at their hands. His thumb was stroking her fingers. Her skin was much smoother than his. Suddenly he gripped her eagerly and looked up.

"I've got it! Lucy, come to mine tomorrow evening. We could be together, and –"

"No. They'll hate me."

"You could win them over! We both would. They'll come round to it. You could stay the night. I'd get you on the bus to town the next morning, come with you."

"It wouldn't be a good idea."

"We could do it." In his mind problems melted away. Lucy won his family over. The united show they'd put on would pull them together, like a formal commitment, making it more likely they'd meet up at a future date than if she disappeared without seeing him again … then he realised another reason she might be wary.

"Oh, and I don't mean anything by it – I mean I don't just – I wouldn't try it on. Nothing would happen – you know."

She grinned. "I wasn't even thinking of that! Of course nothing would happen. I can take care of myself."

"I know. Think about it. If you don't want to stay overnight in one of the bedrooms you could just stay for the evening then I'd put you on a bus or something. I know it seems like a big deal, and a lot to ask … but *please*. I'm sure my family will be nice. We could meet near my house, only go to the party if you feel able to. If you say no I'll understand, or do my best, and I won't raise it again. So it's your call. I'll accept whatever you say."

She stared at him but her intelligent blue-grey eyes were a barrier, not a window. Eventually she leaned her head forwards, eyes closed tight, sighed, and touched her forehead to his. A tingle, echo of the past, the two of them frozen like an art gallery drawing. They stayed that way for a minute before she leaned back and looked at him again.

"Sack it," she said, and a smile crossed her face. "I'll trust you."

They hugged, tightly, and the smell of her made him giddy.

Smiling, Alex made his way to Piccadilly rather shakily, singing to himself.

"So, we'll go no more a-roving

So late into the night,

Though the heart be still as loving,

And the moon be still as bright.

For the ..."

He paused, puzzled, looking up at the moon for inspiration, then carried on once it arrived.

"For the sword outwears its sheath,

And the soul wears out the breast."

He hadn't bothered with Byron for years, thought his interest was dead, but he was wrong. There was room for art after all. He was idly wondering if this poem of Byron's was an ode to maturity, or to hangovers, when his bus came.

He dozed on and off on the way home, grinning every time he remembered Lucy's smell when they hugged. How could a smell make him feel so good, simple particles connecting with his olfactory senses? For once he was willing to just accept that it was a kind of magic.

This time Lucy had a pen and paper in her bag.

"I came prepared to deal with someone who writes everything down," she'd told him.

He'd written bus numbers and times on the sheet for her. She teased him for having all of those details in his mind. "You have a first-class intellect," she had joked.

"I'm working on the other bits," he'd replied.

He was going to meet her so they could walk to his house together.

"Though the night was made for loving,

And the day returns too soon,

Yet we'll go no more a-roving

By the light of the moon."

Life was so full. He tried to be quiet as he let himself into the house and grilled potato waffles. This night was indeed made for loving, he thought, as he dripped brown sauce onto his supper.

Then he swayed up the stairs and fell asleep on his bed still fully dressed.

Drrring! Bell ringing, wound-up tension relaxing, vibrations crossing space and entering the tympanum, turning into beats of a tiny drum, vibrations entering the dream further in, switches flicked, the dream becoming a pattern of bouncing dots, urgent energy, an eye-searing second before his body reached out for the bells to stop them, body memory ahead of consciousness, flailing arm, he muttered, "Why is there a text file?" and opened his eyes, confused as he finally pushed the lever to stop the noise and knew the after-echo was a real vibration finding frustration when each wall bounced it back with a solid hand of rejection. The dream's after-image danced across the ceiling like specks performing a Straussian waltz.

Alex felt rough and dehydrated. He hadn't thought at the time that he was drinking that much, but then again, he hadn't been counting. He had been matching Lucy though; and she definitely drank more than she had in the past.

His head was banging as he stood up and wandered into the kitchen. No-one was in there so he pulled the curtains partway closed (it was *way* too bright). Coffee and toast made him feel better, and a hot shower helped too. Once he'd brushed his teeth and gargled with mouthwash he was halfway human again. Apart from the unsettled tummy. He thought a glass of fizzy health salts would cure it, but it didn't. He eventually realised it was nervousness, not acid.

The front door opened and his mum came in, lugging canvas bags of food shopping.

"Hello day-sleeper, have a good time last night?"

"Yeah, I think so. Just feel a bit rough today. Can you not bang the cupboard doors, Mum?"

"Don't be so soft. Though you do sound croaky. Can't believe you slept in so late. I hope you aren't going to be out of sorts tonight."

His stomach lurched. "No, I'll be fine later. I'm going to get ready for work."

He gripped the kitchen counter tightly, didn't turn round.

"Mum?"

"What, love?"

He could tell her now. Get it all in the open.

"Nothing."

She shook her head. "You're a strange boy."

He was ready to leave for work, pens, papers, Zip disks, notes, a book, fresh-breath mints, pads and printouts neatly put into his bag.

His mum was in the living room watching *Trisha* on ITV, a cup of tea nearby. He hesitated then went in.

"Why are you watching this crap?" he asked.

"There's nothing on the other channels. I just want to sit down for five mins to have my cuppa."

"It'll all be digital one day. Loads of channels to choose from. More than five, anyway. It'll be like America."

"Another of your predictions?"

"Yeah. Mum?"

"Uh-huh?"

"Nothing."

"For fuck's sake, just tell me what it is!"

"Did you get your hair done this morning when you went out shopping? It looks good. Like autumn gold."

"What is it really about? "

"It's about tonight."

"Oh, Alex! You can't skip it again! Absolutely not. I want you here. You'll have to cancel –"

"Mum, button it. I *am* coming tonight. I just want to bring a friend."

"What are you asking for?"

"Because it's Lucy."

She put her cup of tea down slowly. "*That* Lucy? I thought you weren't in touch?"

"True, until the other day. I bumped into her in town."

"Kept that quiet."

"I didn't want to worry everyone. But she's changed. A lot. Not the same person at all. We're friends again. Don't look so worried. I'm in no danger."

She shrugged. "Okay, fine."

"Fine?" He tilted his head. "Aren't you going to argue about it?"

"Alex. You're twenty-eight. You're old enough to choose your own friends, your own toothbrush, your own life and anything else that needs choosing. Apart from clothes, maybe. If you want her to come, it's your lookout. I won't argue about it. My decision is final."

"And you won't be horrible to her?"

"No. Nor will anyone else. I'll speak to them. We're mostly house-trained, you know. Now I want to watch this. They're going to put him on a lie detector."

Alex hugged her. She shooed him off, but happily.

Jane was panting. Despite the heat she hadn't been able to resist going for a run, seeing how much she could push this body, make it live. Plus it had seemed like the weather would break at last. There had been a few drops of rain, but the sun came back, scorching moisture away and leaving everything heavy. It made her feel dense, so the running was harder work, the air less willing to flow into burning lungs. She took off her trainers, tucked the socks into them, then spread her toes on the cool hall tiles for a minute.

A glance at the clock. There was plenty of time for a shower.

The run had been a chance to pound thoughts out as she followed straight lines of decisiveness. Going to the party scared her. The terminal scale to which the lie was growing. The only thing that made it possible was that she knew Lucy never remembered details about topics and people she didn't care about. Jane playing it by ear would probably be as convincing as Lucy's disconnection.

"You're so mean about me," said fictional Lucy, sat in the armchair. She had make-up on, in contrast to Jane's sweaty face.

Jane went to the bathroom and splashed herself with cold water but Lucy followed.

"I'm not always the villain, you know," Lucy continued. "You can't just focus on the negatives. I once missed a party to stay in with him when he had flu. I bet that doesn't fit your image of me."

"Leave me alone. I can do this without you. I'm strong enough."

"Then why didn't you tell him who you really are?"

"Not the right time."

"Yet, conversely, there's never *enough* time, is there? Twenty-three left, Jane."

Lucy looked fainter this time; perhaps it was the light, making imaginary Lucy seem washed out like an old film. Jane snatched a towel and dried herself, glaring at Lucy. "I should never have let you out of the box. You're no help at all. You're just trying to worry me."

"No, I just want you to see that we can do things together."

"Screw together!" Jane flung the towel towards Lucy, but she was gone. It fell to the floor in a heap. "I can do this alone," Jane told it, uncertainly.

There was unsettled energy in the household when Alex got home. His mum was making snacks. Auntie Louise popped round and gossiped. Kelly had escaped on the pretext of her piano lesson. Melinda was helping his mum by dusting. Natalie was reading at the kitchen table. A radio blared in one room and a TV in another.

"Pass me the tin of fruit … no not that one, the mixed fruit … yes, that's it," his mum directed Auntie Louise.

"Should I dust these as well, Auntie Hannah?" Melinda asked his mum, pointing at ornamental crockery.

"What does gregarious mean?" queried Natalie.

"Hello! How's life?" asked a neighbour who came in through the kitchen.

"The heatwave continues – scorchio! News just in, high street chain C&A is going to close all its UK stores, with the loss of over four thousand jobs …" waffled the radio.

"With men and women, does you think that men should marry only one woman? Does you believe in mahogany?" asked Ali G from the telly.

Alex unpacked his bag but didn't feel like doing any research or paperwork. Too unsettled. He checked his watch. Over an hour until he had to leave to meet Lucy.

He went into his parents' room and lay on their bed. The duvet cover was pastel pink, a sure sign that Dad was away. He turned on the portable TV that sat on a chest of drawers at the end of the bed. He wanted mindless distraction.

He found it: a re-run of *The A-Team*, which soon had him laughing at their antics. Natalie must have heard him. She poked her head round the door.

"What's so funny?"

"A programme from before your time. I used to watch it when I was doing my GCSEs. Every week they made a tank out of dustbins and a go-kart, or a bazooka out of a drainpipe and household chemicals. It's ridiculous."

She was dressed in shorts and her favourite baggy shirt she wore around the house, the top few buttons undone. Barefoot as usual.

"Your GCSEs? That long ago, eh?"

"Get out if you're going to be cheeky."

On screen, B.A. Baracus called Murdock a "crazy damn fool!" for talking to an invisible dog.

"Ooh, that's corny. I wanna watch this too. Move over, I'll curl up with you."

She jumped onto the bed next to him so that they lay on their stomachs, propped up on their elbows, heads resting on hands.

"I didn't thank you for paying for us to go ice skating the other night," she said. "You're a star."

"It's nothing. I'm just glad you didn't lose any fingers."

"All present and correct." She wiggled them near his face. Her fingernails were painted with the same vivid blue varnish as her toes.

B.A. Baracus stormed around the set, yelling, "I ain't gettin' on no plane!"

"You mentioned exams," Natalie said. "I've been thinking about the future and stuff, what to do. I'm sick of crappy jobs so fancy going back to college, but stick at it this time, actually stay till the end of the course."

"That's great, if the time is right. I'd be proud of you."

"Are you taking the piss?"

"No! I never do."

"I know that really. I'm just pulling your leg." She elbowed him lightly. He didn't retaliate.

"I just mean that if you really want to do well then you'll put the effort in, study, pass. Especially if you can find a course you'd enjoy. The problem's always when it's just a vague yearning, someone wants a bit of paper at the end of the course but not to work much, they often fail – and hate it. And probably get put off ever trying again later. So it depends on your attitude, and only you really know that. What do you feel, in your heart? Because what you feel there, that's what you have to go with. Always." He spoke without taking his eyes off the screen, but was aware that Natalie was mostly looking at him.

"You talk really nice, Alex. Sorry, distracted."

She thought for a few seconds while Murdock escaped from a psychiatric hospital with the help of Templeton "Faceman" Peck's improbable seduction of a nurse.

"Last time there was tons of other stuff going on, rows with Mum, going out with someone who skipped all his lessons to skive off and smoke weed. But them things are different now. Starting to get on with me mum again, might even move back home, get out of your hair. And I'm not seeing anyone at the moment. Did you know that?"

"No," Alex said, staring ahead.

"Yeah, well, just saying."

"It sounds like you'd do better this time. I can arrange for you to talk with someone from county careers if you want, they could go through courses at the different places."

"I fancy art I think. You lot are arty. Or maybe something like office skills, get better jobs. And English. You could help me with that, I bet."

"You won't need help."

"I know, but *if* I did," she insisted. "I *knew* I was right to chat to you. I like the way you don't tell me what to do; you just help me think clearer. You're an angel."

On the TV B.A.'s milk was being spiked with drugs so they could get him onto a plane. "Thanks, but loads of people would disagree." And probably call him a bore too. *Want career advice? Come to Alex!* He'd be giving mortgage guidance next.

"They're wankers then." She leant over and gave him a soft kiss on the cheek; he could smell her, shower gel and Ribena. "By the way, if *you* ever need to talk about anything, I'll listen. I can be good at that."

When he didn't reply she joined him in watching the programme again. She was close. Her warm thigh and arm were touching his. He did his best to focus on the elite US Special Forces commando unit convicted of a crime they did not commit. In the grand finale The A-Team blasted their way through enemy lines in a jeep, simultaneously outmanoeuvring the military that wanted to arrest them. Natalie was chuckling – and when Colonel John "Hannibal" Smith said, "I love it when a plan comes together!" with a cigar hanging out of his smug mouth, they looked at each other and burst out laughing.

The programme finished and the adverts came on. Natalie rolled onto her back, still smirking at him, and he found himself looking into her eyes. The smirk faded. They stared, but only for a few seconds.

He rolled away from her and stood up quickly.

"Guess it's time to start getting ready. Are you going to be watching any more telly, Nat?"

"No."

He turned it off.

"You don't need much time to get ready do you, Alex? You look fine."

"I've invited someone along so want to dress up a bit smarter."

"Who is it? A girl, I guess, if you want to be 'smarter'?"

"Yes. An old friend from university."

A questioning look.

"Her name's Lucy. We used to go out back then."

"Ah. I think Kelly mentioned her once."

"I bet Kelly didn't say anything nice about her."

"You're right. Just friends?"

"Yeeees," he answered, slowly and unconvincingly. He fidgeted. "Right, better go and get a shower. See you later, Nat."

"Yes. See you later."

He headed for the door.

"Oh, Alex?"

He stopped. "Yes?"

He couldn't read her expression.

"Good luck," she said quietly.

Alex let the door swing closed.

He stood at the bus stop, fidgeting. He sat down on the bench. Two seconds later he stood up and looked at the timetables, trying to work out which bus would come next and whether Lucy would be on it. He couldn't concentrate so he sat on the wall. He jumped down when a bus came round the corner, but it was the wrong one. He sat on the bench again and played with the buttons on his new shirt.

Reflection in the shelter glass. Smart. No reason to have doubts about his tidy appearance. Even his briefs were new ones his mum had got him from M&S.

His digital watch said 19:01. He was sure she would be here soon. But it felt like forever.

A gang of teenagers were making a lot of noise on the other side of the road, yelling and trying to pour beer over one another. They weren't his usual nemeses. These were wearing tracksuit bottoms with stripes up the side, but somehow he didn't think they'd just come from the George Carnall Leisure Centre. He hoped they wouldn't cross over and come to the bus stop.

19:02.

Thankfully they walked on and their shrieks faded.

What if she'd chickened out? No, she'd sounded keen on the phone.

19:03.

Buses are often late in Manchester.

19:04.

A bus came his way, but didn't stop.

He looked at the timetable again but there wasn't another due for fifteen minutes. He slumped back onto the bench and stared disconsolately at some chewing gum on the floor between his feet, and let the sticky minutes stretch by.

"Boo!"

Alex spun, half-expecting it to be the louts from earlier, about to pour beer on him. He was relieved when he saw it was Lucy with a pink bag over her shoulder.

"How did you get here? You weren't on the last bus?"

"I was! But I got off a stop too soon. Just over there," she pointed. "It was funny watching you. You looked like you were on trial." She seemed amused at that.

"I couldn't settle."

"It's me who should be nervous."

"Are you?"

"A bit." A pause. "But let's go anyway."

Alex had been fantasising that she would step off a bus and they would hug. She'd surprised him and now it didn't feel the right time to embrace.

He offered to carry her bag and she accepted. She was wearing a long denim skirt with pockets, and the red top she'd worn when he first spotted her in the pub.

"It's a lovely road, this. I like all the trees and big houses," Lucy said after a while.

Alex looked around. She was right. The pavement was wide enough for trees, some at least a hundred years old.

"I've got a lot of happy memories around here," he said.

"How many people will be there tonight?"

"Loads. Forty, I think my mum said, so more like fifty in the end."

"Fifty! I'll never remember that many names!"

"Don't worry, neither will I. I never do. People bring people. It's fun. Sometimes I get up in the morning and someone I don't know will be having breakfast in the living room, a friend of Kelly's or my mum's. Or relatives stay over. There are quite a few bedrooms. It happens fairly often. People like our house. Friendly. So don't worry."

"I'll try." But her normally smooth brow was slightly creased.

They walked in silence down the Crooked Lanes Footpath which led to his road. There were fields on one side, and blackbirds scurried under bushes at their approach. Lucy looked around her, smiling at each detail, and that changed it in Alex's eyes, too. It stopped being just a shortcut he used every day, and became a magical jade grotto, enclosed under a canopy created by the hawthorn trees on either side which almost met at the top. The breeze seemed fresher. Everything seemed fresher. Being with Lucy transformed things.

They emerged from the lane onto his road. Shapes moved behind the open windows of his house as it filled, music pouring out across the garden towards them.

Lucy had stopped walking. She was staring at the house. Alex halted too.

"You okay, Lucy?"

"Yes. I think so. It's a big house isn't it?"

"Yes. My mum and dad built it when I was a kid. Though Dad won't be here tonight, he's still on the rig, so you won't get to meet him. You never met him, did you?"

Her voice was soft, peaceful, and her eyes had a far-off look in their smoky greyness. "It would have been nice. It's a shame I never got the chance."

"At least you've met my mum, that time she dropped me off at university."

Her peaceful look disappeared. "Yes."

"Don't look worried. It'll be fine, come on. *These legs were made for moving, and the day will end too soon.* My own paraphrase."

She looked at him in silence. He had an overwhelming urge to touch her, so leaned forward and kissed her gently. She seemed tense.

"What's up?" he asked.

She just smiled enigmatically and held her hand to his cheek. Her wrist smelt of perfume, berries.

He picked up her bag and they walked on towards the house.

Alex led Lucy into the kitchen through the open back door. Conversation and laughter spread from every room, partially engulfed by the loud music. Kelly was ladling a glass of punch, the others were chatting or picking at snack food. They made their way through the room, Lucy saying hi and smiling prettily as Alex introduced her. The only nettle in the garden was Kelly, who pissed him off by barely grunting in reply when Lucy spoke to her. He could have happily kicked Kelly up the arse.

"Ignore her," he said to Lucy as they walked away. "We're not all gorillas."

He was aware of close scrutiny from the last person in the kitchen, someone whose eyes were more on Lucy than the baguette she was slicing.

"And my mum, Hannah," Alex said loudly.

"It's good to see you again, Lucy."

"You too, Mrs Kavanagh."

"Did you have a nice journey?"

"Yes thanks. I liked the walk here, especially that lane nearby. And I adore your house."

Alex could tell his mum was pleased by the flattery.

"Well it's lovely to have you here, just help yourself to food and drinks, though I think Alex should put your bag somewhere first, then you can relax more and get to know everyone. We might be playing games later, Monopoly or cards, do you like playing?"

"Oh, Mum!" Alex exclaimed. "She doesn't want to be dragged into the mammoth games you lot play when you're drunk!"

But Lucy disagreed. "Oh yes, especially cards. I used to play a lot with … well, with a group of girls I knew."

"What, bridge? Poker?" Auntie Louise raised her painted eyebrows.

"Not poker, but I know how to play bridge, whist, chase the ace, and snap."

Mum and Auntie Louise laughed. "Excellent! You'll *have* to play later. Alex can watch, he's too much of a spoilsport to join in," teased his mum.

"I'm not a spoilsport. And I thought you didn't used to play, Lucy?"

Lucy gave him a glare that warned "Don't you *dare* start saying I've changed again!"

There was a knock on the kitchen door frame as the next-door neighbours arrived, making it the ideal time to escape.

"Let's take your stuff upstairs. Then we'll get a drink," Alex said.

"Okay."

"Well, past the first line of defences. I told you it would be fine," Alex said. They headed down the hall to the staircase just as Richard and Martin ran from the living room. Richard was holding up an Airfix model plane and making engine noises. Freckle-faced Martin was following with a toy spaceship, imitating machine-gun clatters. They stopped when they saw Lucy.

"Hello, who are you?" Martin asked with the innocent outspokenness of the very young.

"I'm Lucy, a friend of Alex's."

"What's your second name?" demanded Richard, scratching his head, fingers disappearing in thick hair.

"Spiers. So I'm Lucy Spiers in full. Who are you?"

"We're Richard Newman and Martin Horton. I'm Richard, he's Martin. We're cousins. Alex is our uncle."

"I'm pleased to meet you both," Lucy said, mock-formally.

"We were told we haveted to say hello to new people," said Martin, smiling.

"No, Martin, we *had* to say hello," Alex corrected reflexively.

Martin repeated, "We *had* to say hello to new people," slowly.

Then Richard and Martin ran through to the dining room, each calling "Bye, Lucy Spiers!"

"How old is Martin?" asked Lucy.

"Seven."

"Leave school behind, Alex. It's a party."

"Correct English is always imp–" Alex saw she was about to interrupt. "Yes. Sorry."

She relaxed. "I love kids!"

"I don't – though they're not as bad when they're related. Come on."

Alex led her up the wide carpeted stairs and along the wood panelled landing with its framed family photos on the wall. He pointed out who each room belonged to, guessing which were empty.

"We'll just put your stuff in my room for now. It's less likely to be rummaged by any nosy kids playing hide and seek. Most of them know there'd be hell to pay if they touched anything in my room. You can always move it to a spare room later if you want."

Once in his room she asked if she could take her shoes off for a few minutes.

"You can go around barefoot for all we care."

"I just want to stretch them."

She sat on the bed, grimaced, took her mobile phone out of her back pocket. "I'm always doing that." Jabbed a button. Twice. Showed him the blank screen. "It's dead."

"Have you got a charger with you?"

"It's not the battery, I think it's faulty, maybe I banged it when we were out last night. Haven't been able to get a signal since."

"Do you want me to have a look? I've got an electrical soldering iron. Could just be a loose connection, maybe I can fix it."

She shook her head. "Boys and toys."

"I suppose they might not take it back to replace it if I screw up."

"Never mind. I don't need it now." She threw it to one side then looked around as she removed her shoes. "Like a little boy's room."

"Not at all. I got rid of my Danger Mouse duvet cover last year. And at least half the books on the shelves are from after I was twelve."

"My mistake."

"I like your socks."

"Thanks." Jane wiggled her toes in the pink and yellow striped toe socks. "Caterpillars on a big night out."

Alex sat on the bed next to her but she got up and walked over to where she had dropped her bag. She squatted down and rooted, then pulled out a bottle of some fruit juice and wine mix, Cherry Spritzer.

"This is for your mother."

"I told you not to bother."

"I ignored you."

"Well that's all right then. How are your feet?"

"Fine. Just aching from running."

"I could ... give them a rub. If you want. Semi-professional massage."

She just laughed and put her shoes back on.

They returned to the kitchen to get drinks. As people passed, Alex tried to explain who was related to who.

"Well, Melinda's the girl with the pelican T-shirt on, and she's my niece, Richard's sister ..."

A wave, a smile.

"Trudi's my cousin, but Carl – her brother – isn't here tonight because he's on holiday in Tobago with his girlfriend ..."

An eye caught, another smile.

"Auntie Louise is my mum's sister, and married Uncle Harry, so she's a Smith now not a Herriott. Though obviously Mum's not a Herriott any more either because Dad's a Kavanagh ..."

Nodding, lots of nodding.

"Martin's parents are Simon and Helen. Helen's another cousin of mine. She's Auntie Louise's oldest daughter ..."

Pointing, for Jane's benefit.

"Alan is my dad's second brother, he isn't married –"

"Stop!" Lucy interrupted. She was trying not to laugh, and he couldn't understand what was amusing her. "Alex, it's okay. No more, *please*! I surrender!"

"What do you mean?"

"Look, I need to know a few names but not every detail. You're obsessed with connections. It's too much! I'll work it out. Trust me. I have social skills."

"I was just trying to let you know ... so you'd feel more welcome," he said quietly.

"And you've done a good job. I know you meant well, and it's nice. But you're making me feel like I'm in a genealogy lesson! It's not necessary. Your mother said I should get to know everyone but ... just relax."

"Okay. I guess it was a bit much all at once. And I was starting to lose my voice."

She rolled her eyes then helped herself to another drink while he piled mushroom vol-au-vents on his plate.

His mum had taken more food out of the oven and the kitchen filled with people following the hot pastry smells so Alex took Lucy for a wander. Most of the young children were playing "dens" in the dining room so the adults avoided staying there long. Melinda took to Lucy straight away and sat on her knee, chatting. But on being told by one of the boys to get into the base "because the monsters are coming," Melinda scrambled back under the dining room table with the others, letting out a squeal, and pulled the "door" (a chair) closed behind her.

In the living room Uncle Derek and Auntie Pauline were dancing extravagantly to an old Shakin' Stevens song. He was wearing a T-shirt that said "Blow me, it's my birthday" above a picture of a candle. His size meant the T-shirt was stretched tight across his stomach.

Phil and Trudi came over to jokingly apologise for her parents, though Alex suspected that it was more to find out about Lucy. The four sat chatting on the floor in front of the hi-fi, and Suzannah joined them, the first time he'd seen her since the Lass. They were all about the same age, and for once Alex felt part of a group rather than the odd element within one. At one point Suzannah whispered to Alex that Lucy seemed nice. It was the support he'd been hoping for. *One down, many to go.*

Alex's mum called him into the kitchen to help with the trifle. After sprinkling on hundreds and thousands and setting it out with a serving spoon and bowls he got sidetracked by some friends of Auntie Louise's that wanted advice on buying a new PC and were worried about the "Y2K bug" they'd heard about. Alex couldn't help it. He launched into a mini lecture about how it was old news, had been an over-hyped story, and besides, the word "bug" was American, and why had programmers used two digits for years anyway, since it would inevitably lead to event horizon scenarios, and some had called it "The Millennium Bug" which got extra black marks for ignorance because the year 2000 was only the final year of the previous millennium …

When he left them fifteen minutes later they said nothing, faces slack, obviously thinking over what he'd said, and Auntie Louise seemed to be apologising for something.

He found Lucy chuckling at a tale of Uncle Derek's, always a good way to win him over. *Another one suitably charmed.*

"Your uncle was telling me how you used to play with your cousin's dolls when you were young."

"Derek, do you have to embarrass me like this? He probably didn't tell you the full truth, that I didn't just steal Suzannah's Barbie and Sindy dolls to play with on their own – they were company for Action Man. He used to drive them round in his scout car and then they'd make a base behind the cushions on the sofa."

"Oh yes, I remember that," Derek said, scratching his beard. "And didn't you use plasticine to give Action Man –"

"I think Lucy's heard enough! I had an early interest in biology, now let's leave it at that!"

Natalie and Kelly wandered past with some made-up cocktails, multicoloured hedgehogs sprouting umbrellas and straws. No doubt they were a potentially lethal mix of disgusting ingredients.

"Have you met Natalie?" he asked Lucy. "She's living with us for a bit."

She shook her head.

"Natalie!" He beckoned and she came over with Kelly.

"You must be Lucy," Natalie said. "Enjoying yourself?"

"Yes thanks, quite a crowd here isn't there?"

"Uh-huh. Makes it more fun. They're like family to me."

"That must be nice."

"It is."

Alex realised that Lucy and Natalie were staring at each other. It wasn't what he'd expected, and he looked from one to the other, puzzled.

"They're all good people," Natalie said, breaking the silence first. "Look after each other."

"Families should."

"People who care for each other should."

"I'm sure you're right."

"I am. Are you going to be staying with Alex tonight?" Natalie was smiling, neat teeth flashed, but there was something in her tone that made Alex uncomfortable.

"Well, I'll probably stay over. Not sure where, yet."

"Right. I guess you can see how you feel later as to what you do." Kelly was smirking as Natalie spoke. "Well, I'll see you again, I'm sure."

"Yes. I look forward to it."

Kelly and Natalie sauntered off, heads together like conspirators.

"I don't know why they're being funny tonight, Lucy, sorry about that. I'll have words with them both."

"Don't bother. Do you really not know why they're being funny?"

"No, I've honestly no idea. Unless they're drunk."

"You're sweeter than I thought, Alex. Come on, let's get a top-up."

"Okay, but what do you mean?"

"Never mind."

"No, go on, tell me. I'm confused."

"It suits you. But let's change the subject."

Alex grudgingly agreed.

Jane sensed dislike from Kelly and Natalie. She could discern a difference between the two of them though – some kind of protective animosity on one side; and potential threat or jealousy on the other. She wondered vaguely about the latter, but Alex seemed so oblivious that she ruled it out as a possibility.

Whenever she saw him she was drawn to his transparent innocence. It was easy to feel as though she understood him better than he did himself. Conversely, he was rubbish at understanding other people and their motives.

Perhaps his lack of perception was just as well in Jane's case.

They got another drink. Alex was careful to make sure that his was mainly coke rather than alcohol. He didn't want to get drunk again.

The kitchen was temporarily empty. Alex held his glass up to show Lucy the bubbles in the black, explaining that it was an image he wanted to use in an article he was writing about physics. He started leaning closer to her when there was a commotion outside. Richard ran into the room and yelled with childish excitement, "Melinda's chopped her finger! Call an ambulance!" At that eager announcement a wail was heard from the hall; then Melinda shuffled in, crying and holding her finger.

"I've cut myself!" she sobbed.

Alex put his drink down but Lucy had already snatched kitchen roll and was kneeling by Melinda.

"Let me look at that," she soothed. "We'll have it better in no time. Alex, get a first aid kit will you?"

Melinda offered her finger falteringly, and Lucy inspected it while using kitchen roll to absorb some of the blood.

"It's not so bad, darling, we can fix this. What did you do?"

"Cut it on a can," she whined.

"She put her finger in a can of lemonade and turned it round then couldn't get her finger out!" blabbed Richard. "We saw it. Will her finger drop off?" His last few words caused another howl to come from Melinda, and Lucy had to assure her that the finger was safe.

A few adults and children had appeared to see what the fuss was. By now Lucy had the first aid kit, discarded the slightly-bloody kitchen roll and was sterilizing the wound. It didn't look too bad to Alex, peering over Lucy's shoulder.

"I know it stings a bit, but this is a power ointment that makes things all better," soothed Lucy as Melinda winced.

"Power ointment?" she sniffed.

"Yes, it kills germs and makes skin heal, and it can give you good dreams too. You'll probably dream of fairies tonight."

"Will I?"

"Oh yes!"

"And will I?" Alex asked, being silly to cheer Melinda up.

"No, you dafty, only Melinda will dream of fairies, because she's the only one with ointment on!" chastised Lucy.

"Yes! I'll dream of fairies!" stated Melinda excitedly.

By now Lucy had started to neatly bandage the finger.

Trudi arrived, wanting to know what had happened to her daughter. She knelt by Lucy but seemed afraid to interfere.

"It's only a minor laceration, she won't need to go to the hospital for stitches," said Lucy, calmly finishing the bandage. "It'll be fine in a day or two. There you go, Princess! Nearly as good as new! And you won't put your fingers into sharp metal cans again, will you?"

"No, Lucy."

"Good." Lucy kissed Melinda on the forehead, and added, "Off you go."

Melinda had not only stopped crying but was proud of her new, neat, firm-but-not-tight bandage. Trudi kissed her too, then told her to be more careful in future. Melinda ran off to show the other children her impressive war wound.

Lucy passed the first aid kit and bloody tissues to Alex. There was a smell of witch hazel about her.

"Thanks for fixing her finger, she normally whines for ages after anything like that," Trudi said. "It's so hard, you can't be everywhere ..."

"It's no problem, I was already here so it made sense to fix it right away."

"You're really good with children," Trudi continued. "Are you a mother?"

"No." As if she had made a faux pas all three went silent. It was moments before Lucy broke it by saying, "Melinda's so sweet. It was easy."

"And I was impressed at how you did the bandage," Alex contributed.

"I'm trained for it."

"Trained?"

"I mean, it's just from doing first aid courses at work. Didn't think I'd ever use it."

"I've done two first aid courses and still can't remember things!"

"That's nothing new with you!" teased Trudi. "If it's practical, you forget it. If it's useless information about the number of *buga-bites* in a computer, or what ancient Greeks thought of cabbage, you remember it. He was always like that, Lucy."

"Philosophy elevates us! Words and theories aren't —"

"See what I mean?"

The two women laughed at him, but he didn't mind. It was good seeing Lucy fit in.

Auntie Louise and Alex's cousin Helen appeared, clearing the kitchen table and putting the food and drink on the side units instead. A box was put in the middle, and cards removed. The box also contained pens and paper and matchsticks and dominoes and many other bits of gaming paraphernalia. One chair was empty.

"Will you join us, Lucy?" his mum asked. "Then we can play bridge. You could be my partner."

"I'd like to but it might not be fair on Alex to start a game he can't play."

"Don't worry about that, there are loads of people here that he knows! And it isn't fair of him to hog you all evening anyway."

"I'll be all right if you want to play." He wanted his family to like her but hoped she'd decline.

Melinda, ever-observant and quick to capitalise on any opportunity, tugged at Alex's arm. He hadn't even noticed her reappearing. Kids could be like ninjas sometimes. "Will you help me with a jigsaw, Uncle Alex, my new dog one? I can't use my poorly hand."

"That settles it!" laughed his mum. "You can't ignore a niece with a poorly hand when she needs your help!"

"All right, we'll do it on the living room floor. You okay, Lucy?"

"Yes, I'll be fine. Go and play."

So they went next door and set the jigsaw out. Some of the other children joined in, and soon Alex got the kids so engrossed in finding the edge pieces he was able to sneak a peek into the kitchen.

They were all laughing. Lucy was looking at her cards, concentrating beautifully. A pang, that she should look like that. It was a stolen look, so he deserved the pain. He slunk back into the dining room, feeling left out.

After playing with the jigsaw for a while longer the kids got bored. Alex found himself having a wrestling match with them. This involved him staying on his knees in the middle of the floor while the kids laughed and circled round him, taking it in turns to charge forward and try to wrestle him to the floor while others watched the show with gleeful anticipation. He would flip or spin them carefully so they were propelled gently away or received a quick tickle until they screamed with laughter. Every now and again he would let them wrestle him down to a state of mock surrender. It was a universally understood sign for a pile-on.

"Right, time to stop now," he eventually said, surprisingly breathless.

"Aw, no!"

"A bit longer, please?"

"One more wrestle!"

"No, I'm tired now." He looked at his watch. It was coming up to 11pm.

"We're not!"

Trudi's voice cut them down. "Oh yes you are, you're all getting a bit giddy now – especially you, Alex! – so it's time to stop."

Alex hadn't seen Trudi appear in the doorway so wasn't sure how long she had been watching. Yet more protests came from the children but she clapped her hands. "Enough! It's definitely coming up to bedtime for you all. Everyone up the stairs!"

They trudged up the staircase, complaining all the way. Usually some children stayed for the whole night. Others would just be put to bed until their parents left; at which time they would be plucked, still slumbering, and carefully and quietly carried to the cars.

"Give me a hand putting them to bed?" asked Trudi. "Phil and Simon are having an arm-wrestling competition, Helen's too busy playing cards, and Suzannah's on the phone to her boyfriend half the time."

"Sure. I'll read them a story to get them off to sleep as well if you want."

"That'd be a big help. I might even listen to a story myself!"

"Right. You get started and I'll be up in a minute. Just going to check on the gamesters first."

"Check on Lucy more like …"

Alex stuck his tongue out and went into the kitchen.

"How's it going?" he asked the group.

"Your Lucy is thrashing us!" replied Auntie Louise.

"Oh no I'm not! We only won a few tricks, but I don't think I can hold my own any longer, not with this hand!"

"See, she's trying to bluff us again!" said Helen. "Don't listen to her!"

While Lucy was concentrating on her cards Alex's mum looked up quickly, made a secret thumbs-up signal to Alex and winked. "I bet you're annoyed at us keeping Lucy from you, eh, Alex?" she said. "Don't worry, we'll let her go to bed eventually."

Alex blushed and was glad no-one else had been looking. *Still, it was victory three for Lucy.*

He hovered a while longer, reluctant to leave.

"Excuse me for a minute, I need to go to the toilet," Lucy said after making her move.

"And I'd better go upstairs and start reading the stories."

In the hall they stopped.

"Sorry I'm ignoring you a bit," Lucy said. "But I want your family to think of me as one of them."

"I know. You're doing a great job. I can tell my mum approves of you, and once you're tight with her you're home and dry." Their voices were lowering.

"As long as you know why I'm doing this. I'm not that into games. Sometimes we have to do stuff for others. I just love the idea of being welcome in your family."

"You could have been." She shook her head slightly, so he changed the subject. "Are you going to be playing much longer?"

"We're partway through a game. It'd mess things up if I dropped out."

"Maybe after this one we'll go and sit in the garden for a bit? I bet it's nice out there."

"Yes. I'll try and get away as soon as I can. I promise."

"Good."

Alex inclined forward for a kiss, but timed it badly just as she turned away and moved over to the downstairs toilet. He was left leaning towards air. He quickly recomposed himself.

"I'd better go and get the kids settled," he said, too loudly.

One story turned into three. The last one he made up, telling it in a whisper, adding treasure and a map to a story about a boy who didn't like school but ended up with lots of friends. It wouldn't have stood up well to sustained deconstruction but it wasn't bad off the top of his head.

"Well done, Alex, I think they've all nodded off!" whispered Trudi as she carefully closed the door.

"I thought they never would."

"You're good with them. Though I'm not sure about that bit where the boy started explaining the periodic table ..."

"I was stuck for inspiration there. But the kid with a ponytail liked it."

"Yes. I don't know whose she is. What are you doing now?"

"I'll go and see if Lucy is free of the clutches of the card-sharps yet."

"You're not getting to spend as much time with her as you'd hoped, eh?"

"No. I'm tough though. As long as they don't take much longer."

"Good luck then. I like her."

Another one in the bag.

Back into the kitchen.

"You lot are *still* playing?"

"You asked us that only twenty minutes ago," said his mum.

"No, it was nearly an hour ago!" Alex replied.

His mum pointed to the clock. He was surprised. She was right.

Although he was informed which games had been played, who had won what, and how the current one was going, no-one could tell him when they would *finish*. Someone mentioned playing Monopoly after that.

He threw ice into his glass aggressively, letting it plink around like heavy particles, then poured alcohol over the top. Neat this time. He let the cupboard door bang, and Lucy shrugged at him, mouthed, "Not long."

Alex went into the other rooms. Danced badly. Drank without enjoying it. Chatted. Excused himself from a group argument about the likely outcomes for the US elections now that it looked like Al Gore would be up against George Bush. The consensus was against Bush.

Checked a clock. Ground his teeth. Downed his drink.

The evening wasn't going according to plan. He decided to have a lie down in his bedroom, put a lamp on and flopped onto his bed. The soft light made the room inviting and peaceful. Although music from below could still be heard it was fainter, less insistent.

He imagined footsteps. Lucy's. She would come upstairs to look for him, running a hand along the smooth wooden banister sensuously; then walk in and see him relaxing on a wide, soft, inviting bed. Unable to resist, she would step over quietly, reluctant to wake him, but with a floorboard's creak he would turn and see her –

There was a creak. He ejected surrogate Lucy from the bed as his door opened for real.

It was Richard. His nephew stood there brushing thick fringe out of his eyes, hair stuck up all over as usual.

"Richard, what are you doing still up?"

"I woke up and couldn't sleep so went and played on my Gameboy in anuvva room. But I'm bored now. Can I sleep in here, Uncle Alex?"

"No!"

"But you've got lots of room and a blow-up mattress-thing, why not? I wanna stay with you."

"Sorry, Richie, no. Any other time you know I wouldn't mind, but I've got another friend staying in here tonight," though he wasn't a hundred per cent sure of that, "and there won't be room for you."

"I'll be quiet."

"No, sorry. You'll have to go back to the other room. Or you can sleep in the room on the top floor, where the teddies are. There's a bed made up in there."

"That room's haunted," he pouted.

"No it isn't. And here, you can have some of my comic books to read." Alex gave him a few of his childhood *Whizzer and Chips* annuals. Richard's face lit up and he accepted them eagerly.

"Okay, I'll go upstairs and read there. Thanks, Uncle Alex."

"Don't read for long, it's very late. I'll be up in a bit to check you've put the light out," he lied, "and if your mum catches you still up you'll be in trouble."

Richard scarpered, as if mentioning his mother might make her appear in a puff of smoke. Kids were naive about the solidity of matter. The solidity of people.

Alex fidgeted. He scowled at the clock. Nearly midnight. Downstairs.

There were fewer people around now, but conversations and laughter continued their fight to be heard above the music.

Lucy was still in the kitchen but the cards had been put away. Auntie Louise was talking to her. Lucy seemed cornered but smiled at Alex apologetically, apparently trying to end the conversation without being rude.

She hadn't sought him out.

He needed fresh air so clumped across the kitchen, grabbing a glass of something fizzy that had been left on the side. Into the garden. He stood for a moment, letting the fresh warm breeze tousle his hair and shirt. Took a huge gulp. It was disgusting. He felt so edgy. Yet it was over something so petty. Lucy didn't have to hang on to him. She didn't belong to him.

He leaned against a tree. Leaves rustled above him, swishing in the gentle wind. He could see the kitchen door out of the corner of his eye. He would look casual when viewed from there. He used Tennyson as a spell.

Come into the garden, Maud,
I am here at the gate alone;
For a breeze of morning moves,
And the planet of Love is on high.

The stanza finished; Maud did not appear on cue; music and laughter from the house just filled him with annoyance.

He finished the drink with a grimace, stormed into the kitchen, banged the glass in the sink.

"Auntie Louise, I need to speak to Lucy." He took Lucy's arm and led her outside without waiting for an answer, making his aunt's ridiculous fucking cartoon eyebrows rise up.

"Thanks for the rescue!" Lucy said as they moved into the garden. "You have a lovely family, but they would get a gold medal for talking."

"At least Monopoly ran its monotonous course in the end, huh?" he asked with sarcasm.

"We didn't play Monopoly. They were pulling your leg."

"Typical. Were you all joking about me? Forget it, don't answer that one. Why didn't you come and find me when you'd finished?"

"I was going to. Why are you being off with me?" There was a hint of pain in her voice.

"I've hardly seen you tonight. I wanted to spend time *with* you. That's why you came here, I thought."

"Don't you think that's what I wanted too, you idiot!" she snapped back. "Twice I left the games to find you, but I couldn't! I followed you at one point but you were gone! I wasn't avoiding you, I was *right there!* And I thought you wanted me to get on with everyone? So snap out of it will you? I'm sorry, if that's worth anything. I got it wrong."

They could have sat on the bench. Instead they faced off against each other under the tree.

The kitchen door opened, light spilled across the edge of the lawn as Alex squinted at the figure stepping out with a slight wobble.

"Nat? That you?" a voice asked.

"Kelly, go back inside," Alex said.

But Kelly didn't go back in. She came forward unsteadily. "Ooh, should have known it would be you two. How romantic."

"Stop stirring and get inside," growled Alex.

"You tell *me* to get inside? You can't trust her, Alex. I can see right through her." Kelly turned to Lucy. "Are you going to use him again, then piss on him?"

"Fuck off inside!" Alex repeated, stepping forward.

"What, or you'll make me? You're an artistic weed," she slurred.

"I'll take that as a compliment. Though I assume you meant *autistic*, you piss-head. For the last time, fuck off!"

Lucy put a hand on Alex's arm but it wasn't necessary. Kelly turned and went back into the kitchen muttering curses.

"Don't take it out on her," Lucy said, stepping closer to Alex and speaking softly. "I'm fine. She cares about you, that's all. You shouldn't fight about something like that, or one day you'll regret it. I know what it's like to be in that position. I suppose Kelly will be going to university soon, for three years. That's a lot of time when you won't see each other; you don't want her to become a stranger in that time, lose the connection. Trust me. She's part of your life. Keep her in it. Alex, are you okay?"

Alex shook her hand from his arm. "No. That's another thing. I don't want you to interfere! I see it, this nagging, lecturing, correcting. And you know what? It reminds me of how you used to be. I didn't understand you then, and I don't understand you now."

She stepped back. He heard her inhale sharply. When she spoke she sounded hurt. "Why are you being such a dick with me?"

"I'll take that as a –"

"It is NOT a compliment. Not. NOT! Stop reverting to your automatic phrases, and instead actually *communicate* with me honestly, treat me like an adult you care about, not a student in your classes!"

"Honesty, huh? I'm surprised you remember that, Lucy."

She stared at him.

Beyond her some people were looking out of the kitchen window to see the commotion. He wanted to tell them all to fuck off. At the top of his fucking voice.

"It's falling apart," she said, slumping onto the bench.

"Yeah. A washout. I'm going upstairs. See you in a bit." He didn't wait for a reply.

He ran a palm over his face. Paced across the carpet, glaring at his door every time he turned towards it. The noise of conversation from below irritated him and he tried to block it out.

It wasn't long before there was a knock and Lucy came in. She hardly glanced at him, face blank; just walked over to her bag and picked it up.

"I'm sorry I came. I was wrong. Will you at least order me a taxi?"

"You're going?"

"What do you think, Einstein?"

"I think …" He didn't know what he thought. "I think …" He held his head up high but his lip was trembling. She looked at him, saw the weakness. "I'm sorry," he managed to spit out, squeezing his eyes tight shut. "I'm sorry. I'm tired and grouchy and I'm a shit. An arsehole. It's me, I'm blowing it and I don't understand why." He sniffed and wiped his eyes on the back of his hand, then let his knees bang on the floor as he knelt in front of her, looked up, filled with sudden panic that she would turn her back on him and walk out of the room. He wouldn't cry.

Her face betrayed nothing. He took that to be encouragement as he looked up at her, afraid to touch.

"I know what it took for you to come here tonight."

She shook her head but seemed to soften.

"And there I was in the garden, treating you more like a stubborn stain than a guest. I was being horrible. If you hate me, it's justified." He wiped his eyes again. "Please don't go. Not like this."

Finally, she moved; squatting down to his level.

"Alex –"

"Please say you'll stay. This makes me think back – do you know that I blamed everything on you when we split up? But

I'm not even sure of *that* any more. Maybe you saw something in me, something not so nice ... I don't know ... Please stay." He sobbed once, wiped his eyes angrily again.

"Alex, it's okay. Apology accepted." She put her hand on his and he gripped it. "We're both experiencing a lot. These few days, like a whirlwind. It's not just you."

"So you'll stay?" he asked eagerly. "You can have another room, or I'll sleep on the floor in my sleeping bag, but it would be nicer if you crashed in here with me, it's a big bed. I don't mean any funny business, just that we can have a bit of peace, and a bit of time together, undisturbed. There's nothing – *nothing* – I'd rather do right now."

"If I stay, I'll want you to agree to something."

"Sure, whatever you ask. What is it?"

"I'll tell you later. It won't be anything you can't do."

"Why the mystery?"

"Because I don't want a long discussion now. I want to get to bed."

"Okay."

"Should we say goodnight to people downstairs?"

"No. They'll be wrapping up soon, I hope. Let's just go straight to bed. I'm going to do my teeth. There's two bathrooms."

They got up. He gave her a hug and had to force himself to let go.

Soon he was spitting out toothpaste, and raised his face to look in the mirror. Eyes tinged red to match his hair. What interest could she have in him anyway? One more splash of cold water and he returned to his room. Lucy was still in the bigger bathroom at the end of the hall. He could hear the tap running.

He flopped into bed, just leaving one soft light on. And almost immediately dozed off.

Pressure next to Alex. A weight that pulled him from sleep with its gravity.

He rolled over. Lucy. Sat next to him, looking down with a tender expression. Her eyes sparkled.

"So tired," she said.

"So tired," he repeated.

She was wearing a long loose nightshirt that went down to her knees. It had a picture of a sleeping cartoon dog on it.

"Move over, Alex."

He did, and she climbed into the warm patch where he'd been lying.

"I'm sorry again about before," he said.

"It's okay, it's past. Let's never argue again."

"That sounds good to me."

"I'm tired and I have to leave early. Turn the light out and hold me."

The light was dutifully turned off. They moved together and held each other. Her skin was warm, breath on his cheek. Lay in near-darkness, butterflies set free in his tummy. He imagined there was nothing outside the room but the silence and peace of deep night, no world but what they created, tonight.

She was so close. He wasn't tired any more. She knew him. His heart lay open to her. That reminded him of words from the past. Since he'd met Lucy again the poetry he'd loved in university was coming back, like a dream remembered, tender associations, Tennyson's.

So fold thyself, my dearest, thou, and slip
Into my bosom and be lost in me.

Her breath tickled fine hairs, sending shivers down his spine. After everything, she had come back; it proved that love could conquer all.

Their lips moved closer; every touch of her hand electrified his body. Then they kissed and moved together, and the kisses became more passionate. Their bodies touched, and he explored ground once known but assumed lost forever. Off came her nightshirt and his new briefs. Her leg slid across his, smooth, and he touched the softness of her breast, nervously at first, but then with increasing energy they caressed, kissed and explored, until he was lying on top of her, between her thighs. When she spoke it was just to whisper "Yes" into his ear. He fumbled for a condom from by the bed.

Now folds the lily all her sweetness up,
And slips into the bosom of the lake.

For a few minutes he lost himself in her, and it was like the first time they'd had sex together. No, better than the first time. All he knew was that their hot bodies moving together felt right, good, vital and of this moment. They gently rocked back and forth, no hurry, as at peace with each other as they'd ever been. She moaned softly and he approached climax, his focus moving down his torso, concentrating in that point of sensation that spiralled up in pitch from the soft pressure inside Lucy. She held him tight against her with her legs.

Now slides the silent meteor on, and leaves
A shining furrow, as thy thoughts in me.

It felt like coming home.

In the faint orange light of a street lamp her face was cast in shadows. Her eyes were closed as she moaned quietly. She kissed or bit his lips, neck, shoulders, ears, fingers: whatever was near her mouth at the time. Her nipples were erect and whenever he wasn't sucking on them he could feel them against his chest. She wanted him.

He could see her close-up, she was beautiful, more than ever before. Feelings welled up within him, a heatwave, desire for closeness, to get rid of barriers, to twist two into one, a sweet thread of mortality just like the best words in the best order that he always yearned for, *this was poetry*. This was love. And when the point of no return came and passed she held him, panting, eyes still closed.

"Stay in me for a minute," she whispered.

Her heart beat against his chest as he relaxed and lay his head on her shoulder. His own heart also tattooed a rhythm that did not slow for some time. In the silence of that rhythm he felt they were truly one.

At last he withdrew. After disposing of the condom they lay curled up on their sides, as close as they could get, facing each other with legs entwined. He stroked her hair: she held his other hand.

Now droops the milkwhite peacock like a ghost,
And like a ghost she glimmers on to me.
The poetry was over.

"I think I've wanted to do that for days," Alex whispered, as he stroked her face.

"And me. Although I was nervous, too. I even wonder whether I put off coming to bed tonight because I knew this would happen?" She seemed to be talking to herself.

"I wish I'd known it would happen. I'd have been much more relaxed."

She chuckled, and he felt the vibrations against his body.

"I should have seen it," he continued. "Paid more attention to Apollo's first law: 'Know Thyself'."

"If it had been predicting results in science then I'd have trusted you to spot it. People: not so much," she teased.

Something had been niggling at his mind. He couldn't think of how to phrase it so just blurted it out, assuming that they could say anything in the re-found intimacy.

"You made love differently from how you used to …"

He immediately knew he'd said the wrong thing as she withdrew her hand and asked angrily, "What is it with you? Why do you have to spoil the moment?"

"I'm sorry, I didn't mean bad, that was lovely. Different but … better. I felt really close to you this time, I meant."

"What, and you didn't used to feel close to me when we made love?"

An image of a man digging a hole popped into his head. Women were tricky.

"Not exactly, but you did used to – oh forget it."

"Go on, I insist." But she seemed to have relented from her anger slightly.

"Well, you used to take less part, and get less worked up. I'm not saying this to accuse you or complain or anything," he added defensively. "It doesn't matter now. But this tonight was on a higher plane. I felt like we were there together, which is all I've ever wanted. You used to sometimes joke that sex was only for me, remember? That you were doing your 'duty'? But it never felt like it did tonight. Tonight it felt like you don't think that way any more. And it was lovely." He kissed her forehead.

"Was I really that bad?" She frowned, as if trying to remember. "I was horrible back then, wasn't I?"

"No, just ... well, I loved you. But you're nicer now."

"I'm glad you think that. It's been a strange night, hasn't it?"

"Yes. And I'm sorry again for before."

"I warn you, if you apologise again I'll hit you!"

He bit back the urge to say "sorry".

"Despite what you said, you have been nice to me tonight," she continued. "You made me a part of your family. Yet you were never even introduced to mine. That says a lot."

"It doesn't matter."

"It does."

"We can argue about that another time."

She squeezed his hand. "You're not missing much. By not meeting my relations. You're luckier than me, having a large and loving family."

"It doesn't always feel that way."

"It should. They're so full of life. Sometimes life stings, but it's better than numbness." A pause. "Do you ever wonder why we're here, Alex?"

"I think about it. I concluded that we're meant to grow as people and find happiness. Give happiness, too."

"Give happiness – I like that. A focus on others, being selfless. That's the best reason."

They lay in silence for a bit, just touching, as if to confirm that the other was still there, was real.

"You were right," Alex whispered.

"About what?"

"Lots of things. But being obsessed about the past, haunted even – I was thinking about what you said in The Temple of Convenience. You don't know how hard it is to change the way you think."

"I have a good idea."

"Well, being with you again, it's given me a new perspective on things. On what's important. And I can see that it wasn't just you. I've been blaming you, but it wasn't the full truth. Even before you I didn't have much luck with girlfriends. They left, or got bored, or it didn't get started. I'd got used to it, tried to numb myself. Just got even more into other things. And when I met you it was weird, the physical side was one thing but I also sensed hidden depths, like there was more to you than on the surface. I came to believe in you, and started to hope that this was it. The future. Then when it happened … it shattered me. Numb again. Worse than before. That soured the PhD too, I couldn't continue. Since then I've not really wanted anyone else. Don't trust anyone to commit."

She kissed him on the lips but didn't speak.

"The weird thing is, all those questions I had about us splitting up, whether it was because I wanted us to live together, or Ted had made moves on you first, or you were bored, or didn't love me as much, or maybe the relationship had run its course but I hadn't noticed, whatever – they're not important now. Ha! I don't need to know about it any more. Not everything in life needs explaining. And that's the thing I can hardly get my head round – me, admitting that! I mean, it was never even enough for me to know that a toaster worked, I had to know *how* it worked. To leave something unanswered … But I decided I would. Let the questions die. Or float away. *Adios.* So I suppose I just wanted to say: I forgive you. For anything you did. I don't care."

"Wow. Alex, coming from you, that's amazing." They kissed again, more passionately. "I wanted to tell you that, how it's better to move on. This isn't just about me. This is bigger than me. It's about a habit," she enthused. "You could go mad trying to rationalise the past, things like that can stay in you, growing like a fungus, giving out spores of obsession to other parts of your mind. But I never thought you'd be able to really start again, say you don't need to know. Alex, living with uncertainty! Oh, sounds like I'm giving another lecture, don't be mad."

"I'm not. You're right. I was angry just because I'm not used to admitting that someone else could understand something better than me. I was wrong. Don't hit me, I didn't say the 's' word."

"I won't hit you. I'm too happy. This backs up what I've always thought, what I wanted the world to be like. I've always believed happiness doesn't come from facts, it comes from *living*. And it isn't about the past, it's about life now and onwards. You're better than you were. You can let go of the past, of me. Most people couldn't do it, but I could see it in you, this ability. After all that ... We're both sorry. Clean slate?"

"Clean slate."

Their foreheads touched, rested. He shuddered. She was his Jane Morris, perfectly drawn in living lines. He caressed her neck, followed the contour of her skull, ran a finger down to her lips. Upturned at the corners, smiling, like his own.

"That was easy to consent to," he said. "If you'd told me I only had to agree not to ask you about the past again, I'd have been happy."

Her hands stopped roaming. "No, that wasn't the concession for me staying."

"Oh?"

"It's a bit more. It's that you won't follow me when I leave in the morning."

"What kind of request is that?"

"A literal one."

"You're pulling my leg."

"I'm not. I thought we understood each other? That it's best to move on; you can change your life for the better then. Your bad opinion is the last thing in the world I'd want. I wouldn't have done this if I didn't think you were strong enough to deal with it."

He let go of her. "I don't believe this. We've only just worked everything out!"

"That's it. We've worked everything out."

"So why can't we move on together?"

"It wouldn't work. Not every relationship can. It doesn't mean I don't love you."

"This is bullshit." He rolled onto his back, arm on throbbing forehead. "You can't do this to me again."

"It's not the same. We can't be together, there's no future in it."

"Why?"

"You wouldn't understand."

"Try me. You've already said I've amazed you once." He turned back to her, unwilling to touch yet, but hopeful.

She sighed. "I don't want to be put on the spot, but you deserve to know. I made a promise to someone, and can't break it."

"You're with someone else?"

"I will be."

"Someone you love?"

"Not in the way I care about you."

"What, it's not sexual?"

"No."

197

"You make it sound like some kind of arranged marriage or something. Last I heard, women had a choice."

"I'm doing my best to explain, but I knew it wouldn't work. You've got strong principles, can't you accept I'm committed to something else and can't break my word? You wouldn't want someone to break a promise."

"I'd allow it just this once."

"I only stayed because you agreed to do anything I asked. And this is what I ask."

"So, you want to break my heart again?"

"I'm not breaking your heart. I love you."

"Don't say that if it isn't true."

"I love you. It's true."

"If you were committed to someone else, some promise, you shouldn't have done this to me."

"I told you, that's not the same kind of love. It's not what I feel for you. This feeling ... I only have it for you."

"You should have told me."

"Answer this, Alex, completely honestly. If you knew this at the start, that I would only be with you for three days, and that I couldn't stay, but we would end up in bed like this – would you have changed anything? Stayed away?"

After a pause, his "No" was barely audible.

"That's what I thought. It doesn't mean I don't love you. It just means that I can see it now – this was inevitable. We had to do this. Not every relationship can work out. But it's better to end with love than bitterness. Will you keep your word?"

He wanted to shout. To shake her, to throw his pillow across the room. Instead he said, "Yes. I can't believe I'm saying that, but yes. I'm too tired to argue any more. However, I want you to promise me something."

"Only if I can."

"I want you to promise that if your mysterious thing doesn't work out, you'll get in touch?"

"If it was possible then I'd do it."

"Okay. That'll have to be enough."

"Don't think me leaving has anything to do with you. It doesn't. Given every choice, I'd stay. Don't ever put yourself down. You're lovable and loving and loyal, and any girl with a saint's patience would be lucky to have you. You're also a complete geek, yes, but hey ho, horses for courses."

He couldn't help splutter out a laugh. "One day geeks will rule the Earth. Give it fifteen years."

She ran a hand down his damp cheek.

"I'm not crying," he said, with a sniff.

"I know."

He yawned. "I'm just tired."

"We both are."

"I feel strangely peaceful," he whispered. "Who'd've thought it?"

"You'll forget me before long. Just keep the peace in you."

"Never forget you," he murmured sleepily.

"I just mean in sleep."

"Oh."

She put her hand on his forehead, told him to sleep, he was in her arms, they murmured a few more things to each other, sleep nothings, and one of them sounded like she was saying she'd be gone when he woke, he wanted to laugh or tell her he didn't believe her but he was too tired so just grunted. Maybe he imagined it. He was soon asleep.

Jane lay awake. Alex's breathing was the rhythm of slumber. She was alone.

She kissed Alex gently on his cheek. He didn't respond. She carefully slid out of bed. The springs creaked once but didn't affect Alex's breathing. She walked on the balls of her feet to the door and eased it open slowly before slipping out and going into the bathroom at the end of the hall, navigating by the bluish moonlight that shone through a skylight. Only once she was inside the bathroom with the door closed and locked did she turn on the light over the sink. She put the seat down on the loo and sat on it, rubbing her upper arms to stave off the chill. Her bags were by the bath, where she'd left them.

She couldn't go back to bed, sleep, and wake in the morning as if things were normal. Daylight had a way of reducing things, grinding magic against concrete underneath a heel.

She washed in cold water then dressed. Sat on the loo seat again. Rooted in her bag for a pen and the postcard.

How much should she tell? Honesty would make her feel good. She had kept intending to tell the truth. And failing miserably. This was the last chance saloon. On the other hand, it would injure Alex. Undermine everything.

She wrote. Packed her bag. Put her trainers on. Light off.

As she came out of the bathroom she noticed something white down the short corridor to her left. A notice taped to a door. She crept down the hall to read it. "Natalie's room" it said in wax crayon, a child's writing with animal doodles around the edge. Maybe a gift, drawn by one of Alex's nephews or nieces. Jane stared at it.

This was silly. She should go.

Instead she turned the handle and opened the door slowly, hoping it wouldn't creak. There was only the sound of slow breathing from the darkness beyond. She held her breath and stepped into the room, closing the door softly behind her. The breathing did not change. Her eyes adjusted to the dark.

Paintings on walls and old-fashioned furniture. It didn't feel like a young person's room, but it was being transformed on the surface. Clothes on the floor next to black pumps with white laces, one of which lay on its side. Make-up scattered all over a unit by the bed, bottles, nail varnish, open compacts. A mess. Jane smiled. The opposite to Alex.

The shape in the bed moved slightly. Settled.

Instead of being sensible and leaving, she carefully stepped over the things on the floor until she was at the bed. Natalie's head and upper body lay outside of the duvet. She wore a pink T-shirt.

There was a book near one of her hands. A pale cover, bold writing. Soft light came through the thin curtains which hadn't been pulled fully closed; they were slightly tangled as if tugged in an impatient hurry. She could just make out Wordsworth, Coleridge, *Lyrical Ballads*. It surprised her. Something she would have expected to see on Alex's bookshelves, not in Natalie's bed.

Jane nodded to herself, eyes half-closed in realisation.

Pushing her knees against the bed frame for support, to save putting down her hands on a potentially squeaky mattress, Jane bent over the sleeping form and whispered a few words near Natalie's ear. Quiet enough not to wake her, but hoping the words would enter a dream.

She retreated as cautiously as she had come and held her breath until she was out in the hall. This was taking too long.

More creeping. Postcard pushed under Alex's door. Palm to the wall on the other side of which was his sleeping head. He never really knew *her*.

Never would.

She checked her watch. Only two and a half hours to go. Time to leave. She could ring a taxi from the payphone down the road.

Alex gradually came back into awareness. Morning. A sliver of sunlight was shining through a crack in the curtains. It crossed the carpet, ran up the side of the bed, then lay across his legs like a golden stream.

He rolled over to face Lucy, but she wasn't there. He was momentarily perturbed but assumed she had gone to the toilet, or was downstairs getting breakfast.

He slid his hand over to where she had been lying.

Cold.

He sat up and looked at the clock. It was just after 9am. She would have left by now.

He leapt out of bed and flung on his dressing gown. As he fumbled with the knot he spotted something underneath the door. Snatched it. A postcard. One side showed *La Donna della Finestra*. The other was Lucy's handwriting.

Letting out an involuntary sob he slumped onto the bed.

Alex,

You hardly stirred when I got up and kissed you on the cheek. I wanted to just climb back into bed. But I can't. This was a diversion from somewhere I have to go, but believe me, it was important. You are important. This brief time together was beautiful, and if I had the choice I'd want to carry on. But I can't. Just know that I loved you.

Please be happy.

Lucy. x

He stared at these words. He remembered what they'd said last night. He could complain that she'd come into his life just to trouble him all over again: but he didn't feel that any more. There was no anger at all. Just calm. He wasn't used to that feeling.

He loved the girl who had written the note. He'd promised not to follow her. As a man of honour it was a rule that he should keep his word.

Sack it. Maybe some rules were meant to be broken after all.

Clothes were hastily pulled on, watch grabbed and strapped on wrist as he rushed downstairs.

"Morning, Alex, is Lucy up yet? I can make you both some breakfast if you –"

"Wait a minute, Mum!" he snapped, thumbing frantically through the phone book. She retreated to the kitchen.

He found the number and dialled.

"Hello, National Express, this is Lorraine speaking, how can I help you?"

"Hi, can you tell me what times the buses leave for London Kensington from Manchester Piccadilly Coach Station on Chorlton Street?"

"Today?"

"Yes!"

"I'm checking now ... Well, there's no journeys direct to London Kensington today, but you could get the 440 service from Manchester to Golders Green via Birmingham which leaves at 9.30am. After that is the 540 service from Manchester to London Victoria, also via Birmingham. That arrives in London at 3.05pm, and is due to leave Manchester at 10.15am."

"Shit!"

"Excuse me?"

"Oh, sorry. What stand does the 10.15 bus leave from?"

"Ah ... stand B, bay 4."

"Thank you, goodbye." Click. "Mum!"

"What? Is everything okay?"

"Can you drive me to the town centre? Now?"

"What, Urmston or Stretford?"

"No, city centre."

"Why? And what about Lucy?"

"Mum, there isn't much time. Lucy has gone to get her bus. She may already have left Manchester, but if not she'll probably be on one of the next two buses. I'm too late for the first, but the second leaves in ..." he glanced at his watch, "about forty minutes. I know it's a long way at short notice but it'd be the hugest favour I'll ever owe you and it means a lot to me so please please pretty please say you'll drive me."

"I doubt if we'd make it that quickly."

"If we go right now we just might!"

"Okay! No need to shout!"

She took her apron off and threw it on the table, grabbed her car keys, then stopped to look in the mirror.

"Mum!"

"Sorry."

They got in the car, doors banged, seat belts clunked and clicked.

"Where to exactly?" she asked as they pulled out onto the road.

"The coach station in town."

"So what happened?"

"A long story. I'll explain it later. I want to see her before she goes."

"I didn't see her leave."

"No, I think she left early and slipped out so as not to disturb anyone."

"What did you do to upset the poor girl?"

"Nothing!"

They were passing through Davyhulme. Alex saw it as a good sign that there weren't many cars around.

"Well if she catches the bus before we get there can't you ring her or something?"

"If she gets her phone fixed then yes, eventually."

"Ah. Even if it's broke I'm sure you could get hold of her somehow. All that technology and online and things."

"Maybe. Just drive."

His mum looked left and right then pulled onto Chester Road. They were soon passing the purple neon PC World building, meaning they were in Old Trafford, location of various activities that had never interested Alex. Namely football, cricket, and car showrooms. They drove past the shops near United where it was illegal not to have red frontage.

"Can't you go any faster? There's a few straights where you could gain some time."

"I'm already pushing the limits but I'm not doing anything dangerous."

He dared to look at his watch again. Nearly 10am. They weren't even near the flyover yet. He recalculated distances and times. They wouldn't make it.

He slumped.

The day was going to be a scorcher. Scarcely a cloud in the clear blue sky, the sun already hot and bright. It reflected from metal railings and the windows of concrete towers.

He wouldn't make it and she'd be gone.

While at some traffic lights his mum gave his hand a squeeze, still looking ahead.

"We'll get there, don't worry, love," she said.

"I hope so."

They were crossing the flyover now, and would soon be entering the city centre near Piccadilly train station. A few roads from there, via part of Manchester's maze of one-way streets, was the coach station.

"When we get near it don't bother finding a parking space, just pull over anywhere and I'll jump out and run."

"Do you know what stand she'll be at?" she asked, concentrating on the road ahead.

"Yes."

"Good. That'll save time."

They passed Monroe's bar, with its tacky pictures of the screen siren plastered everywhere.

They had to stop. A metro tram was crossing the road. He gritted his teeth to keep from swearing.

Then unfastened his seatbelt.

"Where are you going?"

"We're nearby. I can run quicker and be there in a minute. See you soon!" He slammed the door shut and ran in front of the car and across the road, along past the white modernist structure that was Aytoun Business Library where Suzannah worked, and up Chorlton Street.

As he ran he felt better, his effort getting him closer. The NCP car park edged nearer: the way into the new airport-style coach depot was at the far corner. He glanced at the wire Lowry figures scrambling up the side of Arthur House. You always had to work hard to achieve the summit.

The coach was waiting for her. The display only showed a number 0. Perhaps the other numbers were broken. She checked with the driver – the same one who had brought her – and it was the correct coach.

She'd made it.

The automatic glass doors were open so he plunged straight into the milling crowds in front of the display monitors, narrowly avoiding falling headlong over a badly-placed pile of luggage.

"Hey!" someone yelled angrily as he regained his balance, leaving one of the suitcases skidding across the floor.

"Sorry!" he shouted back without stopping, moving as quickly as he could to the stands.

He was breathless, eyes scanning the chaos frantically. Kids being dragged, cries and yells, clicks of heels on hard-wearing floors. A shaft of sunlight blinded him, eyes watering, smearing the world into a fly's view of human complexity, broken up all incomprehensible. He had to filter it out, and focus: picture the desire, then match that pattern to what he saw.

Jane stood by the storage compartment at the side of the coach, removed a few things for the journey, then let the driver take her bag.

"Ready for a long ride?" he asked as he heaved it into the empty space in the belly of the coach. He had a thick black moustache and a Spanish accent.

"I think so."

"Don't look so sad. I'm a good driver!"

She nodded. It was the best she could do.

He spotted a bus with an open storage compartment on the side. The driver was putting things in.

Then he saw Lucy. Looking upset.

He ran towards her. It felt like he was in slow motion. She turned, saw him. Burst into tears.

He threw his arms around her.

"You idiot, Lucy, how could you leave? How could you?" he sobbed. "You're a part of me. Inside me. Your thoughts, our past, it's all one thing."

People stopped and stared but he didn't care. At that moment he only cared about what he clutched in his arms, holding tightly so she couldn't escape.

"You followed me, even after I told you not to?" Her face was wet against his neck as she squeezed him back, painfully and beautifully tight.

"Of course I did. This is too good to miss. What you said – I think it was just a test of love. I don't care what promises you've made to others. You're going to be mine!"

They held each other until the bus driver interrupted. "Sorry, but can you take your seat, miss? We're about to leave."

"Don't go yet, Lucy, stay a bit longer. Even if you catch a later bus today we've got to resolve all this first."

"I've got to leave now," the driver repeated. "If you aren't on board you'll lose your ticket I'm afraid."

She looked at Alex. They both spoke at once.

"Sack it!" they said, then laughed and clung to each other fiercely before kissing passionately, unconcerned with the world around them any more, just their world, that small circle between two arms. A circle that could not be broken.

A shaft of sunlight was in his eyes, blinding, watering, and all the colour in the world faded away. Just Lucy's face remained, a drawing in fine pencil; living art; it was his.

There was only one other passenger. Someone in grubby clothes. Bearded. Staring intently out of the window and patting his right knee as if listening to music, or agitated.

Jane moved to the back of the vehicle. A long seat to herself. Sat in the corner, feeling the bristly seat material rubbing her leg. The headrests blocked anyone's view of her from the front. A private compartment. She put her bag by her feet and watched the contrasting life outside: some people rushed around asking for directions, or trundled suitcases on wheels behind them in a hurry to find the correct stand; other people sat by piles of cases, resigned and calm. Fast and slow. In and out. Life.

The bus reversed. Beep beep. Goodbye, Manchester.

"I feel like I'm being twisted in two. It hurts," she whispered, to herself.

Twists and turns down boiled city streets. Separated by glass from the life outside; hidden behind it by reflections.

She wasn't surprised to feel weight on the seat next to her.

"Go away," she muttered.

"Happy now you've had him?" asked Lucy.

"Get lost."

"Some sister. You were always jealous of me."

"No I wasn't."

"Yes you were! Wanting what I had, but too timid to take it. I can see through you, remember? You wanted Alex just because I'd had him."

"That's not true." Jane turned to look at Lucy. A talking mirror image.

"You like to think you're so goody goody and I'm materialistic."

"You are. And manipulative."

"You never told the truth to Alex. So who's the real lying bitch?"

"If you were real, I'd slap you." The bus was making a sharp turn, Jane put a hand on the back of the seat in front.

"You wouldn't dare, timid Jane –"

Slap.

Jane's hand tingled. She had expected her hand to pass through thin air.

Lucy looked surprised too, putting her palm to her cheek. No smirk or grin now. "You're so angry, like you hate me," she said, wounded.

"I don't hate you." Jane glanced down the bus, but neither the driver nor the agitated man seemed to have noticed.

"We used to be close once. Long ago. All this over Alex?"

"Not just Alex. You know that."

"But it was after Alex that we drifted apart most. Stopped communicating."

"Yes."

Lucy's eyes unfocussed for a second, seeing into her past instead, a distance beyond the rumbling coach. "Let me tell you about it. Maybe then you won't hate me like you do. Alex is older than us."

"I know."

"Give me a minute, will you? He was doing his PhD when I was just starting my undergrad course. Maybe that was part of it – he was thinking at a different level than me. Thinking about all this big stuff, all these old theories. He was charming and cute and I was flattered that someone who was so obviously intelligent would like me. I'd always been bored with men my own age.

"I soon realised he wasn't as mature as he seemed. I think it was because I started to see flaws in him that I held back a bit, not wanting to get too involved. Not wanting to introduce him to Mummy. Wait and see. You glare at me for that? You think I'm a mercenary bitch.

"But let me even things up a bit. It was sometimes like he wasn't there. Like he was haunted by ghosts and obsessed with the past. At those times I just didn't exist for him. An irrelevance. It was only old thinkers and poets that he cared about. That hurts. There was worse though."

Jane said nothing. Just clenched her teeth tight. Lucy continued.

"He used to go on about his first girlfriend. Even though it was years before, and he hadn't even gone out with her for long. He seemed to think about her a lot, as if he felt he'd missed out somehow. He would tell me details. I'm sure in his mind he was 'being open with me'. But how do you think that made me feel? Knowing how much he'd been obsessed with this girl from the past, someone I could never compete with because she wasn't on the scene? It meant he felt no jealousy about me. I tested that once, a bit of flirting, trying to get a reaction. Nothing. No passion for me."

"So you two-timed him," Jane cut in, unable to hold back any longer. "Spoiled things. With his *best friend.* Couldn't you have broken up in a less hurtful way? Not been such a bitch."

"Ah. Ted. I don't want to discuss this. But you know what? You never share things with me. You don't behave like a sister *should.* You look surprised that *I* should accuse *you* of that? Well it's true. You've never wanted to be close to me or understand me. You just switch off when it's my life. If you'll listen, then I'll tell you."

Outside the bus the road was whitewashed with brightness. There weren't any people walking along this stretch, making the city seem ghostly, buildings just uninhabited shells. The bus hissed as it shifted up a gear.

"I didn't plan for anything to happen. Ted was Alex's closest friend but that doesn't necessarily mean what Alex thought it meant. I don't think *any* of Alex's relationships were as important to him as he claimed. Ted was a nice guy. Much more open and friendly than Alex. We would all go out together. I would be in the background as they talked about their research, but Ted was polite enough to change the topic after a while if I was there, to bring me in: whereas Alex sometimes seemed surprised that I was *still there*.

"It was good to have someone who seemed to understand all that. And I did only think of Ted as a friend. We would go shopping together. I don't know how it started, but one day we held hands on the bus home, and it was sweet. I told Alex, and he didn't mind. I think he was just glad that he didn't have to go shopping with me himself. Ted told me he loved me once, when the three of us had gone to a club with the mature students' union. It was really nice and we hugged. It was just love between friends but it was so good to have a connection and feel wanted. We spent more time together. Ted helped me with a bit of coursework I was having trouble with. He was in the management department. I had tried Alex first, but he was more interested in some article he was writing for the student magazine, some great attempt to popularise physics, he claimed. I thought his obsession was sweet, if naive. However, it's so easy

to see now that Ted and me were being naive too. It seems iron-
ic that you can be at university but not even understand
yourself. So when Alex wasn't around we would meet up. None
of this was quick. We were friends for over a year by this point.

"I'm going on too much. Long – short. Alex was back in
Manchester for a weekend, something with his family. I was in
my second year now. I went out for a few drinks with Ted. We
were back at mine, sat on my bed – not such a strange thing in
the student rooms we had, there were no other comfy options –
and I was tired and tipsy and turned the lamp out. It should
have been obvious what would happen."

"So you had sex with your boyfriend's best friend?"

"Sex? Why would you think we had sex just because we were
in the dark? I'm not a slut. We only kissed. And only for a minute. Then Ted got up. We both felt guilty and said we'd talk in
the morning. He left. I know I was a bit drunk because I didn't
lock the door to my flat or my bedroom door. I wasn't thinking
clearly. He didn't come back though. I was sad. And relieved.

"The next morning he came to see me and we sat on the bed,
talking about it. Saying that we'd had too much to drink. That
it would only harm Alex if we told him. That it meant nothing.
The words sounded convincing, but a minute later we were kissing again. It only lasted a few seconds, but it changed
everything. I realised that we hadn't kissed because of the booze:
it was because we really cared for each other. And the rest you
know. Alex and I split up. He left university."

"And Ted?"

"It didn't work out. He stayed at the uni to teach while I finished my degree and came home, and the distance thing didn't appeal to either of us. It had run its course and we were both happy to let go and move on with no hard feelings. The end. Do you still think I'm so evil?"

Jane shook her head reluctantly. "The whole thing still seems unfair though."

"It was unfair that you got involved. But you know what? You did the right thing."

"You think that?" The bus entered a tunnel, sounds closed in, Manchester blacked out.

"Yes. You were right. He loved you and forgave you and let you go. I'm impressed. Really. You went a funny way about it, playing it by ear. It was unexpected. But the outcome is the thing."

"I know. It still hurts."

"You always wanted to be a nurse, but it doesn't help you now. You should just be happy."

"Easier said."

"You know what, Sis?" Lucy took Jane's hand, and Jane didn't resist. "We're from the same seed. We're the same. We shouldn't fight. And I want to say I'm sorry. You're a better Lucy than I ever was. Thank you."

"Maybe we're not so different."

And they did something that hadn't happened for years. They hugged. Lucy was solid. As the bus rumbled out of the tunnel's darkness the sun came into view, the whiteness so bright it hurt. Jane held up one hand to block it; the rays seemed to bend round her skin so it looked translucent.

So hard to see anything. She could feel though. It felt like they were merging into one as they moved into the light, and she smiled, at peace.

He shaded his eyes, blinked them dry until they adjusted and he could search the signs at the coach points – 1, 2, 3 … And as he got nearer he saw that in reality there was no bus.

He rounded on someone nearby, a tall spotty lad who looked like a member of staff.

"Has the 10.15 for London left yet?"

"Yep. About five minutes ago. Have you missed it?"

Alex didn't answer. The attendant's attention was distracted by a large family asking angrily about compensation.

Alex turned back to the empty stand. The only thing there was a group of pigeons. They took off in a scatter of feathers, as if startled, and flapped up above the bustling crowds and out of the draughty bay entrance in the direction of the sun.

He wiped his eyes on a sleeve and sniffed. All the colour in the world faded away.

Just pigeons taking off.

He wanted the world to be neat stacks that would not topple over.

He was empty.

Everything was connected.

He would keep his word. Let her go. Much as he hated it. Such a huge decision, it made him dizzy. Maybe she would contact him. It would be her choice.

Things swam in his vision again. He gripped the back of one of the rows of metal seats for support, needing the solidity of firmly packed molecules. Someone asked if he was okay and he nodded, but their voice had sounded like it was a thousand miles away.

Sucked down, down into the darkness inside. It was just Alex alone once more. Despite the sunny day this dark place was chilly now, icy even, and everything outside it was a blur. It was hard to focus, hard to remember, hard to think. An explosion of frozen black behind his eyes.

Binary Collisions

"When two charged particles collide it has an effect. It's very likely that if they don't destroy each other then they will exchange energy, and this can change atomic orbits."

Mid-June. Tuesday onwards.

– he was shaking his head to clear it, like waking from a dream, chills running haywire through his body along nerves, synaptic pathways, arteries, courses that can't be stopped once set in motion, inevitable and foregone conclusions, he gasped unable to catch his breath, teeth chattering and brain frozen so it couldn't think properly, dizzying icy pain from above bringing faintness to his eyes as time unfolded. Shivering that continued after he turned it off, seconds to regain normal breathing accompanied by a drip drip drip that was slower than his heart, the heart that started to grind again, unstick, and live.

Late night, cold shower. The best way to forget about problems, despite the inevitable result: physical pain and blue bollocks.

Shoulders tight. He tried to lower them, stiff, stressed. But he was warming up, feeling again. He rubbed the towel vigorously over his body, friction to end the shivering, bring things back to life. The mist in the room cleared, allowing reality to creep back in. He let the pain of the cold fade into the mirrors, alternate worlds where everything reversed. Perhaps one of the reflected Alex images was happy. He hoped so.

He was exhausted. But it was worth it. At least showering at this time meant no fights for the bathroom. No-one banging on the door telling him to hurry. Peace. Time to think.

Thinking didn't help.

He went to bed.

Family trip to Granada Studios Tour, a special treat for his mum (an unrepentant *Coronation Street* addict). It was organised by an insider friend at the studio. Alex had never been. Always meant to do it, and this was the last chance before the tour closed for good. He knew if he didn't go it would piss everyone off.

Good. He skipped it.

That evening, everyone in the living room. People talking about the rides, something to do with the film *Aliens*, a tour of *Coronation Street*.

Digs from Kelly. Residual anger from his mum. She made a comment to one of his uncles about "Alex's girlfriend". Alex snapped that he was single. The room went quiet.

Video playing on the TV, apparently an episode of *Coronation Street*. Then everyone but Alex was laughing when they saw his mum and Natalie badly superimposed onto existing footage in the Rovers Return, that early victim of apostrophe ignorance. People joked that his mum looked like a washed-out hag and sounded like a constipated zombie when she said, "I'm new round here." The spoof mini episode ended with credits.

At last. He could go.

Natalie caught up with him. She said the day hadn't been as much fun without him. She'd missed him.

He felt guilty. It had partly been a treat for her 19th.

Sorry. So sorry. Didn't feel up to it. Excuses. Escape.

The next night. He was combing his hair in the hall. Getting a neat line, deciding he wasn't satisfied, starting again.

"Where are you going?" asked Natalie, leaning over the banister halfway up the stairs.

"To Phil and Trudi's. They invited me for a meal."

"You're lucky, having family that want to spend time with you."

"It's just family social work. They'll feed me, give me a beer, and pretend to be interested while the kids have the telly on full volume. Fantastic evening."

"Sounds quite nice to me."

"You'd be welcome to it. Playing happy families with me as the pitiable spare part."

"Well I'm not –"

"Oy, Nat, get in here and check this out!" yelled Kelly from upstairs.

"I'd best go," said Alex, accepting that a neat line wasn't possible tonight. He waved and left.

Happy couples. Everyone playing happy couples.

Happy fucking couples.

He'd got back from Trudi's. He was a spare part. He didn't seem to fit anywhere.

Leaving for work. He shuffled down the hall, eyes focussed ahead. He had to go out into the sun. He didn't want to.

"Can you pick up some bread on the way home?" He hadn't noticed his mum coming out of the kitchen.

"Bread?"

"Yes. Sliced. I don't know who's stuffing their face with it. White or brown, doesn't matter."

He stared blankly.

"Anyone in there?" his mum asked. As if it was funny.

He couldn't help it. Two blinks and the next thing there were tears running down his face. A fault in the cryogenics.

A worried look crossed his mum's face. She rushed over and hugged him. It was like pressing a button in his back, baby doll, toy robot, press the button to make it speak, "Hello I'm the Tomytronic 5000, be my friend" but he didn't speak, he just sobbed stiffly into his mum's shoulder while she held him, calmed him; when she asked what was wrong he just mumbled that he didn't know.

She hugged him tighter. "It's okay, son. Whatever it is, it'll get better."

The French doors at the back were open to welcome the evening breeze. Natalie and Kelly mixed cocktails in the kitchen. Kelly stirred hers with a pink plastic sword.

"So you don't know what's wrong?" asked Natalie.

"Nah. Don't care either. He's probably run out of ideas for wacky books."

"I doubt it. He's so brainy."

"I am too!" said Kelly, licking the tip of the sword.

No response to that bit. "When are you going out?" Natalie asked.

"In a bit. Sure you don't want to come?"

"Nah," said Natalie, sipping her drink and looking through the doorway at the stairs.

Alex was alone in the house. He sat on the floor dressed only in his briefs, staring at his bed.

It was neatly made.

The sun brightened his room but he shivered.

The bottle of Martini he'd taken from the drinks cabinet downstairs was almost empty. And he DIDN'T EVEN LIKE the fucking drink, let alone *neat*. His mouth tasted like perfume.

He strode to the bed and pulled the duvet off, throwing it onto the floor. There was some form of quantum entanglement messing up lives. He threw the pillows across the room, jaw clenched tight, and a lamp was knocked off his bureau, bouncing on the ground to the tinkle of a broken bulb.

He was a primitive, some atavistic fuckwit holding on to superstitious hopes.

He kicked the bedside table: it banged against the wall, gewgaws scattered across the floorboards; his toe made a cracking sound, pain brought tears to his eyes as he flopped to the floor and put his hands over his foot, rocking back and forth.

The room seemed to spin.

He spied a book of poetry, tipped from his bedside, *Childe Harold's Pilgrimage*. He snatched it and tried to rip it in two down the spine, but the spine was too tough so he bit the pages, tore some loose and spat them out, then threw the book across the room. It bounced off the wall with a lame flop.

He grabbed the bottle, necked the last mouthful and threw it at his bookcase. He cheered when it smashed on the floorboards. "Ha! Didn't expect that, did you?" he yelled. "Fucker! I'm a man!"

Then he started crying, head on his forearms.

"What's the matter, Alex?" a shocked voice asked.

He assumed it was Kelly and sobbed "Fuck off!" without looking up but quick light footsteps crossed the room and a slender arm slipped round his shoulders as the warmth of a body leaned against his.

He looked up and saw Natalie staring wide-eyed at the mess of his room, at his bleeding toe.

He groaned and hid his face again.

"Don't ask," he said.

"I never would," she replied with concern. "But I'd listen if you told me."

"Just go." She was making him feel worse. A man should not be found in his briefs.

"Please don't cry, Alex. You'll make me cry too."

He looked up and saw she was telling the truth. She put her hands on each side of his face as if she would kiss him but he flinched away from her. A pained expression crossed her face.

He saw that same tacky bright nail varnish she liked to wear, and it angered him; anyone classy didn't need such cheap tricks to attract attention.

"What do you want, Alex?"

"Nothing."

Damn her if she wasn't wearing a short skirt; her skinny bare legs annoyed him.

He sensed movement, a twitch, and rested his forearms across his thighs, concealing; he muttered, "Go," but she noticed, understood what he was hiding. Her face knowing, some kind of realisation, she moved his hand aside, his struggle weakened when she touched him; he couldn't look at her face, her legs, her hand, but as soon as he closed his eyes he saw them; it was wrong but she was not clumsy, freed the end and it was not too quick, hand enclosing in firm grip, enclosed friction, his briefs tangled on his erection at first; he even said, "No, Natalie," that many words croaked but not enough to stifle the eager sweltering friction, harder for him, he didn't dare say any more words, it was just hand contact, nothing more, he gritted his teeth and wanted to stop but couldn't, disgusted with himself he started to come, her hands sliding now, he gripped her slender wrist firmly to stop her moving, he had to look at her, had to look at her eyes like melted chocolate.

He wiped his eyes on his forearms, said "Thank you" quietly, pulled up his briefs and stood, passed her a T-shirt to wipe her hands on, he wasn't crying now but he wanted to. Turned away from her while she dried her hands.

"I'm sorry ... I didn't mean that to happen," he said, pulling on trousers too.

"It's okay." Her voice was subdued. It did not sound like Natalie speaking.

"No, it's not okay. I'm messed up. But it's no excuse."

He could hear her getting up, moving.

"I'm sorry too," she said. "If I made you feel bad. I thought it was what you wanted."

He nodded without knowing why.

He took the T-shirt from her. She put a hand on his arm. He patted it weakly, unable to think of anything to say. She tried to smile, then she left his room.

After a suitable pause he finished getting dressed and walked out of the house. Stormed to The Bent Brook pub, sat in a corner facing into the family room, laughing groups making the beer bitter in his mouth, music like tinnitus.

He drank until he puked in the toilets.

"Alex. A word."

His head still ached. He had avoided everyone until now. But his mother had caught him making brunch. Fried mushrooms on toast. Recipe number two.

"Sure, Mum." He plonked himself at the table and picked at the food, not hungry any more.

She sat opposite him.

"I'm not really sure what's going on with you."

Alex moved food around the plate.

"I wish your dad was here to talk to you. I wish he wasn't away so much. I want you to be happy. But today I heard something off Kelly that has got me worried."

Alex laid the fork down. Here it comes.

"She said that Natalie likes you. I love the girl and haven't minded her here, but always thought she was a bit ... provocative, maybe. Which can be a temptation. I hadn't realised she really felt anything for you, or thought she did. But from what Kelly said, Natalie seems to think that you two might be a bit of an item. And I just want to know what's going on there. I care for everyone under this roof and I don't want vulnerable people being hurt. *In loco parentis.* You know what I'm saying, Alex?"

He looked up from his grey mushrooms. "I don't want anyone to be hurt either."

"Good. Just make sure that there aren't any misunderstandings. You're supposed to be the mature one."

He sought Natalie but found Kelly instead. A talkative and excited Kelly who depressed his spirits further. She told him she was "psyched" that him and Natalie were an item. He said they weren't an item, but Kelly just laughed. Natalie was out visiting her mother.

Kelly then said, "It all makes sense now. When you spied on Nat in the shower it was on purpose, eh? Maybe you were just being subconscious."

He told her to fuck off and mind her own business, pleased when the words had an effect.

He was restless until Natalie returned. She chatted with Kelly and his mum in the kitchen. Talked and talked and talked. He needed to speak to her. He paced around the landing. Eventually he grabbed his wallet and strode into the kitchen. There was no peace in this house, nor privacy.

"Natalie, do you want to come for a quick drink with me?"

"Such a gentleman," joked Kelly. "See how he asks someone out without even smiling at them, Mum?"

"I see," replied his mother in a less jocular tone.

"I'd love to." Natalie smiled, showing her perfect small teeth.

"Can I come?" asked Kelly.

"No."

Alex was walking fast, then felt mean as Natalie scurried to keep up without complaining. He took a deep breath and slowed down.

"So, you were at your mother's?" he asked.

"Yes. We didn't argue for once. Just talked about good things."

"I'm glad. What good things?" he asked idly as they passed the garden centre and turned towards Woodsend. He couldn't face The Bent Brook again, even though it was nearer.

She smiled nervously. "I told my mum about you."

"Is there anyone you *didn't* tell?" he snapped.

"I didn't tell anyone what we *did*. Honest!" She sounded hurt.

He sighed. "What did you tell her then?"

"I told her about you – that you're the nicest person I know, and I thought you might like me, at least a little bit."

"I don't even know if I am that nice any more."

"Well, to me you are."

Silence the rest of the way to the pub.

The Fox & Hounds pub. It normally reminded him of a large cottage but today the diamond-leaded windows, bare brick walls and heavy black doors made him think of a prison.

He bought her a half of cider. He just had water. They sat in a bay window seat.

"We're not going out, Natalie."

"Okay."

"I wish no-one knew."

"There's nothing for them to know if we're not going out. I'll say I made a mistake."

He smiled with relief until he looked up and saw she was upset. He felt like he had stolen her personality. The spunky confidence wasn't anywhere. He'd taken it. Somehow he had taken her happiness too.

"Look, this is awkward."

"Sorry."

"I've always liked you, Natalie. I mean that. This is just a bad time to be around me. Things are complicated."

"The girl you –"

"No."

"Okay. I can wait. Maybe I can even help. I promise I won't pester you. But I don't want you to ignore me. That hurts. Because I really do like you."

He reached and put his hand on hers, a ridiculously formal gesture, but she took his hand gratefully and even smiled. He left his hand where it was.

Another day. Alex sat on the patio with some printouts and a set of coloured highlighters. He had a glass of lemonade. He meant to sip it but his gulps had emptied the glass. He swirled an ice cube in his mouth, savouring the cold, then spat it out. It bounced on the paving, broke into two pieces which skidded onto the lawn, then began melting into each other. Joined again. That's what heat did.

He moved to the shade of an apple tree. Cooler. Moments of peace. As the branches whispered above him he watched a bee climbing frantically over some of the remaining flowers, her energetic movements making him feel lethargic by contrast. The pens stopped moving, and before long he dozed.

Kelly woke him when she returned from her piano lesson. She had been walking up the path absent-mindedly humming a tune he vaguely recognised. Chopin, maybe. She hadn't seen him lying in the shade. Her chestnut curls bobbed as she walked, and her usually stern face looked pretty and natural when she didn't think she was being observed. When she wasn't arguing.

He got up and rubbed at the reddened grass indentations on the backs of his legs and arms, marvelling at how impressionable flesh is.

Kelly saw him, stopped smiling, jutted her chin as a greeting, and carried on, almost like a stranger.

(Don't lose the connection.)

The words seemed to come from a dream.

"How was the lesson?" Alex asked, forcing her to stop.

"Good."

"Great." He picked up his pens, mind blank. Kelly fidgeted. "What are you doing now?"

"Revision. As usual. Soon be over though, thank God."

"What, you've done most of them already?"

"Don't you pay attention to *anything*, you fuckwit?" she snapped.

He counted to three in his head, and let it go. "I'm sorry," he said. "What have you got left?"

"Media studies. The one I'm weakest on."

"Do you want any help?"

They both seemed surprised as those words left his mouth.

"Really?" she asked. "This isn't a trick or a joke?"

"No. Genuine."

"Okay. Let me get my things. We could do it outside. You can test me!" She seemed suddenly energised, and rushed into the house. Alex waited at the patio table. He took deep breaths. The current was taking him to unknown waters.

He put down the sheet of paper. "You need to avoid getting connotation and denotation mixed up. Otherwise, spot on. Every definition. Impressive."

"You mean that?" She was biting at her thumbnail.

"Yes."

"I do feel a lot better about it."

"You should. You've worked hard."

She nodded.

"You'll get into the College of Music. *Royal Northern College*, I should say. Kavanagh brains."

She laughed and shook her head, but not in denial. "This is great. You. You're acting like a brother! Spending time with me, I mean."

"I suppose I am."

"I could get used to this!"

"Hey, enough distractions. Let's look at the mnemonics. What seven key concepts make up MIGRAIN?"

She groaned. But happily.

Natalie hung around Alex. Not pushy. Just wanting to spend time with him.

She joined him on the sofa, a light weight and a smile. "This looks good," she said, settling in next to him. "What is it?"

"*Buffy.*"

"Sounds like a hamster."

They watched TV all evening.

He was reading on the bed, an article in a PC magazine explaining how the Melissa computer virus worked.

Natalie joined him with her own magazine, *Marie Claire.* He took it from her.

"Tips for sexy hair? What's sexy hair?"

She snatched it back off him.

He tried to go back to his article but she insisted on reading bits of her magazine out.

She told him a joke she'd overheard in the Arndale Centre.

She asked questions about a term on the cover of his magazine she didn't understand.

Worst of all, she took a perverse pleasure in tickling his feet when he didn't expect it.

He hated laughing whilst saying "No, stop it!" because it just encouraged her.

They wrestled, she tickled his ribs, he surrendered. Then they carried on reading, but this time she was leaning against him.

He was going into town.

"I'll come too," she said. "I need some things."

"I just want to go to my shops and go home."

"It's okay, I won't make you go in too many women's clothes shops."

She kept her word, but instead dragged him into men's clothes shops.

"Try this on. It will suit you, honest."

"What's wrong with the clothes I'm wearing?"

She pulled a face. He decided not to press her.

Walking home with her, Burton bag in his hand, wondering what had just happened. Why hadn't he treated himself to a digital camera? He'd wanted one for ages. He'd seen a Fujifilm MX2700 with 2.3 megapixels and a 4MB memory card for only £335.

Forced to try the clothes on at home, Natalie pointing out to his sarcastic sister and watchful mother that she had picked them for him. She said it proudly.

Late at night. They were on the sofa again. It had been his turn to choose, so they watched *Blade Runner* (seventh time for him, second for her). The VHS tape was wonky at the start, making the picture fuzzy and the sound distorted, but he knew it well enough to fill in the blanks with his mind. One day they'd get a DVD player and he would buy a new copy on a shiny disc and maybe it would be so realistic he could feel he was really there, really in the future.

Natalie was always discreet, and he was glad of that. Only after everyone else was in bed did she snuggle up to him. So close, and warm, and smelling so good. She was sleepy because it wasn't her kind of thing.

Rick Deckard performed his investigation. Tests were done to determine if someone was human or not. Replicants looked human, but were better. Maybe that was why humans were scared of them. Alex empathised.

Natalie had three earrings in her left ear, each one different. Earlier, he'd asked her why.

"I had two, but then everyone else started getting two. I hated it looking like I was the one copying. So I got a third. Plus … well, Mum told me not to."

He felt like touching the earrings now. Metal threaded through flesh. A replicant of his own.

No. Watch the film. He returned to it. He loved it. The dystopian yet haunting world it portrayed where the only remaining beauties were sunsets and love.

But he found himself watching Natalie again instead.

Her eyes would close; twitch; open, as if startled. Pattern repeated. Until this time, when she looked up at him. Caught him staring at her. Squeezed him, smiled, content. She wasn't normally languid like this. Her energy scared him sometimes. Wildcat spiked, sure, uncultivated. But now she was approachable. Dark eyes, small nose, a face with gravitational pull.

His fingertips touched hers, stroked, and they held hands in their private cinema.

He went back to watching the film. Something nagged at his mind, painful but not insistent, not a memory he had to deal with right now.

So easy to slip into it when she looked up again, and he lowered his head to hers. He only intended to nuzzle her forehead, innocent, friendly, but their lips met. Lip and tongue making a circuit, mild current flowing. Gentle caresses while kissing. It was just a kiss, and they stopped, and she hugged him, and it didn't happen again. He turned the film off. They said goodnight on the landing. Both lingered. But he did the right thing. He went to bed.

Alex, lay in bed that night. Restless.

It was only a kiss, he kept telling himself.

Not sex.

It was an accident. They had both been too weak for restraint. Too magnetic for close proximity.

He changed positions, unable to find one that was comfortable.

It wouldn't happen again. He didn't want to complicate things.

And he thought about Natalie, what he was doing. She was wasting her time with him. He was too old for her. Boring. He didn't like clubs or loud music. He was happier with a book than going to the funfair on the common. That's why it made no sense.

And going on like this, it could only be harmful for one or the other.

He gave up trying to sleep. Put the light on, grabbed a book.

Her interest would fizzle out soon.

In some ways she was just a kid.

He tried reading.

It wasn't fair on her, using her as an addictive distraction from gloomy thoughts.

He put the book down again.

He could make it easier for her.

It wasn't as if they had strong feelings for each other.

They were sat at a greasy spoon cafe in Urmston, not far from the train tracks. Natalie's choice. She liked sitting in cafes and watching people. Alex would have rather gone straight home after filling his rucksack with books from the library. In front of him were unattractive things he didn't need: metal ashtray, red plastic squeezy bottle leaking a congealed blob of ketchup, salt and vinegar pots with their white plastic tops that reminded him of nipples. He slid things out of the way and spread books out on the plastic table top instead, deciding what order he would tackle them in. Natalie was alternately sipping from a mug of tea and playing with a mobile phone she'd just bought. Packaging was strewn around, and some invaded his book space. He pushed it back to her side when she wasn't looking.

"Hey, you can make different ringtones on this one," she said, accompanied by irritating beeps from the phone.

"Music to my ears."

"I've not got the hang of it yet. That was random notes."

"*Really?*"

"It has games on too. There's one called snakes. Maybe you could play it with me."

"Maybe not."

"It does something with picture messages too. And look, there's no stuck up aerial, it's all inside." She shoved the grey phone in his face so he couldn't ignore it any more.

"I'm not interested," he said, brushing her arm away.

"You could get one too."

"Why the hell would I do that? I'd have no-one to talk to."

"You could send texts to me."

"I'd rather just talk to you if I have something to say. You live in the same house."

"You've got no imagination."

"I just don't get it. What they're for." He snatched it out of her hand. Looked at the green-lit screen. "I mean, the screen. Teeny. Horrible buttons. No keyboard for typing."

"It uses predictive –"

"Yeah yeah. It just seems so limited." A beat. Thoughts shuffled. "Then again … Maybe they could be useful one day. You know, computers get smaller all the time, faster every year. Moore's law. They might make phones like small computers so they can do useful stuff instead of just banal conversation like you hear on the bus." He prodded buttons, vaguely interested now. "Maybe you could even get the Internet on them. You'd need bigger screens. A better interface. A mouse or some sort of touchpad like on a laptop. Maybe even find a way to make glass panels that can detect where your fingers are, so the screen can be as big as the phone. Then they could actually *do* things. Run little software applications or something. I'd call them Cleverphones." He sat pondering. Then handed the phone back dismissively.

"You write stuff about the past. Why not write about the future?" Natalie asked, sipping from her tea and watching Alex.

"Me? I can't see a thing."

"No, because you've been walking along looking back, old history, a waste of time. Look forwards instead. What's coming? We all want to know that. Then we'd be interested. You've got the brains. Just add some common sense."

He was going to point out the stupidity of all that, but stopped himself. Thought about it.

"See, it's good to spend time together," Natalie said. "I give you ideas." He picked up his glass of lemonade. Observed the bubbles of carbon dioxide rising through the higher density sugar solution, seeking escape. Drank a bit. "Isn't that right, Alex?" she insisted.

A pause. "Maybe we should have a bit more space," he suggested. He didn't want to repeat "We're not going out". It was written as a reminder on most of his actions. "We're friends but … it's difficult. Confusing. I think a break would be a good thing."

"If that's what you really want."

"It's what I think is best."

"Whatever." She scrambled to put things into her carrier bag, shovelled in haphazardly, no care given now to the new phone. She got up and walked out. Alex packed quickly to catch up with her before she got to the bus stop.

Maybe this was good. Good for her. Some space.

It wasn't easy to distance yourself from someone in the same house, but he could try.

He tried.

More time at the library, staring at blank sheets of paper in frustration, willing words that wouldn't come.

Avoiding rooms with Natalie in, sidestepping the family to be on his own, hearing muffled laughter through the walls.

Giving her a half-smile and scuttling off when she tried to start a conversation, then feeling like the Grinch that stole summer.

Even sitting in his space rocket when the kids had left the park, straining his eyes against fading light in an attempt to read a formula.

"I'm not doing this for myself," he said, dropping the papers and resting his chin on the edge of the porthole. He would have liked a response but there were no other crew on his spaceship.

Fuck it. Not any more.

He wasn't in the garden, reading old poetry on the bench by the back door; he wasn't in the kitchen getting a drink, or in the living room watching the silly *Star Wars* programmes with Captain Spock beaming up Spotty.

"Alex?" she called upstairs, a deflated word, despite the air she tried to put into it.

She kicked her trainers off and climbed two at a time. Sometimes he was so engrossed in a book she could watch him frowning at it, unaware, lips moving slightly as he read. It was funny, because the kids who did that at school had always been the thickest ones.

The door to his room was closed. "Go away, I shut you out, pest," it said.

Natalie struggled quickly out of her T-shirt, threw it on the floor and kicked it into a corner of the landing; untucked her vest top, unfastened her hair, gave it a shake, ran a hand up her shin, smooth enough.

"Alex?" She didn't knock, just eased herself into his room, but he wasn't on the bed reading. She squeezed the door handle hard. *On purpose, he knew when I'd come home.*

She was tempted to wait; get into his bed just to spite him. Leave hairs on his pillow. Change the page his bookmark was on. Hang her knickers on the back of his door. He'd have a fit. She grinned, looked up, saw cracks on the ceiling, cracks she'd seen while she lay on the bed with Alex, cracks above and within, cracks everywhere with him …

She knew. Sudden, certain: the sneaky bastard.

The next flight up had no carpet and she relished the thump as the balls of her feet bounced on the wood, letting him know she was coming, each thump a warning and a promise that she understood him and could see through him. She would do what she wanted and not be discouraged. Achieve things. It was her new self. Better self. She was sick of him fucking her around. She would *kick his arse.*

The attic room door banged open. Alex had been staring at it nervously as determined footsteps thumped up the stairs. Natalie looked furious.

"You've been avoiding me and I'm sick of it," she said, arms folded and frowning.

"I –"

"Said you wanted it. But you didn't ask what *I* wanted. You prick." She was breathing fast and glaring at him.

"I did what I thought was best."

"And you know what, Alex? I'm not sure your thinking is always right, especially about important things," she said sarcastically.

He felt like he'd been slapped.

"But –"

"Zip it. You don't want to go out with me, fine. If you don't want to kiss me, that's up to you. You have problems with controlling your hands? Try harder. Or just accept that you fancy me. But don't fuck me about, hot and cold. And don't push me away, leaving me worse off than before. My mum does that. And I hate it. Really hate it." She was practically steaming.

"I'm sorry," he said, unable to match her vehemence but meaning it nonetheless. "I didn't think you'd be bothered."

"Wrong." They stared at each other. "It's the avoidance that pisses me off most. It makes me feel like I've lost a friend. I *need* a friend."

"Sorry. I won't avoid you any more then," he said.

"Good."

He looked down at his fingers. Fidgeted. "I've missed being around you," he admitted, without looking up. "Really missed you. And I've missed having a friend too."

She flopped down next to him on the bed. Sighed. Put an arm round his shoulder. "Then stop being a dick."

"Okay," he replied, slipping an arm around her hot waist. "Consider me dickless. No, I didn't mean that ..." he added once she started sniggering.

Soon she had jabbed him in the ribs, leading to a tussle, then a tickle. Alex got up quickly, otherwise he knew where it might lead. They were friends again. Better to keep it simple.

Alex was trying an experiment in his bedroom. Seeing if he could read a book whilst doing sit-ups. In theory it should work, and lead to efficient use of time, but he had problems keeping the book held at the right distance from his eyes as he went up and down. He was wondering if taping a ruler between the book and his head would help, when Natalie knocked and stuck her head round his door.

"You sure you won't come out?" she asked.

"I don't tend to change my mind." He stayed in a sit-up position, hugging his knees.

"Stubborn."

"Reliable."

"Boring."

"Natalie, I don't even know what drum and bass is. I mean, doesn't all rock music have drums and a bass guitar?"

"You are so out of it, it's unreal. Anyway, do I look okay?" She stepped into the room. A short skirt. T-shirt which showed off her midriff. The skirt was tiny. Black pumps. Bare legs, a lot visible below the diminutive skirt. Make-up. That skirt.

"Yeah. Look fine. Have a good time."

"What's up?"

"Nothing."

"Something is. Your face."

He sighed. "What you look like."

"What? I'm going out. Asked you to come."

"You could wear more."

"It's hot."

"Are lots of people going?"

"It'll be packed. The usual crowd. Wait – you're ..."

"Why are you looking at me like that?" he asked.

"Nothing," she replied, apparently satisfied with *some*thing.

"I'm not jealous."

"Uh-huh." She knelt next to him. Nodded. Smirked.

"I'm not."

"You don't normally lie. You say it is the resort of the common."

His jaw tightened. "Maybe. A bit. Guys will stare."

"Let them. I'm all yours if you want me."

"I'm not happy about it."

"Come with me then. I'll hang on your arm, sugar daddy."

"Don't call me that. I'm too old to go to a party of eighteen-year-olds. I'd feel awkward."

"I wouldn't. I don't give a shit about that. And I was eighteen when I started liking you."

"No."

"Fine. Let's do something else. I'll forget the party. I don't care about it. But give me something."

"You won't go?"

"It's got to be something going out. We spend too much time in this house."

"What?"

"Ice skating."

"No."

"Please?"

"Why? I can't skate."

"That's exactly why. It'd be hilarious! Just thinking of it makes me smile." She stood and did an exaggerated impersonation of someone with wobbly knees holding a bar and taking tiny, unsure steps. She was laughing and he couldn't help joining in.

(Sometimes we have to do stuff for others.)

"All right," he relented. "We'll go."

She knelt and hugged him, excited.

"Not tonight though. At the weekend," he added. "You go out to the drummy bass thing tonight. Kelly would kill me if I stopped you going with her. Have your fun. We'll skate later."

"Promise?"

"My word is my bond."

"And I promise I won't even look at any lads. And if anyone touches me they'll get a slap."

"I believe you. As Mr T would say: 'I pity the fool'."

She walked to the door, shaking her head and smiling. "Madness. You agreeing to go out and *do something* that doesn't involve libraries. Then being jokey. Total personality transplant."

She looked amazing. Happy. Radiant.

He'd done that.

It felt good.

Superlight Matter

"We've seen how matter can be compressed, becoming denser. It is possible to have matter which goes the other way. Think of it as bigger gaps between the Lego bricks. Even when at great size it can remain light. Imagine the implications for engineering, construction, transport. It should be possible, in time, to construct nickel lattice tubes that are over ninety-nine per cent air, so you have strength and lightness combined. Would light matter be weaker? Maybe not. Reeds bend in the wind, and early experiments suggest that superlight matter can resume its original shape after compression, simulating life's ability to recover from trauma. And – what do you want, Kelly? I'm ... [sigh] No, no, It's fine. I'll finish this later. Not a problem."

August. A Monday.

Alex was on the bus, heading home after a visit to the college to discuss the next academic year's course offerings. The curriculum manager had agreed to Alex's idea for changing the syllabus. Alex hadn't expected approval. A good start to the day.

For once he was content to look out of the window, following the changes from flashy city centre commerce to fast food alley and student area, on through graffiti-splashed Moss Side. People, everywhere. Doing things. Lives beyond his own, mixed flavours in a shake and bake.

The plastic edging of the seat was hot from the sun, sticky on his arm. The bus shuddered to a stop. Pneumatic hiss of doors. A group boarded.

Alex automatically compared the number of people getting onto the bus with the number of seats available on the lower floor, calculating the percentage chance he could retain his double seat to himself. Then he saw the Glasgow Smile Man getting on, groaned inside, and quickly reran the calculations to see if he had made an error, but no – there was a chance (thirty-three per cent) that Glasgow Smile Man might sit next to him.

This time he would not give him even the slightest opportunity to target Alex. Full defence.

No eye contact.

Don't do anything that looked interesting (such as writing on a card, or opening the packaging for an item you'd just bought, or having an arm in plaster).

Stick your face into a book, even if you weren't reading it.

Oh, and the most basic defence: no empty seat.

Alex snatched his bag from between his legs and put it on the seat next to him, pretending to scrabble about inside for another pen and tutting to himself. GSM sat next to a teenage girl reading a magazine across the aisle. The bag was hastily closed and Alex sat up, pretending the pen in his hand was a new one, not the one he had been using all along, pathetically brandishing it for people who didn't care.

The bus moved on and he prepared to record ideas and thoughts, but he wasn't into it today. Instead he was remembering a day which had begun with a similar bus journey at the start of the summer, the last time he'd seen GSM. The day when Anne had dumped him. When everything had gone wrong and he'd hit his lowest point. When he'd bribed Kelly to get out of the house and go ice skating so he didn't have to deal with the embarrassment of how she'd found him when she entered his room.

He was going ice skating with Natalie tonight.

As he wrote he became aware that GSM was whispering something to the girl in a low, deep voice that was hard to make out; leaning over her with his messy grey moustache and big sideburns framing a wide face and long nose. She was trying to ignore him, using the magazine as an ineffective shield of words.

He seemed to offer the girl a drink as he whispered. Other passengers minded their own business. Alex doodled. A troll's face.

The girl turned towards the window, cold shoulder to harassment, but GSM just leaned closer.

It was no good. Alex bit his lip. This was his fault. His incredible intellect was too effective. If he hadn't gone to full defence mode GSM wouldn't have sat next to the girl. He didn't plan for this to happen but Alex had to accept responsibility for his powers of understanding human nature so well.

Alex's hands sweated and his stomach churned with fear at the thought of facing the scarred sex-pest. However, he hated the thought of the poor girl mortified. Her face was pale as she tried to ignore GSM and look out of the window.

Alex wanted to tell the menace to "watch it" or "fuck off". He watched the old guy carefully, making sure he didn't put a hand anywhere near the young woman's lap.

No-one else was interested. Newspapers held up, showing articles about fuel protests. A lad with his Walkman on loud, tinny sounds emanating from poor-quality headphones. Blank faces looking out of windows.

Alex put down his pen. Clench/relax, stand/sit, act/hide, what to do … He looked around again. Still no-one else seemed to pay any attention. Oh fuck.

Leaned forward to get up. Sat back. Cursed inwardly. Stood.

Yes, it was true – he was actually *standing up*.

"Erm, hey, why don't you leave her alone?" he said in a disappointingly cracked voice while gripping a smeared silver pole tightly. GSM didn't even hear him at first over the rumble of the bus's engine, so he cleared his throat and spoke again, aiming at forcefulness but still coming out like a nervous first date proposal.

GSM looked up, skin tinted with the redness of quick-to-flare anger. "Fuck off, son," he growled.

Alex ignored him. "Are you okay?" he asked the girl. His heart was racing.

She stood, shook her head, gripping her bag tight, waiting for GSM to let her past. "He's disgusting," she said, indicating GSM with some relief. "Wouldn't leave me alone." GSM moved aside with a grumble, letting her out; she thanked Alex and headed down the bus. Alex retreated to his seat, watching GSM warily, biro in one hand in case he had to defend himself.

The girl was talking to the driver angrily. The bus stopped with a lurch. The driver leaned over his money tray and challenged GSM about pestering the girl. Only now did passengers look up from their books, magazines, bags, anything outside the window. Meerkats from holes.

GSM denied it, saying it was "fussin' about nuttin'".

The bus driver seemed uncertain.

No-one else spoke.

A tumbleweed could have rolled down the bus aisle.

The girl looked near to tears. The driver indicated that she should sit on the seat nearest him.

Alex couldn't bear it. He stood up again. "He was pestering her," Alex shouted to the driver. "We all saw it. He's done it before." Alex sat down neatly. Took out a handkerchief and wiped his forehead.

The driver directed a disgusted look at GSM. "Get off my fucking bus," he told him.

GSM mumbled to himself. Alex looked down.

"I won't tell you twice," growled the driver.

GSM complied, but Alex could see he was receiving a first-class glare from the troll. Oh great. What if GSM became his enemy and wanted to cut Alex's cheeks one dark night, following him off the bus with a gleaming straight razor?

Alex averted his gaze until GSM had descended from the bus and they pulled out. Safe at last. When he looked up the girl beamed a genuinely grateful smile at him.

It was worth it.

Maybe he could get used to this "being a superhero" thing. The Ginger Avenger.

Living room to himself. TV on. Adverts. Watch check. Any time now. Sat on sofa. Excited. Tucked in to recipe number five: Spicy Curry Pot Noodle, served in a bowl over white sliced bread. Trying not to flick sauce onto his shirt as he slurped the noodles.

Time. To himself. This bit of relaxation before facing the unnatural mortification of trying to move on water chilled to 0°C until the molecules slowed down enough to adopt a cold and crystalline state.

Natalie was busy upstairs getting ready. She always took a long time doing that. Could make an evening of it.

Wind down and appreciate the only bit of stable ground for the rest of the evening.

It began. The credits.

Blue logos zooming towards the screen.

Continuing missions to explore strange new worlds.

Sleek white ships with throbbing engines, seeking new life and new civilisations.

Haloed planets and light-speed star blurs.

Boldly going where no-one had gone before, accompanied by swooshing starships and stirring music.

Alex shuddered, involuntary excitement reflex. *Star Trek TNG*. Soon the episode proper began and Alex looked forward to finding out how Picard would overcome the Borg menace from the cliff-hanger at the end of the last episode – would the Borg assimilate more Federation crew members? So scary.

He ignored a shape entering the living room at the edge of his vision. *Focus on the cathode rays*. He tried to ignore the weight that altered the sofa's contours beside him. *Come on, Picard, act, act now! It's not that hard to stand up and make the right decision!*

Fidgeting to his right. But no overt attempt to distract him, ruin his fun.

He watched. More fidgeting, implying nervousness. Oh, and it was looking so exciting too. He glanced at Kelly. She gave him

(*Siblings shouldn't become strangers. Don't lose the connection.*)

a faltering smile.

He sighed. Picked up the remote control.

Turned off the TV.

"I didn't want to interrupt," Kelly said. "I know you like *Star Wars*."

"*Star Trek*," he corrected sharply.

"Sorry. The spaceship stuff."

"Sci-fi."

"Yeah."

She was still fidgeting.

"Are you okay?" he asked.

"Oh, great, yeah, thanks."

He wrapped noodles round the fork. Almost at the soggy bread level.

"What, you wanted to watch *Star Trek* too? I can turn it back on?" Alex asked, sudden hopeful thought.

"No, didn't want to watch."

"Oh. You want something though."

"No."

"What is it? You want to come skating with me and Natalie? I don't mind. I'd have two people to lean on."

"No! Nat would kill me if I came along. She wants it to be just you two."

"Great. What will you do then?" The first soggy forkful had been reached, white dyed yellow, so appetising.

"Oh, erm … Going out."

"Who with? You only ever hang around with Natalie."

"It's someone from college."

It clicked. Coyness, key, open connections. "Oh ho ho!" Alex grinned. "I assume it's a lad?"

"Yeah."

"Is it a *date* date?"

She nodded, defeated *and* relieved. He put down his bowl and gave her a clumsy hug. She hugged him back, tentatively at first but then more firmly.

"Well done!"

"I'm a bit nervous. He's pretty lush. Reminds me of Joaquin Phoenix."

Alex laughed. "You're pretty lush too. Don't forget it. And he'd better treat you well."

"Thanks. I love you being nice to me." She kissed his cheek awkwardly.

(She was his sister. Make the time with her count.)

(It was all working out.)

Alex shook his head to dissipate the unwanted word echoes and reached into a back pocket for his wallet. He should really get checked out for tinnitus. Fumbled through the notes. "Here. Take this. In case he's not a gentleman and you have to get a taxi home after slapping his face."

"Wow! I wanted to ask, but didn't dare."

"You're a leech on the face of society," he said. Then added, with a worried expression, "I don't really mean that."

Kelly laughed and took the money. "You're so funny!"

"I don't attempt to be amusing."

"I know. That's why it is. You're also a complete spaz."

"I'll take that as ..." Sigh. "You're probably right."

"No. Not really. You're much nicer when you don't take your frustrations out on other people."

He resisted the urge to argue with her. He didn't feel so sure of some things any more.

"Hey, now we're getting on again, maybe once I'm in uni you could visit me there?" She pondered. Gave him a calculating look. "But I'd have to be careful about letting you meet any female friends."

He shifted nervously. "Just have a great time tonight, Kel."

"And you have a good night with Natalie. Do be nice to her. She acts tough, but she does care, y'know."

He nodded.

Natalie was excited throughout the bus journey to Altrincham. As they walked the last stretch to Devonshire Road she tugged on his hand, trying to speed up his dragging steps. The ice rink loomed.

"Sure you wouldn't rather just go for a drink?" Alex asked.

They queued. Paid. Got skates. Alex couldn't work out how to close the buckles.

"Here, let me." Natalie did them for him, clacking them closed against the rigid orange plastic. "Now stand up and check they're not too tight."

He raised himself and walked on the carpet a few steps, worrying that one or both ankles would pop to the side and break. It didn't seem right to balance on such slender blades. No bones snapped though.

He shuffled over to the entrance with Natalie. It was packed. Kids whizzing round. Families with children holding hands. Adults dressed in normal clothes, some teenagers in more streamlined garb. Most moved across ice effortlessly. Only a few wobbled. Alex would be in the minority.

Music blared out, pouring over an existing noise of voices and movement, and lights glared over the complex activities. Sensory overload. He had to ignore all that and focus. On standing.

He stopped at the edge of the ice, that untrustworthy surface.

"Did you know that neither the theory of 'pressure melting' nor 'friction heating' can fully account for why ice becomes slippery under ice skates at really low temperatures?"

"You'll be fine," she said.

He stepped forward, immediately found there was no traction, grabbed the bar and shuffled his feet back and forth. Natalie moved past him, slid round to face him. She was wearing leggings and a skirt. Her legs didn't move at all as she stood on the ice, grinning. How did she do that? Why wasn't she falling over?

Shuffle. Shuffle.

"Come on." She slid next to him, took hold of one of his hands. He kept hold of the bar with the other, and they started to move forward.

It seemed to take forever to do that first lap.

"You're too stiff. Like a board. Loosen up," she told him. "Call me greedy but I'd like to do more than two laps all night."

Loosening up wasn't as easy as she made it look.

Many of the people seemed to move to the music. He tried listening to it, to see if it helped. Funky beats and voice, the pace made him want to do better as the singer sang something about asking to see a thong.

"What's this craziness?" he asked.

"Sisqo's 'Thong Song'."

She moved backwards in front of him, holding his hands, giving him more speed and balance, *the look in her eyes so devilish, he really really hoped he could handle it, wiggling her hips till the music stopped like she was living la vida loca.* He was following her, impressed at her skill, her control.

He found himself smiling. He didn't recognise the music – *da na da na* – but he felt it in his legs. He didn't know how to skate – *da na da na* – yet he was having fun. Bizarre.

Slow guitar became rapid beats and rapping about being a "Freestyler".

"Bomfunk MC's," she told him when he gave her a questioning look.

He shook his head. Another world. He told her to move on and did his own shaky shuffle, not rhythmic. She wiggled, heels flicking left and right in time with the music, then turned elegantly and kicked off, moving easily as if in her environment, darting fish in a busy pond, legs powering her.

He hadn't realised that she was so good at something.

He gained more confidence. Not holding the bar at all now, except when he wanted to brake.

A song he did recognise from the telly and radio – the Britney Spears girl, "Oops! I Did It Again". He knew one! Wow! He jutted his head and shuffled faster. He could do this too! He'd worked out you had to slide each foot out a bit, not just back and forth, if you wanted to move forward. Intelligence applied. Simple physics –

Oops! His leg slipped again,
He grabbed for the bar, his balance regained,
Oh baby, baby, that was close.

Off again unshaken, now he was moving faster. He was skating! He picked up speed, saw Natalie waving and singing as she passed him, he waved back, then realised there was someone ahead, a mother and child, blocking him, panic, turn, tried to stop, realised he didn't know how to, tried to reach for the bar, just about touched it when his legs flew forward and he skidded along on his bottom.

No pain. Just embarrassment. And wetness on his arse.

His first attempt at getting up led to another fall. People skated round him. He crawled ignominiously on his hands and knees towards the safety of the edge, worrying about severed digits. Gripped the bar tightly.

Looked right. Natalie sliding towards him. Smiling, the devilish look again. Anger flared, but then dissipated straight away, snuffed by cold.

She was only smiling. She was happy, not mean.

She helped him up. He looked around. No-one seemed to pay any attention, to care or laugh.

He was surprised to realise that it didn't matter.

He could fall on his arse and *it didn't matter.*

"You okay?" she asked.

"Does my bum look wet in this?" he responded, pointing.

She burst out laughing.

"Oh yes! You look like you've pissed yourself."

She hugged him.

Later he took a break. Watched for a bit. Natalie was one of the confident skaters weaving in and out of bodies, natural movement that succeeded because there wasn't too much thought put into it. Relaxed. It reminded him of wild particles pulled and repelled into a rapidly curving orbit. Pattern within apparent chaos.

This whole thing was better than he had expected.

They got off the bus a few stops early on the way home. Warm evening, sky blackening but still with a hint of light. Alex let Natalie link his arm. They took the route down Broadway, silhouettes of spindly birches on their left.

Natalie was talking about her plans for college, but the reminders of it irritated him. The nearer they got to home, the more it grated.

"I can't wait until term starts and I can begin the A levels. I still wish I was doing them at your college. You could have taught me."

"I think you know why that's a bad idea."

"You're embarrassed to be seen with me?"

"Not that, it's just awkward. Tutors can't be seen with their students. I could get the sack."

"Even though we're only friends?"

"It's how it looks."

"I don't care how it looks."

He was uncomfortable on this topic. "You'll soon complain once you start getting homework. College life can be shit."

"You're so negative."

"With reason."

"What do you hate so much?"

"Everything. It's not where I want to be."

"Where do you want to be?"

"Own place. Different job. Why are you smiling?"

"Nothing. What job?"

"Something where the students want to learn."

"I bet most of them do."

They walked in silence for a minute.

"What about teaching at university? Would that be better?" she asked.

"Maybe. You need a PGCE though."

"Well, get one."

"It's not that easy."

"Why not?"

He didn't answer, but she wouldn't let it drop.

"You could get one. Maybe you'd be happier then. Where do you get one of those?"

"College. Or university."

"So you could just do one at your college?"

"Maybe."

"Do it! Then a university'd pay you to do research and stuff, write your articles."

"I'm too busy."

"No you're not!" She stopped, and he had to as well because of the entwined arms. "You know you've got time. I don't know why you won't do this if it might make you happy. Hey, you'd be a student too, we could do homework together!" She laughed but he didn't join in. She frowned at him.

"Come on." He started walking. Their arms were unlinked now.

"Why are you being uptight? It's a good idea."

"I don't want to talk about it," he said quietly.

"But it's a good plan! You should man up and do it."

"I don't need telling what to do." He walked faster.

"I know what it is," she said as she kept up with him. "It's because *I* came up with the idea, isn't it? That's the only reason you might be acting this way. That's it, isn't it?"

"No."

"It is, you know."

Alex was irritated at the volume of her voice.

"It's complicated," he told her, "and you're too young to understand."

She stopped. He thought he heard a deep intake of breath.

"What the fuck?" she said.

"Keep your voice down. There are people in these –"

"I don't give a SHIT! Too young? I know more about life than YOU!"

"I'm not putting up with this," he snapped, walking away from her, eager just to get home now.

He heard her mutter, "You shit," under her breath. He walked on and she ran to catch up with him. They passed an old man but she continued to mutter curses. He knew it was pointless to tell her to stop.

"I thought I understood you," she said. "But you're being horrible. Have I done something?"

"Maybe."

"What?"

"I'm pissed off that you blab everything to Kelly."

"I don't!"

"You told her about when I accidentally saw you in the shower room."

"That was yonks ago, and before anything happened between us! I didn't know it was meant to be a secret!"

"It's probably not all."

"I think you're selfish."

They were nearing the car park of The Bent Brook pub. He wouldn't have to put up with this for much longer.

"I think *you're* the selfish one," he said. "You always want my time."

"You hate being with me so much? You don't care at all, do you? You're colder than the ice."

They were turning left off Broadway, past the small row of shops. Not much farther.

"Can we just drop it?" He was vaguely aware of a small group of teenagers sat on the garage wall opposite the takeaway. They were jeering. He was flustered.

"This needs sorting out right now," she said. "This is important. It changes everything."

More jeering.

"Not here. There's people," he hissed.

"I told you, I DON'T GIVE A FUCK!" she yelled at him. "This is important. They're not."

"Snapperrrrrrr," came the voice of one of the mocking observers.

"Snapper slapper," scoffed another.

Natalie grabbed his arm, stopped him, held it tight. Looked into his face for something, he didn't know what.

A chip thrown, landed on the pavement near his feet.

"Hey ginge, show us your minge," someone taunted. He recognised the voice.

Couldn't stand Natalie's face.

Another chip. Just missed him.

"Stop that," he said weakly, to no-one.

Natalie turned and walked away.

"Ey, darlin', leave him, have a taste of this!" A gesture, possibly lad grabbing his crotch. There were three of them.

He should go home.

Natalie walked on, ignoring everything.

"Yeah, fuck off, you're a slag anyways," shouted one of the lads.

It was like a brain flash. One second Alex had been standing, watching Natalie, the next he found himself facing the three on the wall. He should have known. It was the worst three tearaways who always had it in for him.

"What do your parents think of you?" he yelled at them. "Your attitude, it's pathetic, you'll never get anywhere like this, what do you get from being so horrible?"

They jeered, laughed in his face.

"That girl's worth a hundred of you people, how dare you insult her, I want you to apologise!" He'd never felt so angry as they heckled him, takeaway packaging strewn all round. "Apologise!"

"Fuck off, backpack boy," said the tracksuit-bottomed youth with lines carved into his hair.

"And you, you're a girl, why hang around with these yobs?" he asked Super Perm in exasperation. She gave him the middle finger.

Footsteps running up from behind him. Maybe the fourth gang member. He didn't give a shit any more, he was too angry.

He turned to Floppy Feet, felt like yanking on the blonde hair that sprouted under his woolly hat.

"I want you to apologise. You've insulted my friend."

"Fuck off, mummy's boy." The lad wasn't fazed in the slightest.

A hand on his shoulder. Alex looked, expecting to be punched, but it was Natalie there, telling him to leave it. As he looked away there was movement from Floppy Feet, a blur, hands coming up holding a white carton, a fast movement towards Alex, and everything seemed to freeze, to slow, condensed time in which he felt bizarrely calm, Alex turning to that idiotic cock-sure gurn, and something amazing happened; Alex's hands moved so quickly, both came up the centre and slapped the carton, impulse, body memory from somewhere, causing the contents of the carton to tip backwards and splatter over Floppy instead of over Alex, soggy chips and curry sauce; motions that seemed familiar yet alien to Alex, the chip warrior, the curry force, perfection with two hands, untouchable, while the gooey mess dripped off Floppy's chin and all down his off-white jacket leaving a stunned face.

Everyone looked shocked, including Natalie.

"Didn't expect that, did you, arse-wipe?" asked Alex. He leaned forward, feeling strangely intimidating. "The laugh's on you, you floppy-footed fucker. And you can stop staring too, Tram Line Twat and Super Sperm." Alex jabbed his finger towards them. "Anything to say? Didn't think so."

While they were still surprised at this turn of events he grabbed Natalie's hand and dragged her after him, feeling certain that the three would follow, renew their attack.

Round the corner, down an avenue, still hauling Natalie until she pulled back, broke her hand free. He was ready for her anger this time. He faced her.

But she was laughing. "Super Sperm?"

"You're not angry?"

"Tram Line Twat?" She burst out laughing again. "Where did *that* come from?"

"Pet names."

She was holding her sides, shaking her head, and Alex couldn't help joining in. He realised something.

"Huh. They don't scare me any more."

"I doubt anyone would. You were like … Nic Cage."

"Don't exaggerate."

"Well, Austin Powers then."

"I'm sorry, Natalie."

"What about?"

"Me being a dick. Before. A number of times before, in fact. You're right. Everything you come up with. Good ideas."

"You mean it?"

"Yes. And that was the last time I'll be like that. I'm certain. It's all so clear to me now."

They stared at each other, lit by orange street lamps and surrounded by flickering TV lights in the windows of semi-detached houses.

"You're the best friend I could have," he added.

She seemed to make a decision. This time she grabbed *his* hand and pulled him.

"What?" he asked.

"Just come with me. I wasn't going to do this, but ..."

She led him towards the main road then got her mobile phone out. Rang someone. Gave her location. Said thanks. Hung up.

"What is it?" Alex asked again, confused.

"You'll see."

She refused to answer any more questions. So he stopped asking.

She shivered. It had cooled down now. He put an arm round her shoulder.

Part of the mystery was solved when a taxi pulled up and they climbed into the back. She told the driver the name of a road not too far away. They set off.

Natalie squeezed his hand and smiled at him. He felt detached, but in a good way. *Let it roll.* Street lights flicked past the windows, distance metronome. He didn't even bother paying attention to where they were.

(Nearly blew it.)

The car pulled in and they got out.

(But there's a second chance, sometimes.)

The taxi left them on a side road not far from Urmston. They were next to some flats covering three sides of a grassed area. Across the road were houses. Natalie took his hand and pulled him towards the flats. The path was well lit with neat bushes and a few mature trees that could look nice during the day. The flats themselves were severe – dark brown brick extended to three floors, banks of curtained PVC windows facing down. An air of scruffiness made him worry about what was going on behind the curtains. He imagined drug sellers, and rooms piled high with TVs.

"Don't pull a face, they're quite nice inside," she said.

"What, are we visiting a friend of yours?"

"Sort of."

They approached one of the entrance doors. She pressed a buzzer. After a few seconds a man answered.

"It's me," she stated to the grille above the button. "I'm with Alex."

"Come on up," came the crackly voice. A buzz and a click. Natalie opened the door and led him in.

In his mind he saw broken lifts, litter, and steel reinforced doors. Maybe even a junkie on the stairs. But it was clean, if spartan. Neat mailboxes without graffiti. A bicycle that was just leaning against the wall, no padlock.

Alex followed her up to the first floor. She knocked on one of the doors.

The man who answered was smart: styled blonde hair and short stubble, wearing a loose top and jeans. Around Alex's age. Natalie gave him a hug and a kiss on the cheek.

"Alex, meet Rhodri," she said.

Rhodri smiled, shook his hand, a firm grip and direct look into Alex's eyes.

"Pleased to meet you, come in." Welsh accent to match the name.

Not a single mum then. But maybe something else. Alex weighed up how many seconds Rhodri had kept his hand on Natalie for.

"You too," replied Alex, looking round uncertainly.

"She talks about you a lot."

"Are you a friend of hers?"

"I am here, y'know," she cut in. "Yeah, Rhodri's been a friend since he came here from someplace with a funny name."

"Llantwit Major."

"Whatever. I come here sometimes."

"I see," said Alex.

"Nat's great, always there when you need her."

"Is that so?"

"Yeah, love her to bits."

"Right."

"Do you want a drink?"

"No thanks."

"Where's Sara?" asked Natalie.

"In bed. Best not to wake her. I'll have to keep this visit as one of our secrets, or she'll have a fit in the morning."

"Ah. Okay to show Alex round? Only be a few mins."

"Be my guest. I'm going to make myself a drink. Something strong." He left through a doorway, glimpse of kitchen.

Alex stared at Natalie.

"Don't ask too many questions. I'll tell you when we get out. Don't want any big debates here. I just want to know what you think."

Alex eyed the room. It had a relaxing feel. Wood flooring with thick rugs. Comfy-looking sofa. Glass coffee table. Soft lighting.

"What am I looking for, exactly?"

"Whether you could live somewhere like this."

He looked at her with mistrust. "A flat?"

"A nice flat. Something I've had on my mind. There's one going on the floor above, same layout. No more questions now. Just look."

She took his hand, pointed to an alcove full of CDs and toys. "See, shelves built in for all your books."

Pulled him to a pair of doors opposite the kitchen. "Can't go in the small bedroom, Sara's asleep, but look ..." she opened the other door, put a light on revealing a wood-framed bed with green floral bedclothes, white slippers by the bed, a chair supporting a pile of woman's underwear, purple satin bra on top.

"Don't stare at those, perv, they're Elinor's. She's lovely."

Towed across the flat, small bathroom this time. It smelt floral. Toothbrushes in a pot. Cartoon towel on the rail. Toys around the bath. "I think the one above has a shower too."

The last door was the kitchen. Rhodri had his back to a jumble of breakfast cereal packets, hands clasped round a mug of coffee.

"Not a bad size are they?" he asked.

"No, it's surprising," replied Alex. "Bigger than –"

"They look from the outside," Rhodri finished in unison with Natalie. "Won us over, too."

"Rhodri works in the planning department of the council. Has lots of clever ideas for making towns nicer."

"Don't win all my battles though," he said. "Otherwise I'd like my job more. You going to stay? Elinor gets home from Gregg's soon." He addressed the last bit to Natalie.

"Nah, would like to see her but I need to talk to Alex."

"You look dazed, man. I don't like being dragged around houses by Elinor either."

"Ha ha," said Natalie. "He's fine. Still need me to watch the poppet tomorrow?"

"Just for a few hours."

"Cool. I'll text you."

Outside.

"I bet he thinks I can't string a sentence together."

"Yeah. The flat?"

"He seems like a good bloke."

"Yeah. And the flat?"

"Isn't it expensive?"

"Not really. £225 a month, furnished. It's not far from your family. By the bus stop, easy for Urmston Library."

He rubbed his eyes. "You want us to live together?"

"Bloody hell, you're supposed to be the one with the brains," she muttered. "Yes! Don't look so worried. We can just do it as friends if you don't want to be more serious. The one above Sara's room would be mine, I guess. If we'd been together then you could have used it as a study, lock yourself in. And I'll pay my way. There's a few pubs near here, I'll get a job in one. Go to college part-time."

Alex couldn't process all the data. Not because the situation was too complex, but because it kept changing. Kept flipping between the now, and a past; memories of suggesting something similar to a woman; the hurt that followed. Here things were reversed. He was the one being asked. Someone else's happiness depended on him. His assumptions about Natalie going back to live with her mum were as flawed as most others he'd made.

"I think we both want to do this," Natalie said.

He looked at her, but not like he usually did, as if marking an essay. No, he looked properly this time, and *saw* her.

"And you've got to do things. Grab them when you can," she said eagerly. "Gotta look forward."

He perceived the shape within, just for a second. She had hope. It spread; he could almost witness electrons moving through the magnetic field between them, following lines of force, beautiful things everywhere, sharing, changing both of them in the process, the covalent bonding of life.

"I won't ask you again if you say no. Won't have hard feelings, but I won't mention it ever again."

"I'm sorry, Natalie. Sorry for being a dick so many times. Sorry for messing you around. If you forgive me for the way I've acted then … yes. Let's do it."

She gave him a hug, face lit up. Sudden seriousness as she said, "But you've got to be nice to me, Alex. Or I'll go."

He nodded, she smiled again, and he hugged her back. Just a hug. Just bodies in close proximity, so he could smell her, chemicals igniting. Just arms around her, but it shared warmth. Just a kiss when their lips touched, but it felt right.

Home. Natalie in the shower. She called to him through the door. He rushed down the hall.

"What?"

Water hissing inside. "Need a clean towel. Can you get me one?"

He opened the fresh linen basket. Took one out.

"Got it. I'll leave it outside the door."

"It's not locked. Just come in. Nothing you've not seen before, long, long ago …"

"No!"

"Well, just reach in, drop it inside. I can't come out in the hall, can I?"

He hesitated. But her logic made sense. Opened the door ajar, reached in, felt the steamy warmth. Heard the shower turn off. Imagined her grabbing his arm, yanking him in. Dropped the towel and closed the door quickly. Heard her laughing at him.

Catching up on press-ups he'd not done earlier. Head to left, head to right. Sit-ups, panting. Then some new squats he'd seen Mr Motivator do on GMTV, just to shake it up a bit.

It was bedtime, yet he was full of energy.

A knock. He said nothing, a test. Another knock.

"Come in," he invited, content.

Natalie. In pyjamas.

"Hey," she said.

"Hello."

"Can I?" She looked towards his bed.

(Don't follow all the rules, be spontaneous. This is life, y'know.)

He nodded.

He had his arm round her as they snuggled up.

She reminded him of a contented cat.

His bedside table had one of the RHIC newsletter printouts. He looked down at Natalie. Back to the newsletter. Picked up the newsletter and opened it.

"What?" asked Natalie. She swatted the newsletter aside. "I'll rip the bloody thing up!"

"Joking," he said, dropping the newsletter to the floor and pointing at her.

"Oh. You got me. I'm not used to that."

"I know. But it is interesting."

"Bollocks."

"It is! They did several experiments where some people thought it would be the end of the world. It wasn't. It was just gold particles being smashed apart."

"Gold particles? They're wasting gold?"

"No. The particles are so small. Over twenty years they'll use less than one gram of gold. That's just one small gold ring."

"I'd rather have a ring."

"You've got to see the beauty of it though! Gold particles colliding at the speed of light, golden fireworks that teach us where we came from, fired along precise magnetic tracks, collisions inevitable."

"Fired from a gun? What if they hit people?"

"It wouldn't matter. They're so small. It would be like two gnats colliding. A ghost's caress, so light you'd hardly notice it." He touched her arm with his fingertip.

"I felt that."

He did it again, even lighter, just a brush of fine hair. She took hold of his hand.

"I'm tired, but I've got to tell you this," she whispered. "I just want to say that I love you. Even if you don't love me yet. I still do." She said the last with her head on his chest as she hugged up to him, not expecting a response.

He held her, quiet, until the pattern of her breathing changed, slowed, descended into sleep. Alex didn't feel tired at all. For a moment he thought about all the jobs he could be doing, all the articles he was behind on. He could slip his arm out. Maybe get up without disturbing her.

He looked at her face as she slept. He was really seeing her.

He shook his head, rebuking himself, and relaxed.

(Sack it. Let her sleep. There's always tomorrow.)

He turned off the lamp, and smiled in the dark.

Cold Fusion

"Nuclear power stations use nuclear FISSION. Blasting atoms apart and collecting the energy. The downside is radioactive waste, so it's a dirty form of energy. Nuclear FUSION is what goes on in stars, where the high pressure and high heat environment causes atoms to merge into newer, more stable forms of matter. Energy is still released but it is much cleaner. Our Sun fuses over 600 million tons of hydrogen every second. But it's no mean feat to replicate conditions at the heart of the sun. Cold fusion is the hypothesis that fusion could be possible at room temperature. But if we dream of cold fusion we're dreaming of something we can't have. It's like wishing for the past. It's a dead end and you have to move – What? I'm busy! Recording, what do you think? No, it's in the – just get it from the suitcase! Argh! Holidays are horror shows – stop laughing at me – It means … You're trying on that swimsuit now? Wow … It means … Screw this, it'll keep. [Click]"

Four months later.

Alex leaned over the icy handrail of the bridge, looking down into the murky waters of the ship canal forty feet below. His breath turned to fog with every exhalation. His raincoat, bought for style, was useless for insulation.

Holy protons, it was *cold.*

He found it hard to believe that the water down there hadn't frozen yet. His fingers were numb. But the water was still liquid, defying logic. It gloomed blackly, relieved only by the occasional reflection from a street lamp.

It was a long drop down there. Someone falling in from the bridge would probably be a goner. They would plunge into the dirty arctic water, then straight down into the stinking muddy slime of centuries which is supposed to be at least ten feet deep. It would suck you down, trap you, and you'd drown, body cryogenically frozen. Even if you were seen, and someone called for help, you'd be dead before it arrived. Anyone foolish enough to dive in after you would suffer the same fate. And so would end every problem.

Of course, if you *weren't* spotted your body would eventually bloat and decompose alongside the tyres, shopping trolleys, broken bicycles, shoes, cans and bottles that generations of dirty Mancunians had discarded into the waters.

Who'd want to be swallowed up in the past like that?

A wry smile spread across Alex's lips as a stanza of Tennyson floated into his mind.

Break, break, break,

At the foot of thy crags, O sea!
But the tender grace of a day that is dead
Will never come back to me.

Twenty-seven words. Seventy-two, backwards.

He moved away from the railing, hand slipped into his pocket. A hard angular lump. He withdrew his small collection of Tennyson's poetry, always his favourite. Sometimes dead days *could* return. Ever since he'd rediscovered his old poetry books he'd felt the urge to read them again. It was as if they'd woken something long lost. It was a good thing. He should never have denied it.

There was beauty everywhere. So much.

And always sadness too.

A few months ago he'd got a letter from London. An old friend from university had included a page of obituaries from a newspaper, with one highlighted.

> **SPIERS, Lucy Jane** *On 18th May, 2000. Services at*
> *OUR LADY OF VICTORIES, 235a Kensington*
> *High Street on Tuesday 23rd May at 3pm.*

It didn't connect at first, seeing it typed out like that. She'd never used the name Jane, and hated seeing it on university forms. The friend said he'd heard it was a stroke, but it had been misdiagnosed at first. By the time doctors realised, it was too late.

The bit that really got to him though was that the obituaries above and below hers had longer entries, detail about the person and who they'd left behind, giving a taste of lives worth living.

Lucy's was tragically pared back: nothing about being the "beloved daughter of so-and-so", or her history, or anything that made it look like she'd been a real person, someone who'd touched lives, for better or worse.

Alex hadn't thought about Lucy with anything other than anger for a long time, anger which orbited a dense core of questions. But when he read the obituary he realised it was all mysteriously gone. Instead there was just grief and something else. *Love.* It didn't matter that he hadn't seen her for six years. It was still there. It didn't die.

He cried that day. Didn't tell anyone why. It was something just between him and Lucy. He'd wished that she knew that.

Then he took a postcard he'd been using as a bookmark, a picture of one of his favourite paintings, *La Donna della Finestra*. The back was blank. He couldn't remember when he'd got it but looking at it made him feel strangely sad, despite its beauty.

On that card he wrote a note to Lucy. Partly to help himself,

(fortiffy himself)

but also to make it clear that he remembered her, and that scrap from a newspaper was not the final word. She *had* lived. She *had* been loved.

Then he'd taken it up to the attic room when everyone was busy, creeping amongst the antique dolls and the old wooden furniture, avoiding the floorboards that creaked the most. He'd knelt by the rocking chair, where the skirting board was loose. A narrow gap behind it. A secret compartment. He'd hidden the card and let go of the past.

Maybe someone would find it in a hundred years. Maybe not. It didn't matter.

He wished the world was better organised than this. But there was only so much you could do to hold back the chaos.

A car beeped its horn and Alex was pulled back to the present, breathing exhaust fumes from the busy road behind him. He turned and watched one driver mouthing insults and shaking his fist at another. Then both idiots drove off.

They should all just chill out. He grinned and pulled his hat down tighter.

He'd found the hat in this same canal during the summer. Floating there like a black jellyfish. On a whim Alex had fished it out, held the dripping thing at arm's length until he worked out what it was. Apart from being wet it seemed to be in good condition. New and unfaded. A Kangol. Someone's history, lost but re-found. Alex had slipped it into a carrier bag and taken it home. Washed it and dried it and, on an even crazier whim, worn it. No-one took the mickey. So he kept wearing it. The brim kept the sun from his eyes in summer, rain from his face in autumn, and the top of his head warm in winter. A heat-retainer that was also cool. He liked that. Wordplay making impossible physics possible.

Footsteps approached from the direction of the Stretford Metro. He turned to see her.

"How was college?" he asked.

"Fine. But I need your help – I have to start an English essay. Poetry," replied Natalie.

"I'll help you. In return you can read over my new PGCE assignment."

She wrinkled her nose girlishly, and he paused, confused as he felt a twitch of memory.

"What's up?"

But it was gone. "Nothing." He shook his head. "And I was only joking about having to read my work."

"I know. But wait – I've got something for you."

"Not more clothes?"

"Shut up. You look loads better since I became your stylist and made you get a haircut. But anyway, no, it's nothing like that." She rummaged in the bag slung across her waist. "It's only second-hand," she said, passing him a compact gadget. "I know we can't waste money but I saw it in a shop and thought of you. All those notes you're always writing."

Alex examined the small pocket memo. Pressed eject and a tidy little tape popped out. It closed again with a pleasing click.

"I thought you could record all your ideas on it, save you losing any. For that big book of physics you keep talking about. It might get you started. It needs batteries, though, I didn't have any spare." Her face was expectant as she looked up at him.

"It's absolutely brilliant," he said slowly, slipping it into his pocket. "I've always wanted one. You do have good ideas, Nat."

She beamed at him. "I'm glad you like it. Come on, let's go." She took his hand. "Fuck, your fingers are freezing, you must be numb."

"I don't mind the cold."

She rubbed his hands between hers for a few seconds, transferring warmth, then linked her arm through his and led him to the bus stop.

"Maybe we should go on a holiday. What do you think? Can we go on a holiday next summer? Go away together? Greece, like some of those musty philosophers you write about? You get to see all those crumbling things from the past. And I get sun, beaches, bikinis, cocktails."

"Greece is a bit far. What about Wales?"

"Wales!"

"I've never been abroad. I need to start slowly."

"All right. Wales." She rolled her eyes, but it was just a show. He could sense her happiness as she squeezed him tighter.

They crossed the busy road. She was warming him up. He remembered something, laughed to himself.

"What?" she asked, but he just shook his head.

Last night he'd been explaining dating systems in his study, and how the new millennium would begin in a couple of weeks. Natalie had only been paying half of her attention, more interested in choosing where to put decorative candles in their flat.

"Another millennium? Wow, I get two of them!" she'd said cheerfully. He'd been drinking water; had gripped the glass tighter. But when he'd seen her face, so gleeful, happy, those chemical changes popping in her brain – he could learn from her too. Something inside him had creaked, shifted.

(A year is an arbitrary number. Not everything needs analysing.)

"Oh, I've got something for you, too," he said as they reached the bus stop.

"Oh yeah?"

Her hands were hot when he took them, kissed them, ignoring the people stood around. Then he kissed her properly, her mouth warm, sweet as cider. When they stopped he whispered three words in her ear, surprising himself; she locked eyes with him and said, "I know. It was just a matter of time."

The street lights were burning orange and yellow, and Alex thought he could feel a cool breeze coming from somewhere, could hear it whispering through the branches of the tree to his left. It was a beautiful end to a beautiful day, and it was good to be alive.

Acknowledgements

Thank you for buying this book. Without you, there is no point in writing. *Diolch yn fawr!*

1001 110 / 11001 1111 10101 / 11 1 1110 / 10010 101 1 100 / 10100 1000 1001 10011 / 10100 1000 101 1110 / 11001 1111 10101 / 1 10010 101 / 1 / 111 101 101 1011 /, 1 1110 100 / 10100 1000 1001 10011 / 10 1111 1111 1011 / 1001 10011 / 100 101 100 1001 11 1 10100 101 100 / 10100 1111 / 11001 1111 10101 / 10100 1111 1111.

About The Author

Karl Drinkwater is originally from Manchester but has lived in Wales for half his life. He's a full-time author, edits fiction for other writers, and was a professional librarian for over twenty-five years. He has degrees in English, Classics, and Information Science.

He writes in multiple genres: his aim is always just to tell a good story. Among his books you'll find elements of literary and contemporary fiction, gritty urban, horror, suspense, paranormal, thriller, sci-fi, romance, social commentary, and more. The end result is interesting and authentic characters, clever and compelling plots, and believable worlds.

When he isn't writing he loves exercise, guitars, computer and board games, the natural environment, animals, social justice, cake, and zombies. Not necessarily in that order.

If you enjoyed this work then please rate it or leave a review on the seller's website or www.goodreads.com. Thank you.

Find Karl Online

Website: karldrinkwater.uk
Facebook: facebook.com/karlzdrinkwater
Twitter: twitter.com/karldrinkwater
Newsletter: bit.ly/newsletterkd

Also By Karl Drinkwater

2000 Tunes

Mark Hopton's an outsider obsessed with Manchester music. He knows the dates, facts, band members, lyrics, histories and places. He can join them in complicated webs of association because he knows the secret: everything's connected. Music's his escape into a better world.

Oh man, he needs that escape. His dad's in prison, his psycho brother's only one step away, and they're twisting his melons trying to make him risk his freedom by smuggling drugs. It ain't easy saying no when family and their shady contacts can be bone-breakingly persuasive. Heaven knows he's miserable now.

The summer sun does bring one ray of light: he secretly admires Samantha, a beautiful Welsh girl at work. Watching her is like listening to music, it strengthens him, she's his wonderwall of true faith. He's happy with that. Love is fool's gold.

Meanwhile, Samantha's been caught up in a hedonistic lifestyle of cigarettes and alcohol with the 24 hour party people but now she's had it up to here with Mancunians. Cheaters, weirdos and two-faced scummers, the lot of 'em. When the drugs don't work it's time to grow up but no-one's going to take her for granted again. Don't look back in anger? Screw that. She's never been one to walk away.

2000 Tunes is a meditation on life, family, friends, growing up, and following your dreams.

Appendix: Butterflies

Alex's full poem is reproduced here. Butterflies don't live long. A brief time here, burning brightly, then they're gone.

The Butterflies
By Alex Kavanagh

I loved you in cool honest darkness, at night,
When we were together my fire burned bright.
Each day I was reborn, my heart leapt anew,
And then it was night-time and thoughts turned to you.
We lay in near-darkness and your smile set free
All of the butterflies living in me.

The shadows grew longer, the nights grew long too,
The love we made cooled now, the fires were few.
I wondered in silence, in silence I cried,
I hid the tears from you yet each night I died.
We lay in near-darkness, I searched for your smile:
All of the butterflies rested awhile.

My need just grew stronger, so I came to you
Unexpected and cold in the moon shadows blue.
I looked through the window and felt my blood freeze
As you sweated and rutted in Venus' foul breeze.

You lay in near-darkness, I clenched tight my coat:
All of the butterflies stuck in my throat.

Alex's poem follows the three stanza pattern of Byron's *We'll Go No More A-roving* – a connection not consciously recognised by Alex. He also didn't recognise his poem's value as doggerel.

Discussion Questions

If you're reading this as part of a book group then here are some potential questions to consider.

1. What happens just before and after the chapter Broken Parities? How does it relate to what happens while Alex is doing press-ups at the start of the novel?

2. Why doesn't Jane appear before or after the chapter Broken Parities?

3. What are the themes and concerns of the novel?

4. What is the significance of the novel's name?

5. How do the chapter names relate to the events of those chapters?

6. What is the relationship between the chapters Superdense Matter and Superlight Matter?

7. How many elements of Alex's behaviour, character and interests label him as geek? What are they?

8. Why is Alex such a disaster area at the start of the novel? Has he improved by the end? In what ways?

9. Does Alex deserve to be happy? And after the novel ends, will he be happy?

10. Do you think Natalie is making a mistake in pursuing Alex?

11. What is the significance of Hannah's casket in the art gallery/museum?

12. If you could meet any character from the novel and ask them a question, who would you choose, and what would you ask? Why?

You will find information relating to some of these questions in the Cold Fusion 2000 FAQ: tinyurl.com/cf2kfaq

Lightning Source UK Ltd.
Milton Keynes UK
UKOW04f0144030917
308452UK00003B/42/P